hidden truths

THE SHATTERED HALO SERIES BOOK 2

PATRICE ASHLEY

6 YEARS AGO

LOOKING around the small garage that our band has called home for the past few years, I take a deep breath. The smell of motor oil and mildew fills my lungs as I commit it to memory.

"Dude, what the hell are you doing?"

I look over my shoulder to see two identical faces looking at me with a mixture of annoyance and confusion.

"I'm memorizing everything about the space so I can talk about it in our documentary," I tell Ezra and Kai, my best friends.

"Don't you think you're getting a little ahead of yourself?" Kai teases as he starts loading our instruments into the back of the SUV he shares with his twin.

"I don't know. I have a good feeling about today," Ezra adds. He's been in a really great mood for the past few days, and I decided it's because he must have a sixth sense about our impending success story.

"See? Manifest with us, Malikai!" I shout and then cough from inhaling all the dust that's being kicked up by the twins. Kai just glares with those piercing blue eyes and resumes dismantling Willa's drum set. He hates when we use his government name, so naturally I do it whenever possible.

"Are you going to help us or just stand there?" Ezra asks as he starts folding my sister Bellamy's keyboard stand.

"Careful with that!" Kai yells before running over and wrapping the keyboard in a blanket and then gently folding the stand. Ezra raises his eyebrows at his brother but says nothing.

"I'd be more worried about damaging Willa's drums," I mutter. Willa is part of our band and one of our best friends, but she's also scary. The tiny blonde has no problem speaking her mind and cutting down grown men with a few choice words.

"So, no helping us, then?" Ezra asks again.

"I have to go pick up the girls," I shrug, like I would help otherwise. Spoiler: I hate manual labor.

Kai sighs, wiping the sweat from his brow and causing his dark, curly hair to look even more messy. Girls love it.

"Just go get them and make sure they make it to the gig on time," Kai mutters as he lifts Belle's keyboard and gently places it in the back seat of the car.

"It's in the woods. We're not being paid. And we're performing in front of a bunch of probably drunk high school graduates," I point out.

"I thought you said this was our big break," Ezra teases, taking Willa's drum kit from Kai.

There's a party in the woods of Summer Bay, our small

Maine town, every summer. It's always the night after graduation and it's always packed with the current grads and returning alum. It's a great way to get our music out there to our peers and then hopefully spread the word.

Kai, Ezra, and I all graduated two years ago. Willa and Belle just graduated last night. We formed our band, Shattered Halo, four years ago. It started as just something for the five of us to do together, since we all enjoyed music. We slowly learned that we all had a passion for it and tonight is the first time we're performing in front of an audience that isn't our parents.

I'm the lead singer and the face of the band. Kai plays guitar and Ezra plays bass. Willa kicks ass on the drums, which I was honestly pretty skeptical about considering her lack of height, but that girl will prove you wrong the minute you doubt her. Then my sister is on keys, but her real talent is in writing and composing. One of the songs we're playing tonight is a Bellamy Griffin original.

"Go get the girls," Kai grumps, obviously over me standing there and not helping.

"Aye aye, Captain," I say and salute him before taking off to collect the rest of the band. I hear Kai grumble and Ezra chuckle as I run across the street to my house.

"You look nice. Where are you headed?"

My mom startles at my question, having not noticed me sitting on the couch.

"Callahan! Must you sulk like that?" she huffs at me. My mom looks just like my sister. Dark curls and deep blue eyes, but where Belle's eyes have warmth, my mother's are ice cold.

"I'm just waiting for Belle and Willa. I wasn't trying to scare you."

Mom runs her hands down her blue, knee-length dress, flattening out the non-existent wrinkles before bringing her eyes to mine.

"Your father and I have been invited to dinner with the future governor and his wife," she replies, a bit of her inner snob showing with the lift of her nose.

I lift my eyebrows in surprise. "James Wolfe?" The election hasn't even happened yet, but my mom has recently become close with his wife. She won't stop bragging about it.

"Of course. Who else would I be talking about?" she snaps. I just shrug her off. The maybe governor is Maverick Wolfe's dad. He's a year younger than us, but we all go to the same college, and he's become close friends with Ezra. So we've become friends by default. He's a cool guy, but his dad is kind of a dick.

"Where is Dad?" I ask, looking around for him.

"I'm here!" My dad yells, rushing into the living room from the kitchen as he straightens his tie. My dad is warm in all the ways my mom is cold. As I was growing up, their differences always confused me. Even now, I still can't see how they fit together. "Good luck with your gig tonight, Cal," he says, smiling at me and patting my shoulder.

"Thanks, Dad."

"Keep an eye on your sister. We can't have her doing anything embarrassing," my mother orders before leaving the house. I roll my eyes. Belle would break out in hives if she ever broke a rule. Mom should be more concerned about me, but that's never the case. Probably because I'm a guy, as fucked up as that is.

My dad sighs and shakes his head before looking at me. "Keep an eye on Belle to make sure no one tries to take advantage of her. Not because she could ever do anything to embarrass us."

I nod, and my dad squeezes my shoulder before following my mom out of the house. He's always trying to re-word the cruelty that spills from his wife's mouth, like he thinks we believe she doesn't mean it the way it sounds. Too bad she means every word.

I check my watch and see it's getting close to the time we need to leave. I already saw Ezra and Kai leave their house. That was almost twenty minutes ago.

"You're going to be late to your own graduation party!" I yell toward the stairs.

Belle and Willa make their way down the stairs in what looks like matching black dresses, while Belle argues with my statement. I just walk out to my truck, knowing they'll follow me.

Belle is nervous the entire drive. She's lucky it was only about five minutes, or I would have left her on the side of the road. Or at least threatened it. As much as my mom telling me to babysit my eighteen-year-old sister annoys me, I wouldn't actually leave her anywhere alone.

I hop out of the truck the moment I put it in park, needing to get away from all the nervous energy.

"Hey Cal," some leggy brunette greets me, batting her eyelashes. "Can't wait to hear you sing tonight."

"Thanks, babe." I can't remember her name, so I go with

a generic pet name just to be safe. She lets out a high-pitched giggle that has my balls shriveling. She tries to grab my arm, but I slip out of her reach. "I have to go get set up and do some sound check stuff. You know, band things."

She giggles again in a way she must think is cute, but I have to fight the cringe. "Find me after," she says in a flirty tone. I nod and quickly walk away.

"Took you long enough," Kai mutters. He and Ezra have all the instruments set up and are currently plugging in amps, lighting, and anything else that requires power. We're using portable batteries that Willa's dad has from their camping days.

"Where are the girls?" Ezra asks, looking around me.

"I drove them here."

"And left them in the parking lot?" Kai asks, disapproval clear on his face.

I roll my eyes. He's always been protective of Belle, but I swear it got worse when we went away to college. "It's a two-minute walk, and you can probably see my truck if you move a little to your left."

I leave him to his overprotective nature and start getting my mic set up how I want it. The minute I sing a couple of practice notes, people pay attention. I can hear the quiet descending and feel the eyes on me. It's part of why I love this. My voice makes people listen.

I look at my band, making sure they're in place and ready to bring the house down. Figuratively, since we're surrounded by trees and zero walls. Belle's hands are shaking above her keys. Ezra is pale, but Kai and Willa are both serious-faced and ready. I lock eyes with Willa and nod. The next moment, she bangs her sticks together, and the music starts.

I open my mouth and the lyrics flow. I'm in my element like this, on the stage, lights blaring down on me, fans ensnared by my voice. It gives me a sense of power that I don't have in other aspects of my life. They hang on to every note and octave. It's a high that can never be matched.

"You've been great, Summer Bay! We are Shattered Halo!" I shout once the last note of our ten-song set fades. I'm covered in sweat, some of which has been dripping into my eyes and making them sting. But not even that discomfort can take away from the crowd that's clapping and screaming our names right now. Bras are even flying at us. I manage to catch a nice lacy black number before stepping back and helping the twins unplug everything.

I assume we'd normally have more time to bask in our glory, but since we're in the woods on a makeshift stage, we all agreed to get our instruments back in our locked cars as quickly as possible before celebrating with our peers. We're halfway done before I notice Ezra isn't with us or helping. I'm about to open my mouth and complain to Kai about it, but I quickly shut it when I remember I did nothing to help them set up.

The moment Kai hits the lock button on his key fob, making sure our instruments are safe, I'm high tailing it back to where the party is. I'm not as big of a man-whore as I make myself out to be, but I won't say no to a congratulatory blow job.

I find a group of girls, some of which I recognize from my graduating class, and make my way to them. They're all huddled together, probably trying to keep warm. It may be June, but it's still cold once the sun goes down, and their dresses are barely covering anything.

"Don't worry ladies, I'll warm you up!" I shimmy my way in and wrap my arms around two of them. They giggle as they all get closer to me.

"You were ah-maaaa-zing," the girl to my right, who I'll be calling Blonde One, says.

"Like the hottest singer there is right now," Blonde Two says to my left.

I'm smiling like a fool at all the compliments, waiting for the other two girls to sing my praises.

"You were kind of pitchy, and your cover of Fortunate Son was subpar at best," the girl across from me says. My jaw drops. I hear the others gasp and Blonde Three elbows her. "What?" she mutters. "It's the truth."

I take her in for the first time. She's not wearing a dress like the rest of them. She's smartly dressed in jeans, black boots, and a tight pink sweater. Her red hair is a mess of curls, and her green eyes slice right through me. She'd be breathtaking if she hadn't just insulted me.

"Is that so, sweetheart?" I ask in what I meant to be more of a sarcastic tone, but it comes out gravelly.

"Why did you pick Fortunate Son? It doesn't have the same sound as everything else you sang," she asks, seeming genuinely curious.

"It was my grandfather's favorite song. He died the year before we started the band. My sister, she's the one on the keyboard —"

She scoffs. "I'm aware of who Bellamy is."

"Right. Well, to answer your question," I say, frustration

bleeding into my tone, "my sister and I chose that song to honor him."

Firecracker, because that's what she is, tilts her head, seeming to look for the truth in my words. She must find them because the side of her lips twitch up in a small smile. Then she turns on her heel and leaves me with Blondes One, Two, and Three.

I barely hear what they're saying to me. My mind is scrambled by that entire conversation. I mean, I know she was right about my pitch. Even I heard it, but I didn't think anyone in the crowd of teenagers was going to notice that. I start to growl when I think about her critique of Fortunate Son. That one is too personal —

"Oh, you like that, huh?" Blonde Two interrupts my thoughts. She's rubbing my chest in a way that she apparently thinks I like. Is that a turn on for guys? I kind of like my nipples played with, but she isn't doing that. It's like she's trying to clean a spot from my shirt.

"Let's go find somewhere more private, babes," I say, leading them into some dense trees.

"What the fuck is that supposed to mean?" I hear from somewhere to my left. The tree coverage is too thick, and night has fallen, making it hard to see anything other than what's right in front of your face. "I can't!"

I know that voice. It's either Kai or Ezra. Judging from the anger, I'm guessing it's Kai. The guy has been in a mood since sound check.

"You can't be fucking serious!" I hear Kai yell. Deciding this is a private chat between him and not me, I lead The Blondes far enough away to give him his privacy.

A rough hand jerks me away from sucking on Blonde Three's neck.

"What the fuck?" I grumble, coming face to face with Kai.

"Have you seen Ezra? I can't find him." The concern in his voice has the anger quickly leaving my system.

"Not since we loaded your car." I think back for a moment, trying to get the blood from my dick back to my brain. "Actually, he wasn't there for that. So I guess I haven't seen him since we played."

"Fuck," Kai says, running a hand through his messy curls. "Willa said the same thing."

"I couldn't find him in the parking lot or near the picnic tables," Willa says, as if she was summoned by speaking her name. I jump a little at her appearance out of nowhere and she just laughs at me.

"I'm going to go ask Belle if she knows where he is. Can you guys start looking near the river?" Kai asks, and I grimace. I hate the river. The water is too fast, and it smells kind of gross. Kai doesn't wait for a response before he goes to find my sister.

"We can go get a group of people to start searching the woods. I have a flashlight in my car," Blonde Two offers. I forgot they were there and now I kind of feel bad for not learning their names. They seem nice.

"That would be great," I tell them. They straighten their dresses and head off as a group.

Willa snorts and shakes her head.

"Shut up," I grumble. "Let's go look in the river."

"He better not be in the river. We won't be able to see him," Willa says, eyes wide from the implication of my words.

"Shit. I didn't mean it like that. I just hate the damn thing, but I'll search near it for Ez."

I grab my phone from my pocket and turn the flashlight on. The area around us is covered in leaves and red plastic cups. As we make our way toward the sound of the rushing river, the crowd and the scattered cups thin. There's no sign of Ezra.

"Are we sure he didn't walk home?" I ask, assuming Kai already checked if he has us searching, but wanting to ask anyway.

"Yeah, Kai called home, and his mom said he wasn't there. He's been calling his phone nonstop too. Ezra isn't answering."

I shake my head. Ezra doesn't wander or take off without telling anyone. If anything, he's probably the most responsible out of all of us. Which is making me feel uneasy. Any buzz I had left from the show or the beer I was drinking has been sufficiently smothered.

I look over my shoulder and see Belle motioning for us to follow her and Kai. I grab Willa, and we quickly catch up to them. Belle had seen Ezra in a small opening in the trees, but that was hours ago. At least it gives us a starting place.

"What do you want us to do?"

I turn around to see Blonde One with a flashlight in her hand and a group of people behind her, including Firecracker.

"Split into groups, but don't go too far. These woods go

for miles, and I don't want anyone else getting lost tonight," Kai says, his voice tight with barely restrained emotions.

We take off in groups, all screaming Ezra's name until our voices are hoarse, our feet hurt, and the sun begins to rise.

***

Three months. It's been three fucking months and not a single word on Ezra. We're supposed to go back to school soon. How the fuck am I going to do that without him? Kai isn't even considering it. Belle and Willa still went shopping to get things to decorate their dorm with, but I think it was a feeble attempt at keeping things positive.

My phone dings, letting me know I have a new email. I check it quickly, expecting it to be my advisor. I emailed him, asking about the withdrawal process. I haven't officially withdrawn or even made that decision, but I want the information in case I need it.

"Holy shit," I mutter as I read the email I just received. "Holy shit!"

It wasn't from my advisor, it's from one of the many record labels I sent a video of us performing to. I took a risk and sent in the original song. The one Belle wrote. And one of them responded.

"Belle?" I scream as loudly as I can so that she can hear me no matter where she is in the house. "Where are you?"

"I'm here," she says, making her way to where I'm standing in our parents' rundown kitchen. I miss the yellow walls and worn wooden cabinets when I'm at school. Belle and I made a lot of macaroni in this room.

Ever since she and Willa watched Practical Magic and wanted Midnight Margaritas but were way too young to drink, Midnight Macaroni became one of my best ideas. "What's up?"

I explain the record deal to her at the same time I text Kai and Willa.

> Guys, you need to get to my house right now.

KAI

> I was about to go check the train station and the hospitals again.

I cringe. We've been checking everywhere we can think of on repeat for months.

WILLA

> I can be there in two minutes. Kai, I'll go with you after we go see what Cal needs.

KAI

> K.

Once everyone is here and I finish explaining why and how this deal came about, I take in their faces. Willa looks shocked and Kai is glaring at Belle for some reason. Okay, not exactly what I was expecting.

I open my mouth to complain about the lack of excitement, but Belle speaks before I can.

"I'm out."

Her words feel like a slap. "What? What do you mean? You can't miss the opportunity!"

"Then don't! You don't need me to do this," she fires back.

"You wrote the song they want!" I yell, completely blown away by her lack of understanding.

"Keep the song, Callahan! I'm not taking that from you. This isn't what I want. I can't do this without Ezra. I just. . . I can't, Cal." I see the plea in her eyes. She needs me to understand. I quickly glance at Kai and see she won't be getting the understanding from him. He looks angry. I don't know if that shocks me or not. He's been in a constant state of anger for the last three months.

"Let her go, Cal. She said she doesn't want to be with us anymore. Just leave it," the anger in Kai's voice is almost tangible, but there's so much pain woven into it too. From the look on Belle's face, she's only noticed the anger.

"What about Ezra? You're just going to do this without him?" she asks, knowing how painful her words were and not seeming to care. What the fuck had happened between the two of them? They used to be so close.

"Ezra is gone. You heard the cops. He ran. Just like you're doing."

I flinch at Kai's words. Yes, the cops ruled Ezra a runaway, but none of us believe it. That's why we still search. Why we look under every rock and behind every dumpster. Kai is the one leading most of the searches. His words are out of anger, meant to hurt like a dagger.

"What the fuck, Kai?" Willa yells, jumping up to her feet. I grab her and pull her with me back into the kitchen.

"I think they have some shit they need to work out," I mutter under my breath. Willa nods but keeps her eyes on Belle.

Once we're out of their range, she turns to me. "Can we even do this? Without Ezra or Belle?"

I think about it for a moment. "I already knew we had to get another bass player. We could go without a keyboard player." I hated saying those words, like I was fine replacing my best friend and making my sister's role disappear. But what else are we going to do?

Willa nods, her brows drawn together in a frown, like she's thinking the same thing I am.

"I know a bassist," Kai says, entering the kitchen calmly like he didn't just have a fight with Belle.

"Who?" I ask, choosing to ignore the fight if he was. At least for the moment. I sure as fuck will be bringing that up later.

"Mav. He and Ezra would practice together sometimes," Kai supplies.

"How did I not know that?" I ask, more to myself than anyone. Kai shrugs, knowing the answer is because I was busy trying to maintain my barely passing grades, so I didn't flunk out. It's not that I'm stupid. School just didn't interest me, and I couldn't pay attention. But like the good friend he is, he doesn't call me out on it.

"Too busy chasing women," Willa says.

I wag my eyebrows at her. "Jealous?"

She makes a barfing sound, which makes Kai laugh. I feel my shoulders lower, thankful that the mood is less tense.

We spend the rest of the afternoon on a call with the label. They agree to our only demand. That Belle and Ezra be allowed to return to the band, if or when, they so choose.

By the next day, Kai has convinced Maverick to join Shattered Halo, and we all sign on the dotted line. And just like that, we're rock stars.

one

CAL

NOW

"WHERE IS SHE?" I demand, not for the first time. My voice is dripping with frustration. Every muscle in my body is tense, and my hands are clenched so tightly into fists that my nails are digging into my skin.

"I'm sorry, Mr. Griffin, but we need to wait for the test results before allowing you to see her," the nurse tells me again.

"You can't call me and tell me I have a fucking daughter and then not allow me to see her!" I yell, slamming my fist against the desk and causing both the nurse I'm speaking to and the one sitting next to her to jump.

"As I've told you before, we called on the request of the mother. Since she can no longer give consent, we need to wait for the tests to confirm you are, in fact, the father of the baby."

I take a deep breath, trying with everything I have left in

me to keep my composure. The last thing I need is to be thrown out of the hospital before figuring all this out.

"I've got them expediting it, Cal. We'll have the results within the hour."

I turn to see my lawyer, Frank, still sitting in the chair in the waiting room. I called him the moment I got off the phone with the hospital. I hadn't even made it out the door before I had him agreeing to meet me here.

"Do I want to know how much that cost me?" I ask, taking the seat next to him and trying the breathing exercise I learned in yoga that one time Mav talked me into going with him.

"He wanted a signed guitar from Kai," Frank says, still tapping away on his phone.

I snort. Frank is the only one who knows I'm here. I can't wait to tell Kai I have a daughter and that I need one of his guitars. There's no way that won't go well. Him and Belle have been blowing up my phone. They're looking for me, but I can't talk to them right now. So my phone is off.

"Callahan? What the hell is going on?"

My eyes shoot up to meet my dad's. "Dad?" I turn to glare at Frank, who just shrugs without even bothering to look at me.

"You needed support," he says simply.

"That's why I called *you*," I mutter, standing to greet my father. I hear Frank chuckle. We both know he's great at what he does, but the man is not warm.

My dad wraps me in his arms and some of the tension instantly releases. Dad has been and always will be my biggest supporter. I should've called him myself, but I haven't been able to tell anyone what's going on. I'm too overwhelmed.

He releases me and turns to Frank, holding out his hand. "Thanks for calling me."

Frank takes my dad's hand and nods. "It's good to see you again, Jason."

"Now, are you going to tell me what's happening?" Dad asks, turning his attention back to me.

I sigh, rubbing the back of my neck, my nerves taking over. "I might have a daughter."

Dad's eyebrows shoot up to his hairline, and his eyes are so wide I'm afraid they'll fall right out of his head. He regains control of his expression as he processes my words. "What do you mean, *you might* have a daughter?"

"We're waiting for the DNA test to confirm before they let me see her," I explain, feeling both embarrassed about the situation and angry we're even in it. I should've known. Someone should have told me. This shouldn't be the first time I'm learning I'm a father.

"The mother doesn't want to let you see her?" My dad asks. It's a fair question, but it puts a lump in my throat.

"She died. Overnight. Hemorrhage." Frank supplies when he senses I'm having trouble answering. "The hospital hasn't been able to contact any next of kin. So until the baby is confirmed to be Cal's, we have to wait out here."

"Who was she?"

Shame floods my system as I shrug. My dad looks disappointed but is waiting for me to speak before he says anything. He's always been good at letting us plead our case before he gives his judgement.

"They won't tell me that either. I didn't know anything about a baby until a few hours ago."

Dad's expression softens. "You're going to be a great dad, Callahan. Whether that day is today or years from now."

I nod, holding back the tears threatening to spill. It's not that I mind crying. Honestly, I find it pretty cathartic. I just know there's going to be a lot more emotions playing out soon, and I need to keep it together for now. For my daughter. Something in my gut tells me she's mine, and I haven't even laid eyes on her yet.

"Mr. Griffin? The test results are back. Would you like to come meet your daughter?" the nurse I've been borderline yelling at for hours asks me with way more compassion than I deserve.

My dad squeezes my shoulder and leads me down the hall after the nurse. She leads us to a nursery with several babies sleeping soundly in their little bassinets.

"Have a seat in that chair, and I'll bring her over to you."

I nod at her instruction and sit where she told me to, too shocked and scared to form words. I feel my dad still standing by my side, his hand on my shoulder to steady me.

"Here's your perfect baby girl," she whispers before handing me my daughter. And she was right. The most perfect little girl I've ever seen is cradled in my arms.

"What's her name?" I whisper, scared to wake any of the babies in the room.

The nurse gives me a sad smile. "Her mom didn't give her a name yet."

"Do you know her mom's name?" Dad asks.

The nurse carefully pulls out my daughter's foot from

the blanket she's wrapped in. I consider tugging my daughter closer to me but realize how insane that seems. This woman is a nurse and has been caring for my daughter while I couldn't.

"Her name was Bailey Young." I realize she was reading it off the anklet around my daughter's leg.

My eyes go wide, and I gently remove the pink hat from my daughter's small head. "You have your mama's hair," I whisper, letting the tears finally fall and carefully touching the bright red hair on my baby's head.

"You remember her?" my dad asks, emotion thick in his voice.

"She worked sound for us on part of the last national tour. Bailey was fun to be around and didn't want a relationship any more than I did." I shrug, trying not to be angry that she kept this from me. There's no point in being angry with the dead. "I wish she told me," I whisper.

"It's okay to be angry," my dad says, reading my emotions on my face. "But you need to be grateful too. Bailey gave you a gift. This little girl is a gift."

I nod, unable to take my eyes off my daughter.

"We have bottles and formula we can send you home with. Diapers too. You'll need to get a car seat before you can take her home. I can also give you a list of suggestions for cribs and other baby essentials you can get when you have a chance," the nurse offers.

"The car seat should be here. Frank probably has it with him right now. I ordered it to be dropped off the moment I got here."

The nurse seems surprised but doesn't say anything. She

just hands me a folder with paperwork in it. My dad takes it and skims it over.

"You need to name her," he says, pulling out the paperwork to register the birth with the city.

"Cora," I say immediately.

"I like it, but how did you come up with that so fast?" Dad asks, smiling down at his granddaughter. I can see he's itching to hold her, but I can't give her up just yet.

"I was looking at names on my phone while I was waiting. I really liked Cora."

"Cora it is. Any middle name ideas?" he asks, filling out the paperwork for me.

"Cora Bailey Griffin," I say, and my little girl smiles up at me. From my hours of reading while in the waiting room, I know that it's probably just gas and not an actual smile, but I decide to ignore that information.

Once the paperwork is filed and the hospital officially discharges Cora, we're on our way home.

I was taking my daughter home.

Holy shit.

MY HEELS CLACK as they echo through the mostly empty halls of the radio station I've worked for since college. This is the last broadcast until we shut down for good. The station declared bankruptcy yesterday and sold off everything so quickly that my head is still spinning.

"Harlow! Wait up!"

I turn to see my best friend Jo running towards me. Her sneakers are nearly silent on the concrete floors. Her blonde hair is whipping in her face since she's running like she's being chased.

"I have an idea," she huffs, out of breath from sprinting to me. "Best one I've ever had."

I raise an eyebrow, unconvinced. She's had multiple ideas since we found out about our impending unemployment and none of them have been great. She pitched us getting jobs at a circus just an hour ago. She thinks my red hair means I won't need a wig to be a clown, making the initial investment into our new career cheaper.

"Hear me out before you say no," she pleads, still trying to catch her breath.

"Only if it's actually in our skill set this time. Otherwise, I need to finish cleaning out my office."

"Actually, this one is to your skill set, not mine. But it could be exactly what we need for our goals." The smile Jo gives me is part smug and part wicked. She waves her phone in front of my face, which kind of makes me want to smack it out of her hand, but I refrain.

I roll my eyes and put my hand out for her phone. Reading over the job posting, I can't help worrying that Jo has hit her head or something.

"This is a nanny position."

"I know!" she says with excitement. I scrunch my brows, completely confused. I thought our goal was to have a true crime podcast. No diaper changes involved.

"How is this my skill set?" I ask slowly, trying to gauge her mental state.

"You babysat throughout high school and college."

I nod slowly, hoping she'll elaborate.

"Plus, I just talked to your dad," she smiles. That evil glint in her eyes is what tips me off. She's messing with me.

"Oh? And what did my dad have to say about this nanny position?" I ask, going along with whatever this is.

"That this position is actually for the daughter of Callahan Griffin." The triumphant smirk on her face when she sees the shock on mine is annoying as hell.

"I have a lot of questions. First, how did you get my dad to tell you that? He never gossips with me. Second, since when does Cal have a daughter?"

"Harrison and I are besties." I roll my eyes, and she

ignores me. "I actually texted him to see if I could take over your position as his assistant since you said you didn't want to work for your dad again. He sent me job listings in the area instead."

I laugh. My dad isn't great at saying no to me or to Jo, so he redirects. "And that led to him divulging information?"

"Well, not exactly. He said the nanny position was for a new client of his. And I know his new client is Shattered Halo. You told me you've seen Belle and Willa recently and since you didn't mention either being pregnant, I ruled them out. Maverick has been photographed in bars with different women, so probably not him. Callahan, on the other hand, hasn't been spotted in months. So by process of elimination, it's his child."

I blink at her. Sometimes I forget how smart she is when she acts like a fool most days on purpose. Her logic is sound. I helped my dad over the winter while the show was on hiatus and met with both Belle and Willa a few times to go over Ezra's case. Cal becoming a father never came up, but why would it?

"You can use your connection to them to get the job and then find out more about Ezra. You know your dad won't give up anything. If we can break the case and figure out what happened to him before it hits mainstream media . . . I mean, that would be huge, Harlow. It would send our podcast straight to number one."

I graduated with Willa and Belle, but we weren't exactly friends. We just swam in different circles. We're friendly enough when we come in contact now, but I'm not sure that's enough to get me a job as a nanny. Especially considering I don't really know Cal at all.

"We haven't even named the podcast or put out any episodes yet," I lamely point out. It's a good idea. I need a job, and it would put me directly in contact with people who have information on one of the biggest cases to ever hit my hometown. It's even bigger now with how famous Shattered Halo has become. The twin brother of the lead guitarist going missing right before their big break was and still is a huge story. Ezra was declared dead a lot faster than most in the true crime community would consider being a fair amount of time. There are so many conspiracy theories about how that happened or where Ezra really is right now.

"Harlow. You know this is the best idea I've ever had," Jo pleads, folding her hands like she's begging me to agree to her plan.

I sigh and pinch the bridge of my nose. I know she's right. It's an opportunity we really can't pass up. "What do I need to do?"

Jo claps and jumps like she just won the lottery. I glare at her until she stops. The smile never drops from her face.

"I was thinking you could text Belle or Willa and see if you can get in that way. I bet it would be a quick way in."

I pull my phone out and pull up Willa's contact information. She gave it to me the first time I met with her and my dad. I don't have Belle's, so I'm hoping this will be good enough.

Hey Willa, this is Harlow Ray. This is kind of out of left field, but the radio station I work for just shut down, and I was wondering if you had heard about any job openings around you guys. My dad wasn't any help, and I don't really want to work for him again if I could avoid it.

I hit send, feeling slightly guilty for twisting the truth. It wasn't entirely a lie, but enough of one to hopefully get me an interview without seeming suspicious.

WILLA

Hi Harlow! So good to hear from you! I'm sorry to hear about your job. Is there any chance you have childcare experience?

I smile, knowing I got the in, but keeping my phone from Jo when she tries to look. I'm still annoyed by the way she explained this idea of hers.

I do! I babysat all through high school and college.

WILLA

Great! Can you come in for an interview tomorrow at 10am?

She sends an address that's about thirty minutes from my dad's office in Boston.

I'll be there! Can you give me more information? Did you have a baby? I don't babysit adults lol.

WILLA

No babies for me! And don't worry, no adult babysitting. I promise you'll get all the information if the interview goes well!

Sounds good. Thank you so much!

"I have an interview tomorrow at 10."

Jo squeals and hugs me tightly. "This is it, Harlow! We're about to have all our dreams come true."

I smile. She's right. This could be exactly what we need.

three

CAL

"THIS IS GETTING RIDICULOUS, CALLAHAN," my sister grumbles as she shuts the front door of my house. The latest candidate wasn't the right fit. Just like the previous forty weren't. "You need to find someone soon. We can't take Cora to the studio with us, and we need to record soon."

I roll my eyes. "That woman was at least eighty and kept talking to the plant behind you because she couldn't see us."

"Yeah, and what about all the other people we've interviewed? You've found something wrong with each one of them." My sister gives me a look like she's exhausted. And she probably is. Cora has been grumpy lately and not sleeping well at night, so Belle has been helping me overnight. Kai isn't too thrilled with me for stealing his girlfriend, even though she's my damn sister.

"I just want the best for Cora. I can't leave her with just anyone. Hell, I trust you more than I trust anyone, and I still get stressed when you watch her without me." I sigh and run my fingers through my hair. "Maybe I can get those

29

headphones you see on kids at car races that block out the noise and just strap her to me."

Belle slaps her hand to her face and groans. "Absolutely not. No. You know that won't work and even if it did, it won't long term."

"But —" My rebuttal is cut off by my front door opening and Willa stomping in.

"I have the solution and she should be here in . . ." Willa looks at her watch while I grumble about her letting herself in under my breath. "Seven minutes."

I glare at Willa, but she just flicks her lilac hair over her shoulder and sits next to my sister on the couch. Willa has helped just as much as Belle when it comes to Cora. So, as much as I want to complain and tease her, I keep my mouth shut.

The doorbell rings and Willa pops right up from the couch with a smile on her face. Now I'm suspicious. She's far too happy. Even Belle is giving her a confused look.

"Five minutes early!" Willa says, walking past me to answer the door. She looks over her shoulder and winks at me. Fucking winks. What the fuck? Willa and I argue like siblings. We don't do winks.

"Are we being pranked?" I whisper to my sister. Belle just shrugs. If I was confused before, now I'm terrified.

"I'm so happy you said yes to the interview!" Willa says to the red-haired bombshell she's leading into my home. The woman's hair is a deep red, not the more orange color you usually see, yet something tells me it's her natural color. Her body has curves in all the right places and the moment her green eyes lock on mine, I'm done for. Something about her is familiar, but I couldn't have met her before. I would remember someone that looks like her. Fuck, she's beautiful.

"Cal!" Belle shouts. I swing my attention to my sister. She's trying to hide a smirk as she raises her eyebrow at me.

"What?"

"I asked if you remembered Harlow. She graduated with Willa and me," Belle says, apparently not for the first time. I look over to find Willa looking smug, like she knew exactly what my reaction to this woman would be.

The beauty standing in front of me, Harlow, is looking at me with a strange expression, almost disappointed. Have I met her? No. That's not possible. She saves me from an awkward question by shaking her head and forcing a smile.

"He wouldn't remember me. We've never met."

I hold out my hand to her, and she takes it. Her hand is much smaller than mine and so damn soft. "Callahan Griffin," I say, introducing myself. Even though I'm sure she knows who I am if she knows my sister.

"Harlow Ray."

My eyebrows shoot up, recognizing the last name. "Harrison's daughter?"

This time, her smile is genuine. "Yup!"

Harrison has been working on Ezra's case with us. He's also the former sheriff who was on the case when Ezra initially went missing. He quit when it was clear Ezra's case was being mishandled. Kai and Belle recently hired him to hopefully find out what really happened. None of that explains why his daughter is currently in my living room.

Willa clears her throat and looks between Harlow and me. I follow her gaze and realize I still have Harlow's hand in mine. I drop it quickly and let out an awkward laugh.

"So, uh, what can I do for you, Harlow?" I ask, running my hand through my hair, probably making it look messier than it already was.

Harlow cocks her head to the side and studies me. "Hire me," she says with a confident smile.

I'm so distracted by how her smile lights up her beautiful face that it takes a moment to process her words. "Hire you?"

"As the nanny, Callahan," Belle says, bumping my shoulder as she comes to stand next to me.

"You want to be my nanny?"

"Well, I was kind of hoping to be your daughter's nanny. I'm not really qualified to watch adults," Harlow teases.

Willa snickers, not even trying to hide her amusement.

"Do you have childcare experience?" Belle asks. Thank fuck for my sister. Since I can't seem to get my brain to function right now, I need someone to ask the important questions.

"I do!" Harlow says, happily handing over a sheet of paper. I take it and look down. It's her resume. I read through it three times, fully aware that the silence is awkward, but when it comes to Cora, I'm not willing to just hire anyone. Even if that person took my breath and every brain cell away the moment I laid eyes on her.

Belle snatches the paper from my hand and starts asking the standard questions she's asked everyone that's come to interview. I hang on to every word Harlow says. She babysat through high school, was a nanny in college. She took a child growth and development class one summer between semesters. The only reason she's unemployed is because the radio station she was working for just shut down.

Everything she says seems genuine and impressive. Which immediately makes me wary. It shouldn't. She's done nothing to earn my distrust, but when you're in the spotlight like I am, it's hard to trust anyone.

"What's your plan?" I blurt. Three sets of eyes turn to me. Three sets of eyebrows are scrunched in confusion. This is why I let Belle ask the questions.

"I mean, what's your plan career wise? You can't be planning to be a nanny forever if you were a producer on a radio talk show, right? Are you going to get a job in a week and leave?" I ask.

Harlow blows out a breath and shifts on her feet. I haven't even offered to let her sit. I'm such an asshole.

"Honestly?" she asks, and I nod. "I'm not sure. I think I need a break from all that. I loved my job, but it took up all my time, and not in a good way. I ate breakfast, lunch, and dinner at my desk. I took my phone to the bathroom so I could respond to emails as I peed. I would get calls in the middle of the night from the executive producer about the latest celebrity bullshit that broke and needed to be added to the morning show."

"We totally get that," Willa says. "Our last label worked us to the point of burnout and then told us to keep going."

"I need something different. I love working with kids. Do I think I'll be here until your daughter turns eighteen? No, but I think I can at least help you for now. I want to spend time with my dad until I figure out my next step."

That could be anywhere from a month to several years. I chew the inside of my lip, thinking. I trust Harrison, which makes me want to trust Harlow. Just from instinct alone, I don't feel like she's someone that would sell stories to the media to make a few bucks. But that's only half of it. She needs to be good with Cora too. What if Cora loves her, and she doesn't stay? Shit, this is hard. As if she knows I'm thinking about her, Cora's cries echo loudly through the baby monitor.

"The star of the show is awake from her nap," Belle jokes, making her way up the stairs to get my daughter.

I look over at Willa. Her expression is soft and understanding. I know there must be a look of panic on my face because I can feel how rapidly my heart is beating against my chest. I haven't let anyone that's interviewed even lay eyes on Cora, and now Harlow is about to meet her. Belle didn't ask, but I know she wouldn't be getting Cora if she didn't feel comfortable with Harlow. Next to me, my sister is the most protective of my daughter.

Harlow must read my expression. "I can leave if you want."

My eyes flick to hers, and I can see the indecision there. She wants to stay, probably needs the job, but she doesn't want to make me uncomfortable. And that alone is what has me shaking my head.

"No. Stay and meet her. She just hasn't met anyone outside of family, and it makes me nervous," I admit. Harlow smiles softly and nods. "Willa is family," I add, even though she didn't ask. "Maverick and Kai too."

Harlow laughs and fuck does that laugh do something to me.

"Family isn't always blood. I get it."

I look over at Willa to see her smiling smugly. I roll my eyes and flip her off, which just makes both women start laughing at me. Great. There's two of them now.

"Cal?"

I look over my shoulder to see my sister holding Cora. I immediately take my girl into my arms and snuggle her, smelling that baby smell you always hear people talking about. It's a real thing, like a fucking drug I need a hit of. It calms me, just like holding her close so I know she's okay does.

"Hi baby girl. How was your nap?" I whisper softly into her hair. Cora just makes a bubbly gurgle and snuggles into my neck. "There's someone Daddy wants you to meet." Cora lifts her head and manages to hold it for a few seconds before crashing back down onto my shoulder. My girl is practically made of Jell-O when she first wakes up. She's almost six months old now and it feels like time is just flying by.

"Hi sweet girl. My name is Harlow." I can hear Harlow's voice from behind me where she moved so she could see Cora, but I swear I can feel her presence. Like I'd know where she was no matter where she stood in the room. "Can I?" I hold Cora tighter for a moment and then let out a slow breath. I hand her over to Harlow with less reluctance than I thought I would have.

Cora immediately grabs Harlow's curls and drools on her shirt.

"Shit," I mutter, trying to pry tiny baby hands off Harlow's hair. Babies are superhuman levels of strong, and I'm not having a ton of success. Harlow just laughs and shrugs me off.

"Don't worry about it. Babies love to grab, and my hair was right there for the taking. Wasn't it sweet girl?" Harlow coos, and Cora smiles a gummy smile at her. My girl is smiling, and my heart fucking shatters.

Belle hands Harlow a bottle and a burp cloth. "Want to come sit with her on the couch so we can fill you in on the details of the job?"

Harlow nods and follows my sister. I look at Willa, who is smiling a genuine smile. She loves Cora, too, so I know seeing that smile made her happy too.

I watch as Harlow sits and starts feeding Cora, a small smile playing on my lips at the sight. But only for a moment. Then shock hits me, and I freeze in place. My baby girl has bright red hair, and it looks like it's a shade or two lighter than Harlow's. They look like mother and daughter sitting there right now. Where Harlow's eyes are green, Cora's seem to be turning the same shade of brown as mine. But other than that, they look so similar. It's like a punch to the gut, and I can't move or look away.

"We'll be right back!" Willa yells and grabs me by the elbow, dragging me to the kitchen. "What the hell happened?" she whispers.

"Cora and Harlow, they look . . ." I can't even get the damn words out.

"Yeah, I noticed that too. Is that going to be a problem?"

I bite my lip and think about it. "No," I say eventually. "It just threw me. Reminded me that Cora doesn't have a mom. That she'll never know Bailey."

Willa nods. She knows how broken up I was about Cora's mom. I was sad Bailey died, but I was destroyed knowing Cora would have to grow up without her.

"Cora has so many people that love her. So many people to support her as she grows. Maybe Harlow can be one of those people too," Willa says. "Just don't fuck her and ruin everything."

"I'm not going to fuck the nanny! Jesus, Willa." I make sure to sound offended even though I definitely wanted to fuck the nanny the minute I saw her. I can't though. I won't risk ruining things for Cora by having someone to look out for her while I'm at the studio.

Willa just snorts and makes her way back to the living room. I follow to see Belle and Harlow laughing at something as Harlow burps Cora. She's a natural. There's no doubt about that.

"What have you explained?" I ask Belle, taking a seat in the chair across from the couch.

"Just what our recording schedule will probably look like, and that Dad is here on the weekends, so she'll have those to herself."

"It's a live-in position. I need help at night. To be completely honest, that's been the worst for me. Cora has never been great at sleeping and now that she's getting older, it seems to be getting worse. I think she might be getting a tooth." I leave off that I've been in tears with her every night the past two weeks.

Harlow smiles down at Cora. "Does your mouth hurt, sweet girl? I bet it does. Don't worry. We can do all the snuggles until it feels better. And then, guess what? Once you have all your big girl teeth, you can start having yummy food!" Cora gives her that big gummy smile again and makes a cute noise that sounds like agreement. My heart can barely handle watching them.

"Since you'll probably be stuck with a lot of night shifts until that tooth comes in, my dad is going to work remotely so he can be here to help during the day. He lives close by, but not in this neighborhood. He'll come over in the morning or whenever you need him. You guys can work that out yourselves. He's super flexible and loves having Cora, so don't ever feel like you're bothering him if you need his help or want a day off," Belle explains. Apparently, it's a forgone conclusion that I'm hiring Harlow. I mean, I am, but it would be nice if they checked with me first.

Belle explains the salary and then leads Harlow on a tour of my house, pointing out where everything and anything she would need is. I follow along and watch them. Cora's tiny hand is holding on tightly to Harlow's finger, and her wide brown eyes are staring at the beautiful woman with something that looks like admiration.

"When can you start?" I ask the moment the tour is over and we're back in the living room. Belle's eyebrows raise in surprise. I'm sure she thought I was going to come up with an excuse for why Harlow wouldn't work out at the last minute, and I bet I could if I wanted to. But with the way my little girl is looking at Harlow right now, I know she's picked her nanny for me.

"Tomorrow? My lease on my apartment was up last week, and I moved in with my dad temporarily. As much as I love him, I don't love moving back home."

"Tomorrow it is. I need to run a background check, but that will be back by the time you'd be alone with Cora. We can help you move anything you want into one of the guest rooms later this week, and then you can shadow me for the day. That way you can learn Cora's routine," I say, reaching to take my baby girl back into my arms. As much as I love the way Cora took to Harlow, I still want her with me. It feels like my heart is outside of my body, and I have trouble being away from her for more than a few minutes. Willa keeps making fun of me for it, but I won't apologize. Especially if I'll soon have to be away from her for hours at a time.

Cora snuggles right into my neck, which is her favorite spot, and my heart slows back down to a normal rhythm.

"What time does your day start?" Harlow asks.

"Usually around six in the morning. Sometimes she lets me sleep until seven, but not recently. You don't have to be here that early on your first day, though."

"No. I'd like to learn her full routine, and I can't do that if I miss some of it."

I nod. "I'll call down to Gary at the gate and have him put your name on the list, so you're always allowed in. I'll have a key made for you by tomorrow and a credit card by the end of the week to put any expenses related to Cora on. If you have any questions before the morning, you can always shoot any of us a text."

"You will have to sign an NDA," Willa adds. "We can't afford to trust anyone with how public our lives tend to be. Please don't take it personally."

Harlow nods but looks pale. "No, I get it. You don't want the press getting their noses in your lives, especially with a child involved. And what better way than to pay off the nanny to get all the juicy gossip?"

Belle laughs. "I forgot you still had to deal with all that in radio. It's usually print we have to worry about, but I suppose gossip travels via all channels."

"It's the stations that play all the trendy stuff you really have to worry about. Those DJs love to break a celebrity story. They're bigger gossips than old ladies in hair salons." Harlow is still pale, even though she seems to understand better than most people what our lives are like.

I reach out with the hand that isn't holding my daughter and grab hers. I don't even think about it. It's like some inner part of me needs to comfort her. "You're safe and out of the spotlight here. The community is gated as you know, and I've kept the knowledge of Cora's existence out of the media so far." Harlow squeezes my hand as she listens. "I understand if you've changed your mind and don't want to work for someone in the spotlight."

Harlow smiles before dropping my hand. I instantly feel the loss of her warm skin against mine. "I didn't change my mind. I just panicked for a minute. I don't want to accidentally tell my dad or my best friend something when I'm just talking to them about my day."

I nod at her explanation. "The NDA is to protect Cora. Your dad is going to know you're working for me. Especially since he's working with us on Ezra's case, which I'm sure you know. He's also signed an NDA because of that. I don't know about your friend, though. We can talk about that more."

"Do you have anyone that needs an assistant?" she asks with a laugh, like she's joking.

Willa raises her eyebrows. "Actually, yeah. Can you send me her info? Is she actually qualified, or was that a joke?"

"She worked with me at the station. She was the vice president's personal assistant," Harlow says with a small shrug. "I was just joking, but if you actually know someone, I'm sure she would really appreciate it."

Harlow agrees to send Willa her friend's information

and then reminds me that she'll be here at six the next morning before taking her leave.

"Holy shit, you hired a nanny," Belle says with a giant smile on her face. She pats my arm before heading for the door. "I have to get going. Kai bought a car seat for Cora to put in his car and wants to take it to the fire station to have it installed properly." She rolls her eyes as she leaves, but I smile. It's nice having friends that are as insane about your daughter's safety as you are.

"You're welcome," Willa singsongs as she follows Belle out.

I roll my eyes are her back and snuggle my daughter. All I can do is hope I made the right choice for her.

four

HARLOW

"EARTH TO HARLOW," Jo says, waving her hand in front of my face.

"Sorry," I mutter.

"Where did you go? All I asked was how the interview went."

"Good. I start tomorrow."

"Then why do you look like someone kicked your puppy?" she asks, moving closer to me where we sit on my childhood bed. She's currently staying in my dad's guest room while we sort through our lives. It made the most sense since her parents are in New Mexico, and we didn't want to be apart.

It's weird being in this bedroom. My dad didn't move here until I was in college, but he took all the stuff from my room and set it up here. I think he wanted me to feel at home when I came to visit. Which I appreciate more now that I've been here for a few weeks. I kind of wish I didn't have a twin bed, though.

I sigh and flop backwards. "I have to sign an NDA. I don't

know how I'm supposed to dig for information on Ezra if I can't even share it. What's the point?"

"I think they'd be more than forgiving if we figure out what happened to him," Jo points out.

"Sure, but not publicly and before they even know."

Jo shrugs. "So we don't do it that way. We tell them first and then go public."

"And you think they're all going to be fine with that?"

"Maybe. Maybe not, but they're in the public eye. Ezra's case is huge, not only in true crime circles but also in the music industry. It's going to be out there and it's going to be picked apart. You can convince them that us breaking the story will be the best course of action."

"That's if we're even able to do that. There hasn't been any progress in years. My dad is on the case now and was the lead on it from the start and even he doesn't know what happened. How the hell am I supposed to figure it out?" I ask, seriously questioning this genius plan of ours for the first time.

Jo shrugs again, and I have the urge to pinch her. I don't because I'm that good of a friend. "They could easily say something in passing that they don't even realize will help the case. Just pay attention."

She makes it sound so simple. I sigh and stare at the ceiling.

"What else? There's something else going on."

"I just feel like I'm somehow taking advantage of a five-month-old. That's really fucked up, Jo," I admit.

"Maybe you can take advantage of her really hot and famous daddy," she says and makes a bow-chica-wow-wow sound. I don't hold back my pinch this time, and she yelps.

"He's the biggest player and always has been," I mutter, a bitterness to my tone I know she doesn't miss.

"If you don't like him, then there's no conflict. We can deal with the NDA when and if we need to."

Jo's phone chimes, and she looks down at it with a frown. "Why do I have an email asking me to interview to be Maverick Wolfe's personal assistant? Is this fake?"

"Oh shit. I gave Willa your information and told her you were looking for an assistant position. I didn't know who it was for," I say, jumping up from my bed so fast I got dizzy.

"Harlow! Now we can both spy!" she yells and does a weird little jig.

"Can you stop phrasing it like that? You're making me feel guilty, and I haven't even done anything yet," I say, glaring at her with my hands on my hips so she knows I'm serious. "Plus, you don't even know if you'll get the job."

Jo snorts. "Of course I'll get the job. I'm the best."

I roll my eyes at her but laugh. She's probably right.

But I can't help that lingering feeling of guilt that's eating away at the back of my mind.

<hr>

I'm on my second coffee of the day already as I pull into Cal's driveway. I'm used to early mornings, but I didn't get much sleep last night. A sudden case of nervousness kept me awake all night. I guess it's good practice for being up with a teething baby.

As I'm taking in the large home and its beautiful yard, the front door swings open. Cal is standing there without a shirt, gray sweatpants hanging low on his hips. I'd spend more time taking in his abs and the light dusting of dark chest hair if it wasn't for the panicked look on his face.

I quickly get out of my car and head towards him.

"Help," he says before running back into the house.

I run after him, thinking the absolute worst. I'm holding my breath as I take in a red-faced and screaming Cora. Cal picks her up from the portable crib quickly, patting her back and trying to comfort her.

"What do I do? She didn't sleep at all last night. She's so angry, and her face is red, and I think she has a fever, but putting things up her butt seems wrong, but her face is hot, but that could be because of the screaming, and I read somewhere that a fever could be from the teething, but other places said that was a myth and —" I hold up my hand to stop him.

"Start from the top. She hasn't slept?" I ask. He shakes his head. "When did she last eat?"

"I can only get her to eat maybe an ounce at a time, and she just threw up the last bottle." His eyes are wide with complete panic. "I was going to call Belle or Willa, but honestly, they know about as much about babies as I do. My dad is out of town on a business trip until tomorrow." He tries bouncing with Cora to calm her, but I reach out to stop him. If she threw up, bouncing isn't going to help. "What do I do?" Cal's eyes are pleading. He's terrified.

I gently take Cora into my arms, a little surprised he lets me. "It's okay, sweet girl. Let's figure this out." I ask him a few more questions, not really liking the answers. No wet diapers since last night. Can't lay her down, and she only really relaxes while she's on his shoulder.

"I'm not a doctor, but I think she has an ear infection. I'll take her temp while you call her doctor." I watch all the color drain from Cal's face, but he nods. The best way to take a baby's temperature is rectally. So I get his reaction. He'll need to get over it, though.

I head up to the nursery and dig around the drawers until I find the thermometer. Once I get her temp, which she was very unhappy about me taking, I bring her back down to her dad. "102.6," I tell him, and he relays that to the doctor he's on the phone with.

"They can take her at eight when they open but said to go to the hospital if she gets worse," he tells me once he ends the call. I check my watch and see it's a little after six.

"I'm going to try to get her to slowly drink her formula. Can you get her stuff ready so we can leave when we need to?" I left out the part where I meant leave for the hospital if we need to, but I know it's at the back of his mind, and I don't need to send him over the edge by mentioning it.

I manage to get Cora to keep down about two ounces in the ninety minutes I spent feeding her slowly. Cal stays next to me the entire time, leg bouncing as he watches his daughter.

"You're coming with us, right?" he asks while I put Cora in her seat. The little girl is not happy, and she's screaming at the top of her lungs to let us know. If I'm right and her ears hurt, reclining like this will make the pain worse, but there's nothing I can do about it.

"I can if you want me to."

"Please," he says, his hand grabbing mine. I squeeze his hand in return, it's clear he needs the support if he's seeking it out in someone who's practically a stranger.

"Let's go." I grab the diaper bag that Cal put by the door

as he grabs Cora in her car seat. None of the panic has left his eyes. I grab his arm and squeeze lightly as we make our way to his car. He gives me a small smile.

Cora screams the entire drive to the doctor, and I can tell Cal is about to lose it. He's running on no sleep and one hundred percent panic. The moment he parks the car, I get out and take Cora from her seat, hoping having her in my arms in a more upright position will help her feel a little better.

"Go check her in. I'll meet you in there," I tell him as I rub Cora's back and tell her she's going to be okay. Cal nods and runs into the building.

I CLOSE the door to the nursery as quietly as I can. After the first dose of antibiotics and a little bit of infant Tylenol, Cora finally fell asleep. Harlow was right about her having an ear infection. I know I would've ended up in the Emergency Room with Cora and absolutely freaking the fuck out if it wasn't for Harlow.

"She went down?"

I nod at Harlow as I enter the kitchen where she's sitting on a stool at the island. "Coffee?" I ask as I grab mugs from the cabinet.

"Please."

"Eventful first day." I try to joke, but it falls flat. Both the doctor and Harlow have reassured me that Cora wasn't minutes from death, and I need to stop feeling guilty, but I can't. I'm her dad, and I panicked and did nothing for her. Harlow had barely put her car in park before she fixed everything. I'm not sure I can even drink the coffee I'm making with the way the guilt, frustration, and annoyance are swirling around in my gut.

"Cal?" Harlow's voice breaks through the war in my mind.

"Huh?"

"I was wondering if I could ask you some questions before I officially start. Seems like you zoned out there for a minute." There's a hesitant smile on her face. Like she's worried speaking too loudly or gesturing too quickly will set me off. I probably traumatized her from how anxious I've been all morning. The noble thing to do would be to let her back out of this job, but I can't. I've trusted no one else out of my immediate circle with Cora, and even though I don't know Harlow all that well, I already feel like I can trust her.

"Sure," I say, sliding the hot coffee in front of her. "I have milk and sugar if you want."

"Both please."

Once she gets her coffee to how she likes it, which looks less like coffee and more like tan milk, I lean across the island and wait for her to start her questioning.

"I read through everything Willa sent over. She said that no one knows about Cora, and you're trying to keep it that way for as long as you can." She bites her bottom lip, like whatever she's about to say next is making her nervous.

"That's not a question," I point out, smiling into my coffee. Something about this woman puts me at ease.

"Cora's mom. Is she in the picture? Do I need to worry about her showing up looking for her? Or your mom? You mentioned your dad being around a lot but didn't mention her. Am I confined to the house because of that? Like if I wanted to take Cora shopping with me or something, can I do that? My dad obviously must know about her, right? Or can I not talk to him either? What about Jo? She's interviewing with Willa and Maverick today. She knows about Cora. Well, kind of. She read over Willa's texts with me before I interviewed." All her questions come out sounding like one big anxiety induced sentence. So I hold up my hand to stop her.

"That was a lot of questions at once, Harlow." I chuckle as I watch the pale skin on her face and chest turn a bright red.

"Sorry. I just really don't want to have blown this opportunity before it's even started," she says quietly.

I stand up straight and have to consciously make an effort to stop my jaw from dropping. Making my way around the island to take the stool next to her, I make sure she's looking at me before I speak.

"Harlow, the only thing you've done is cement your position. You knew exactly what to do. I'm Cora's dad and all I managed to do is scream and cry right along with her."

Harlow snorts, and that causes a smile to break out on my face for the first time today. I try to answer her questions the best I can. "Cora's mom died after giving birth to her. My dad is very involved in her life and the best Papa to Cora. My mom, on the other hand, let's just say she is unaware I have a child, and I would like it to stay that way for as long as I can." Harlow nods along, paying close attention to every word. "You're not a prisoner here. If you need to take Cora to the store or wherever you need to go, I trust you to do that. Just don't go shouting 'this is the daughter of Callahan Griffin, lead singer of Shattered Halo' while you're out."

Harlow laughs, and it's the most perfect sound I've heard. "That's fair enough. What about my dad and Jo knowing?"

"Your dad is trying to see if Bailey, Cora's mom, has any family. So he's fully aware of her. As for Jo, if she's as good as you say she is, she'll be working with the band and probably you in part, so she's going to know anyway." I scratch at the stubble on my jaw and sigh. "I know how it sounds. I don't want Cora to be a secret, but I'm trying to give her a good childhood. One as close to normal as I can. I can't do that if the media makes it their job to follow her entire life."

I watch Harlow's shoulders visibly relax and a small smile bloom on her face. "You're a good dad, Cal. I know this morning has you doubting it, but you're going to great lengths to allow your child to be a child and there's a lot to be said about that."

Her words go straight to my heart, and I feel it crack. I've spent most of my life keeping women away from me emotionally. I saw what my mom did to my dad. He loved her with everything he had, and she used him for his paycheck and his ability to give her things.

I'll have to try harder to keep Harlow out if she can get to me that easily. It's barely her first day, and she's already seen what I keep under my carefully crafted mask. Taking a deep breath, I slip that mask back into place. Harlow watches, and I can see the confusion on her face.

"You can take the rest of the day off. Hopefully, tomorrow will be closer to normal," I tell her, giving her a big goofy smile before leaving her in the kitchen.

six

HARLOW

THAT WAS WEIRD. Does Cal have more than one personality? I swear even the shade of his eyes changed.

Ok, maybe that's being a little dramatic, but it was strange.

I'm about to start my car when my phone rings. Willa's name comes up.

"Hey, Willa."

"Hi Harlow! Jo is great! I was wondering if Cal would let you go long enough to meet us at Mav's. I wanted to go over some things with Jo that will overlap with your responsibilities." Willa's voice is cheerful. Jo must have really put on the charm at her interview.

"I can do that. He actually gave me the rest of the day off, and I was about to leave. Which house is Maverick's?" Their houses are all together in a row on the same street, but I don't remember what the order is.

"Two down. Mine is the one to the right of Cal's, Belle and Kai are to the left and Mav is right next to them."

"Got it. See you in thirty seconds."

Willa laughs as she ends the call.

Thirty-two seconds later, I'm parking my car next to Jo's. Maverick's house is in the same style as the rest of them, but he has a lot more plants than they all have combined.

"Hurry up, Harry! Willa is waiting for you to eat the brunch she ordered!" Jo yells from the door. I roll my eyes at the nickname. She only uses it when she's in a good mood, so I ignore my retort and follow her into the house.

It's decorated in dark greens and soft creams with touches of black and gold. It's actually really warm for how large and open the design is. I'm impressed. I didn't expect a single rock star to have a house that feels cozy. I catch Willa watching me and she smiles.

"Kai and Mav used to have black and white houses. They thought they were cool or something," she tells me, laughing like a sister who thinks her brothers are idiots.

"They were cool!" Maverick yells, coming to stand next to Willa and offering me his hand. I shake it and smile at him. It's nice to be starting a job surrounded by familiar faces. Even if we weren't close in school, we weren't enemies. "It's good to see you again, Harlow. Under better circumstances this time."

Willa raises an eyebrow and looks between us.

"The last time we saw each other was part of the search party for Ezra," I explain, lowering my eyes. Even though part of the reason I accepted this job was to get close enough to them to get more information, I have no intention of hurting them. If I can help it, anyway.

"She helped with almost all of them. She was in the group with me and Kai," Mav elaborates. The smile on his face is tight. We divided into three groups early on and just kept them the same to make it easy for everyone.

I watch as Willa reaches for Maverick's hand and squeezes it. He looks at her, shaking his head as he does, as if he's trying to shake something off. I guess losing a best friend would do that to someone.

"Anyway, I'm glad you could make it. Your dad should be here soon too." Willa turns and heads for the dark green velvet couch that Jo is sitting on.

"My dad?" I ask Maverick. He shrugs.

"Willa is very efficient when she wants to be," he says like that explains everything. I'm not used to being this confused, and it's taking a lot of willpower not to express my annoyance. Instead, I head to the couch and take the seat on the other side of Jo.

"So, what's going on?" I ask when no one offers any information.

"I got the job," Jo says, not looking up from her phone or seeming overly excited about it.

"You were a lot more enthusiastic when Harlow got here," Mav says, grinning at her.

"She's my best friend," Jo says, like that's an explanation, and I guess for her, it is. To her, a job is a necessity, but friendship is a privilege.

"We'll be friends in no time, you'll see," Mav says, grinning even wider. Jo just snorts in response. Willa looks completely confused, and I know I do too. What the hell is happening between these two? They've known each other for like an hour at most.

I open my mouth to ask, curiosity getting the best of me, but the doorbell rings, cutting off my questions. Willa blinks quickly but gets up to get the door. I catch her glancing back a few times, her brows drawn so closely together it looks like she only has one.

My dad saunters in a moment later. His red hair is turning white and the wrinkles at the edges of his eyes are the only things showing his age. His expression is serious until he spots me. The hardness in the professional gaze he has perfected over the years softens, and he quickly scoops me into a hug.

"I didn't know you'd be here," he says before kissing the top of my head. "What are you doing here, Jo?" he asks as he spots her.

"I just got a job as the band's personal assistant," she explains before standing and wrapping my dad in a hug. Once she lets go, Mav holds his arms open for her to hug him next. She scrunches her nose like he smells bad and takes her seat. Mav just laughs.

Willa's eyes are as big as saucers as she watches him. Her mouth is hanging open. It takes her a moment to realize we're all staring at her and waiting for her to tell us what this impromptu meeting is about. She quickly snaps her mouth shut and clears her throat.

"To get everyone up to speed, Jo is the band's personal assistant, Harlow is Cora's nanny, and Harrison is our private investigator." We all nod. I told my dad about my new job last night since I can't help him with his admin stuff as much now. "You've all signed an NDA and since this is a rare instance where there's a father-daughter duo and a set of best friends, I thought it would be best to let you know that you can share any information between the three of you. It would be too hard to regulate otherwise."

"What do you guys get up to that you're so worried about?" Jo asks with a frown on her face.

"Honestly, not much," Mav says with a shrug.

"It's Cora. Cal is trying to keep the media from being aware of her for as long as he can. He wants her to have a normal childhood," I explain.

"Cora is most of it, but there are a few other things. Things Harrison is aware of that I'm sure we're not going to be able to keep a secret if you guys are here all the time," Willa says, looking at Mav with something like sympathy in her eyes.

"As you girls know, I'm looking into Ezra's disappearance. Some of the trails I'm following, well, they could be dangerous if anyone became aware." My dad has his serious face back on, and I can tell he means it. Something he's looking into is cause for concern.

"Uh, shouldn't Kai be here if we're talking about his brother's case?" I ask. He's been at all the other meetings my dad has had about Ezra. I know because I'm the one that scheduled them.

"Nope. Kai is aware. This isn't new information," Willa says with a shrug.

I look around the room. Jo is focused on my dad, waiting for whatever scrap of information he'll give. But Mav's playful spirit seems to have left the building and Willa is watching him closely. Interesting.

"Kai and Ezra's dad worked as a naval intelligence offi-cer. He fell off the grid soon after Ezra, but because he divorced his wife and liquidated his assets, everyone assumed he didn't want to be found. That he may have not been dealing with Ezra's disappearance well," my dad says, leaning forward to look between me and Jo.

"And what? Left to become a mountain man?" I scoff. The side of my dad's mouth twitches, and I know he wants to smile. He's one of the few people that have found my snark entertaining.

"He could have if he wanted to. He also had the skills to become a completely different person, and we would've never been able to find him."

Jo's eyes widen, but I keep from reacting because I know this isn't the information they all seem worried about. So I nod at my dad to continue and this time, he does smile. I'm his daughter through and through and he knows it. I got my curious mind from him, and he taught me how to read people.

"I believe that's what he did. I think he found Ezra and made sure neither of them would ever be found," my dad says, watching my reaction.

"And?" I ask, raising my brow. We played this game when I was a kid. My dad would start telling me about cases he made up, and I had to find the lie or get more information. I loved trying to guess who the bad guy was. It was like an interactive game of Clue.

My dad laughed, confusing everyone except Jo, who has seen us do this before. "There's a big player. I don't know who yet. All the records are sealed. If Ezra was just a missing person or a runaway, those records shouldn't be sealed. He wasn't underage, so it has to be something bigger. Even the judge who declared him dead has been scrubbed from the official records."

"So be careful and pay attention to my surroundings

because you don't know who the villain is, and I'm in the middle of it just by working for the people closest to Ezra."

"That's my girl," my dad says with a proud smile and then turns his attention to Jo. "I'm kicking over rocks and poking hornets' nests. So I need you to pay attention. Report any and every single thing you see that could help me. Someone is paying too close attention to you at the gas station? Tell me. You feel like you're being followed? Call immediately."

Jo nods, an almost scary determination in her eyes.

"This might be overstepping, but I care about Jo like she's another daughter. Harlow is moving into Callahan's and will be safe behind guarded gates and high-tech security systems. But what about Jo? She'll be more visible."

Jo frowns. "I'm not going to be in danger, Harrison."

"Maybe not, but whoever this is, they have power. A lot of power. I shouldn't be having this much trouble getting to these records," my dad says. I watch his hands and see a small twitch. My gaze moves to his face and see another twitch.

"What are you lying about?" I ask, not in the mood to try to get it out of him in private. It'll be easier to get the truth with more eyes on him.

His eyes meet mine, and I hold his stare, letting him know I'm not letting this go. He sighs and rubs his hands over his face.

"Someone knows I've been looking. They've been trying to hack into my system and erase what I have." I smirk. My dad is old school, anything that's on his computer is also in paper form in triplicate.

"And?" I ask again, knowing this isn't all.

He holds my stare again, probably regretting teaching me everything he knows. "There have been a few threatening notes in the mail."

"Dad!" I explain at the same time Mav leaps from his seat.

"I can't let you work on this case if it puts you in danger, Harrison," Maverick says, his eyes holding a secret terror that breaks my heart.

My dad just holds up his hands and shakes his head. "I'm doing this. Even if you fire me. This is the case that made me decide to resign as sheriff. It's the case that showed me how broken the system is. I need to solve this as much for myself as for you." The look in my dad's eyes as he says 'you' while looking at Mav is sad. Did this case hit Maverick hardest? I thought it would be Kai, but now I'm not so sure.

"I love Ezra. He's the love of my life, and I want to know what happened to him more than I want to take my next breath, but I won't let it cost you your life too," Maverick says, the determination in his eyes can be felt throughout the room.

I look at Jo, who manages to keep the shock off her face; I don't. I inhale sharply and try to stifle it with my hand. Unsuccessfully judging from the four sets of eyes now staring at me.

"Uh, that's a secret," Willa says, looking like she's having trouble deciding what to do after the bomb my dad dropped.

"NDA. Right," I mutter, embarrassed.

"I'm not embarrassed about my sexuality. I just

promised Ezra we would tell everyone about us together, and that's a promise I intend on keeping."

"You're photographed with a lot of women," Jo says, looking pretty skeptical. She has a point. All the guys are seen with different women constantly. At least until recently, anyway.

Mav just shrugs. "I'm attracted to both men and women. Ezra was the first man I was ever with, and he'll be the last. No matter how our story ends."

Jo watches him for a moment before nodding. She's just as good at reading people as I am. Whatever she saw in his expression has her backing down from commenting more.

Willa clears her throat. "Jo, if you want to stay in my guest room, you're welcome to it. I could use some company."

I watch Jo open her mouth, and I know she's about to refuse. I whip my hand out and over her mouth. "She would love to, Willa. Thank you." Jo glares at me, but nods before I remove my hand.

"What about you, Harrison? I have guest rooms you can use," Mav offers.

"Thank you, but I'll be fine," my dad says. I don't bother arguing with him. I'd have better luck convincing a tree it was a fish.

"You didn't cover *his* mouth," Jo mutters next to me. I ignore her.

"How do you know it's not Kai and Ezra's dad trying to stop you?" I ask. I know their dad called Kai and told him to stop looking. I was the one who transferred the notes on that meeting to my dad's computer system.

My dad shakes his head. "If this was Gavin Irons, there

would be no trace. Everything would just be gone. Whoever this is, they're sloppier, likely less experienced."

"Maybe you should be looking into anyone that hires interns or new graduates. You could probably narrow it down to government or maybe law enforcement. If they're going this aggressively after Ezra, he must have done or seen something, at least in my opinion."

"Maybe we should've hired you," a deep voice says, startling me. I turn to see Kai and Cal standing at the end of the couch. "Sorry, I didn't mean to scare you."

"It's ok. I get lost in my thoughts sometimes," I tell Kai.

"I just get lost," Cal says, laughing, but it doesn't reach his eyes.

"Where's Cora?" I ask him.

"Belle is at my house with her," he says, smiling like it's normal for him to be so happy.

What the hell? Does he have a twin too? Not that he was grumpy this morning, but I swear he was a different person. No one else seems to notice, so I'm just going to assume it was all the panic of the morning and not some weird dual personality.

"How is she feeling?" I ask him.

"What's wrong with my girl? Does she need me?" Willa asks, looking genuinely concerned.

"She's still asleep," Cal says, giving me a small smile before turning to Willa. "How come you never ask if I need you? I need a foot rub and homemade cookies and at least three consecutive hours of sleep."

Willa scoffs and rolls her eyes. "What are you two doing here, anyway?"

"We can't visit our favorite person?" Kai says with a smirk.

"Aww, I miss you too," Mav says.

"He meant Harrison," Cal says, laughing. He has dark circles under his eyes, and he needs to sleep badly, but I can see where he would want to get out of the house for a little.

"I was at Cal's with Belle when I saw Harrison's truck drive by. We would've been here sooner, but it took a lot of convincing to get Cal to leave Cora," Kai explains. Cal just shrugs.

"She has an ear infection. I didn't want her to wake up without me there," he says, almost embarrassed. Which I find strange considering how openly panicked he was just an hour ago.

"My girl! Is she in pain? Why didn't you call me? Does she need me?" Willa asks again, moving to the door like she's going to go check no matter what the answers are.

"She's fine, Willa. Harlow actually handled it better than I did. Got her to the doctor and picked her prescription up at the pharmacy all while I freaked out in the backseat," Cal admits. Everyone laughs at him, but I just want to give him a hug.

"So what's the meeting about?" Kai asks.

"Harrison is receiving pushback and threats," Mav says with a look at my dad that says he's not sorry for tattling.

Kai's eyes widen, but my dad speaks before he can. "I know the risk, and you won't stop me from taking it. With or without your money, I will be finding your brother. It's up to you if you want to help me or not."

Kai sighs, and I see his shoulders sag. It's been six years

since his brother went missing, and you can suddenly see the weight he carried because of it. "Understood."

My dad stands. "Come on, girls, let's get you all packed up and moved in. Today." My brows shoot up, and I glance at Cal. I wasn't supposed to move in yet.

"This is the safest place for you if your dad is being threatened. Plus, I could probably use your help with Cora overnight." Cal says.

"You guys go handle that. Jo has a list of responsibilities, and she can go over anything that overlaps with yours with you," Willa says, ushering us out the door.

"Holy shit, there's another person here," Cal says, causing everyone, except me, to laugh. I know he's trying to lighten the mood, but I think I'm in information overload. He notices and bumps my shoulder with his. "You don't have to move in today if you really don't want to." His voice is a whisper.

"No, I should. Plus, I want to help with Cora."

He nods. "I'm home for the rest of the day. Shoot me a text when you're on your way, and I'll get everyone to help move your stuff in."

"Thank you," I say softly, not sure what to make of him right now.

He opens my car door for me and shuts it once I fasten my seatbelt. I spend the drive back to my dad's, wondering how much of the world Callahan Griffin is balancing on his shoulders.

"I told you to let me know when you'd be back so I could help you," Cal says, grabbing my suitcase right out of my hand. He tries to get the bag I have slung over my shoulder, but I move out of his reach.

"This is all I have. I moved everything into storage when I gave up my apartment."

Cal nods and tries to grab my bag again, but I'm faster. He rolls his eyes and mutters something about being surrounded by stubborn women.

"Come on. I'll show you to your room and get you set up with the security system."

The room he leads me to is bigger than my old apartment. It's beautiful. The walls are a soft mauve, and the floors are a light gray. There's a king-sized bed covered with a white comforter and a bunch of cute throw pillows in shades of gray and pink. Off to the right of the bed is a small sitting area with an overstuffed gray couch and matching armchair. I look up and do a double take at the ceiling.

"Is there wallpaper on the ceiling?" I ask Cal. He looks up and shrugs.

"Yeah. That was Belle's idea. If you don't like it, I can always change it."

"No. You're not changing your house for staff," I say, staring at the floral wallpaper. It's white with flowers in a slightly darker shade than the walls. "I actually kind of love it."

I look over at Cal to see a genuine smile on his face. He gestures for me to follow him. "This room has an en suite bathroom," he says, showing me the bathroom that includes a large clawfoot tub. I'm definitely going to be using that a lot. He shows me the walk-in closet attached to the bathroom, which could fit a queen-sized bed. I don't know how I'm going to move out when the time comes. I'm already spoiled.

Cal stands in the doorway, his hands in the pockets of his jeans, rocking on his heels as he looks at me. I really look at him for the first time in the whirlwind of a day I've had. He really is handsome. He has dark hair and dark eyes that could easily make him seem cold and intimidating, but they don't. I thought he was handsome when I was in high school, but he's on a whole different level now. The muscles clearly defined under his shirt and the way his jeans hang low on his hips has me almost drooling.

I shake my head to dispel my thoughts. I can't have the hots for my boss. Not only do I need this job, but it would also jeopardize my future plans with Jo.

"Harlow?"

I swing my eyes up to Cal's and see him looking at me with a smirk, his tongue slowly running over his bottom lip.

Shit. I've been caught ogling him.

Perfect.

Great first day, Harlow.

"I asked if you wanted to relax before dinner. I'm ordering pizza since we've all had an eventful day," he repeats, the smirk still on his face, and I swear I see a twinkle in his eyes. At that moment, I remember this man is used to being checked out by women. Women much more attractive and successful than me. That thought is sobering, and the smile that almost crossed my face is lost.

"Yeah, that sounds good. Pizza is good." I break the eye contact when I see Cal's smile fall.

I make my way over to my suitcase. I need to keep my

hands busy because the urge I have to apologize to him for literally no reason is making me angry.

"Right. I'll let you know when the pizza is here," he says, and the confusion in his voice has the words 'I'm sorry' so close to the surface that I have to cough to tamp them down.

"Sounds good," I say instead.

The moment I hear the door click shut, I throw myself backwards onto the bed. Of course, it feels like a damn cloud. I let out a sigh and stare at the flowers adorning the ceiling. Cal has always had a personality that attracts people like flies to a flame. The type of personality I used to think was an act.

Or maybe it was safer for me to think it was an act than to acknowledge that he's genuine. I've only spent one day with him and between the way he is with his daughter and how much he clearly cares for his friends . . . Well, it's obvious that there's more to Callahan Griffin than I assumed.

Maybe that's why I keep having the urge to apologize to him. For assuming the worst when he hasn't done anything to deserve that. Being a man-whore isn't a crime.

I roll onto my stomach and groan into one of the fluffy pillows. It's going to be a lot harder to dig for more information on Ezra if I care about Cal.

I think back to the night Ezra went missing. I was with a group of girls I knew from school but wasn't really friends with, when Cal approached and immediately started flirting. My walls went up, and I went into defensive mode, using my sarcasm and sharp tongue to keep him out. I guess I could use the same strategy. I just need to be more subtle about it. I can't outright attack the man I work for, but I can't let him in either.

This is a job, and I need to remember that.

seven

CAL

"STOP LOOKING AT YOUR WATCH."

I glare at my sister. "It's not a crime to know what time it is."

"It should be a crime considering you just stopped in the middle of a song, *again,* to check your watch," Belle says with her hands on her hips.

"I need to make sure Harlow hasn't texted me! What if something happened to Cora, and I don't know about it because I'm over here singing about how much you love Kai? Which is a little weird, if I'm being honest."

"I didn't write this one specifically about Kai. It's more of a broad love song that people can relate to," Belle defends, but I catch her glancing over at Kai and smiling.

"Gross," I mutter.

"Let's break for lunch and get back to it in an hour," Jon's voice comes through over the speaker in the sound booth. He's been great as our manager, way better than the last one. He never yells at us for arguing with each other, although I bet he wants to.

I don't argue. Instead, I rush out of the booth and grab my phone to text Harlow.

How's Cora? Does she miss me? Do you guys need anything?

HARLOW

Who is this?

Hilarious.

HARLOW

I know. Thank you.

Harlow…

HARLOW

Cora is great. We just had lunch and now we're going to relax and watch Ms. Rachel until naptime.

I bite the inside of my lip. Do I know I'm being ridiculous? Yes. Harlow has been with Cora and me every day for the past two weeks. Cora adores her, and Harlow is a natural with her. It's just hard to be away from my daughter. She's the most important thing in my life.

Did you give her any solids? Food before one is just for fun. I read that. So you don't have to. She could choke or something. Maybe you should just stick to formula when I'm not there.

She had her six-month appointment yesterday, and the doctor said we can slowly introduce purees.

HARLOW

Cal, she's fine. I swear. She had her bottle
and some pureed peaches. She really liked
the peaches and there was zero choking.

A picture comes through next with Harlow smiling and Cora looking at her like she hung the moon. *Fuck.* My heart squeezes. My little girl really does love her nanny. And Harlow has done nothing but prove how qualified she is to take care of Cora. I need to stop hovering. Well, I'll try to stop hovering.

Give her a kiss for me and tell her Daddy
loves her.

HARLOW

Yes, Daddy.

Fucking hell. This woman is trying to kill me. If I realized how much sass she could fit into that small body, I would have reconsidered hiring her. Probably.

Harlow…

HARLOW

Would you prefer, sir? Yes, sir.

Sir? Daddy? Captain?

Oh! How about Sir Captain Daddy?

"Are you growling?"

I look up from my phone to find a smug-looking Willa standing next to a confused-looking Mav.

"Why did you talk me into hiring this woman? She's trying to drive me up a wall!"

Maverick snorts, catching on to what Willa was so smug about.

"That's why I love her so much. She's perfect for Cora, and she drives you crazy," Willa says with a huge grin on her face.

"You're kind of an evil genius, you know that?" Mav asks her.

Willa just keeps smiling as she takes Mav by the arm and leads him away.

> I'm not a captain. I'm the lead singer. If you're going for nicknames, at least get my job right.

HARLOW

> Sorry Vocal Daddy.

> Are you trying to get fired?

HARLOW

> Cora would never fire me.

> Cora doesn't make the rules.

HARLOW

> I disagree. She babbled at me earlier, and I'm pretty sure she was saying she wanted to play with her blocks. So we played with her blocks. Cora girl is the boss.

I laugh out loud. Harlow isn't wrong. The moment Cora started making noises that could be interpreted as anything at all, she became the boss.

HARLOW

> Shouldn't you be leading the singing instead of being a helicopter parent?

She sends a picture of Cora asleep in her crib. Probably to get me to relax and leave her alone. But she's annoyed me too much for me to let her off so easily.

> Shouldn't you be more respectful of your employer?

HARLOW

I'm sorry, Vocal Daddy. I'll do better.

> Harlow…

HARLOW

I'm going to go clean up a little. See you later, VD!

I groan and rub my hand down my face. I asked for that. I really did. I need to trust her, and she's not going to let me forget it.

I walk in my front door and hear the best and worst sounds in the world. The first thing that hits my ears is the belly laugh coming from my daughter, but that's immediately followed up by the most off-key rendition of "Wheels on the Bus" that I've ever heard.

Making my way into the kitchen, I see Harlow on her knees, holding Cora under her armpits as they dance along to Harlow's singing. Cora is smiling and laughing so hard it puts a smile on my face. I've been grumpy all day, and this was the best thing to come home to. It was my first full day away from Cora since I brought her home, and I definitely could have handled it better.

I stay in the doorway, watching. They haven't noticed me yet. My dad is at the stove cooking dinner and Harlow's back is to me. Cora has just recently started wanting to stand. She obviously can't do it herself yet, but she loves it when she can hold your hand and bounce. The sight of my happy daughter just proves how much I didn't need to worry.

Cora catches sight of me and screams "da!" It's not dada yet, but it's close enough for me.

"Hi baby girl," I say as I make my way over and scoop her into my arms. She snuggles into my neck, and I kiss the top of her head. "How was your day? I hope Harlow didn't hurt your ears with her singing."

Harlow scoffs and mutters, "Says the guy who sings the pitchiest version of Fortunate Son."

I freeze and look at her. Her eyes are wide, realizing I heard her. Then I smile. I haven't sung that song in years. Six years. And there's only one person that's ever insulted me over it.

"Firecracker," I say with a laugh. I watch as her cheeks turn the prettiest shade of pink. But she crosses her arms and stares me down, like she's readying herself for a fight.

"Vocal Daddy," she says with so much sass it makes me want to spank her.

Nope. Don't get turned on by thinking about spanking the nanny, Cal.

"Care to explain that one? Or should I not ask?" my dad says, looking at me with amusement in his eyes.

"Harlow was just trying to get herself fired earlier," I explain.

Harlow laughs and so does my dad. Even Cora giggles along with them.

"Traitor," I mutter to my daughter, who just smiles and grabs my cheeks with her pudgy little hands.

"Dinner will be ready in twenty minutes," my dad says, turning back to the stove.

"Today really did go well?" I ask Harlow. The look on her face that said she was ready to fight me once I realized I knew who she was softens.

"I promise, Cal. We had a great day." She squeezes my arm and rubs Cora's back before moving to help my dad with dinner.

I watch the two of them work in tandem, like they've been doing it for years. Neither of them seems to remember I'm even here, so I take Cora with me to play until dinner is done.

Hours later, when the dishes are clean and Cora is asleep, I can still feel the warmth of Harlow's palm on my skin.

"What are you watching?" I ask, making Harlow jump. I laugh. She's really easy to startle, and I've been doing it at every opportunity. If only to hear the cute noise she makes.

I take the seat directly next to her and steal some of her popcorn.

"Hey! Get your own!" she complains, hugging the giant bowl to her chest and trying to move it out of my reach. I just laugh and steal some more. "Cal!"

"I love when you yell my name, Firecracker," I tease. Her

face turns that shade of pink that I'm becoming so fond of. "Why didn't you tell me that we've met before?"

"Honestly?" she asks.

"Always."

"I didn't think it mattered or that you would remember. It wasn't exactly memorable. Especially considering the events of the rest of the night."

I grab another handful of popcorn and think it over. "Yeah, you're right. But you imprinted yourself in my brain in a way few others have been able to."

She snorts. "It's because I insulted you, isn't it?"

I laugh loudly. "You might be onto something with that."

"Did you come in here to steal my popcorn?" she huffs as I steal more of it.

"No. I came in here to watch tv with you," I admit. "But I have to tell you, this show looks strange."

Harlow laughs, and it's the best kind of song. "It's a reality show," she says, and I groan. "I know I know. It's so addicting, though."

"Explain it to me," I say around a mouthful of popcorn.

She glares at me and sighs. "It's called Senseless Love."

"Harsh."

Harlow laughs again, and I smile, watching the joy on her face. "They pair people up that are missing a sense."

"Like common sense?" I ask, knowing I'll get a glare and laughing when I'm rewarded with one.

"Like touch, taste, smell, sight, or hearing."

"Okay," I say, seeing the appeal. "So explain these two."

"The woman, her name is Hailey. She's been nose blind since she was a child. The man, his name is Jordan. He has all his senses, but he has a medical condition that gives him horrible halitosis."

I throw my head back and laugh. "So she can't smell his breath? That's actually genius."

"Exactly! Last season there was a deaf woman that was paired with a man who thought he could sing opera. Spoiler, he could not."

I'm laughing again. I laugh more with this woman than I do with anyone else. She brings out something in me that's been dormant for years.

"How many seasons are there?" I ask.

"Four," she answers, eyes squinting like she's trying to figure out a puzzle.

"What?"

"You're going to want to watch this with me now, aren't you?" she grumbles.

"Yes. And you better not watch it without me." She rolls her eyes, but smiles.

"Fine, but you're making the popcorn next week."

"Deal."

HARLOW

WATCHING Cal panic every morning before he leaves for the studio is getting exhausting and it's month two. I've already done this every morning for a month. I'm tired.

"You have everything you need, right? Diapers? Formula? What if she gets sick? Did I leave her pediatrician information?" He asks, pulling at his hair. It's sticking up all over the place from him pulling on it for the last half hour.

"Callahan!" I shout, getting his attention and making Cora giggle. He stops at the sound of my voice but smiles at Cora's. When I'm certain I have his attention, I continue. "We have more than enough of everything and even if we didn't, you gave me a credit card for that exact purpose."

"Right, but what if you need to leave —"

"Car seat is in my car that you took to the fire station to have checked."

"Her doctor —"

"Which I've been to. On my first day."

"Okay. Yeah. Right."

"Are you going to be like this every day? How long does

it take to record an album?" I ask, trying to make a joke, but I'm actually curious if this is how every morning will be going.

Cal plops down onto the couch, elbows on his knees, face in his hands and sighs.

I set Cora down in front of him with her blocks and take the seat next to him. Placing my hand on his thigh, I squeeze gently.

"What are you feeling?" I ask. He turns his head to look at me, and I almost gasp at the anguish there.

"Cora already doesn't have a mom and now I feel like I'm abandoning her too. Not that Bailey abandoned her. But I'm leaving her for a long time. I'm missing a lot of time with her. What if I miss her first word? Her first steps? Her first anything?" His gaze is pleading with me to give him answers.

"She may not have a mom, but she has a dad who would do absolutely anything for her, and that's so much more than a lot of people have. Plus, add the family you've created around her, and she's one lucky little girl." I smile softly when the corner of his mouth turns up slightly. "And if she tries to take her first step without you, I'll push her back down."

Cal fully laughs at that. I grab his hand, making sure he's still paying attention to me. And he is definitely paying attention. His gaze snaps to where our hands join, but he doesn't pull away. Instead, he wraps his fingers around my hand and squeezes.

"The only thing you can do as a parent is your best. Not every choice you make will be the right one. Not every piece of advice you give her will be helpful. You're going to fuck up. It's just how it is. But you're also going to do so many things right. You love that little girl, and you'd give your next breath to make her happy. You're a great dad, Cal."

"Thanks, Firecracker," he whispers, a small smile on his face. I wish I could take some of his pain away, but I don't think there's much that can take away the guilt parents feel. Especially single parents.

"How about this?" I say, coming up with a compromise. Cal raises an eyebrow. "What if Cora and I go to the studio for a little? I'll take her stroller with me. Jo and I can take her to walk around Faneuil Hall Marketplace when you break for lunch, and then I'll take her home at naptime."

"Really?" he asks, face brightening as a huge smile breaks out on his face. I just nod and laugh at his excitement.

"Do you want to come see Daddy at work, baby girl?" Cal asks Cora, scooping her up off the ground. She lets out an angry cry at first, but she soon catches onto Cal's excitement and starts squealing with happiness. She's just happy because her dad is happy.

Their happiness is infectious and soon my face is hurting from how hard I'm smiling.

I have Cora strapped in a carrier on my chest as we watch the band get ready. I'm behind the glass with their manager, Jon, and the producer who introduced himself as Geoff. Jo is behind me on a red leather sofa, answering emails on her phone.

Cora's eyes are wide as she takes everything in. She

seems especially interested in all the switches and lights on the equipment that Geoff is sitting in front of. He keeps glancing over his shoulder at her like she can somehow reach twenty feet in front of her and mess with his settings. Which really only makes me want to mess with them myself.

"We're ready when you are," Cal's voice comes through the speaker. Cora screams with excitement when she hears her dad's voice. Everyone laughs at the sound. Well, everyone except Geoff who is now glaring.

Who glares at babies?

"It gets loud in here, and I need to be able to hear the music in order to adjust. Not really a great place to have a whiny baby," Geoff says to me.

I smile sweetly. "That's very true. I hope you can't hear yourself whine through those headphones," I say, pointing to the ones around his neck. He scoffs as his face turns an angry shade of red.

"I will not have this in my studio!" Geoff bellows, standing from his chair. Jon steps forward, like he's going to physically restrain the man.

"Not your studio," Jo says calmly, not even looking up from her phone.

"Excuse me?" Geoff bellows, again. Does the man have a normal tone of voice?

"Not. Your. Studio." Jo repeats, still not sparing him a glance.

"I'll have you know —" There he goes, bellowing some more.

"No. I'll have you know," Jo says, putting her phone down and standing slowly. Geoff's mouth is open, and he's so red he's almost purple. "This studio space is being rented by Nep-Tunes. You work for Nep-Tunes. An outside company owns this studio."

"While I'm here, it's my studio, and I do not want you or the bitch with the baby here!" Geoff is practically screaming now. I have my hands over Cora's ears. The window is one way, and I'm guessing no one can hear us because they're all in there, just tuning their instruments and talking.

Jo laughs. I know that laugh. This man is in trouble. "Do you know who owns Nep-Tunes?"

"Logan West," Geoff scoffs at her, like she's some stupid little girl.

Jo smiles wickedly. "Very good. Now do you know the name of the lead singer of Shattered Halo?"

"Is this a fucking joke?" Geoff says, face still purple, but at least his tone has calmed down.

"I've never been accused of being funny." Jo crosses her arms and waits.

"Callahan Griffin," Geoff bites out like it's painful.

"Good boy. Now, as I'm quite sure you do not know, Callahan Griffin is cousins with Amelia West. They grew up together. Very close."

"West?" Geoff pales now, and I can't help but find it interesting how quickly his face changes colors.

"Yes. Amelia West. Beloved wife of Logan West. Cousin to Callahan and Bellamy Griffin," Jo says, making a show of checking her nails and not bothering to look at Geoff any longer.

"I — I —" Geoff stutters. "Does the baby really need to be here?" he asks eventually, still kind of yelling, but now I'm wondering if that's how he always sounds.

"The baby? Yes. You? No," Jo says, flicking her hand in dismissal.

"You can't —"

"I very much can. And if anyone in that room finds out how you just spoke to an eight-month-old, you'd lose more than just your job."

Geoff's doing his best interpretation of a fish as he looks between Jo and Jon.

"You should probably leave," Jon says with a shrug.

Geoff storms out, slamming the door. Cora starts crying at the loud sound. She stayed quiet the entire time Geoff was yelling, but I think she just found his antics amusing. The door slamming was too much, though.

"It's okay, pretty girl. Let's watch your daddy sing," I tell her, swaying back and forth to calm her. Once she's settled, Jon gets on the mic, pressing a button that allows him to speak to the band.

"Geoff had to step out. Let's work on the third track and take it from there."

"You got it," Cal says, taking his place behind his mic stand.

"I'll turn the volume down, so it isn't blaring in here," Jon says, smiling at Cora when she blows raspberries at him.

"No need. Willa grabbed these when Cal told her Cora would be here," Jo says, handing over a small pair of head-phones. I raise an eyebrow in question and Jo just shrugs. "Apparently, Cal was being so difficult about hiring a nanny that everyone just assumed Cora would be at the studio every day with them."

I laugh as I position the headphones over Cora's ears. She seems confused and grabs at them, but I distract her with a teething cracker. I kiss the top of her head and watch Cal start singing.

I don't know what I was expecting. I've heard their songs, his voice. Of course, I have. They're the kids from our small hometown that got out and made it big. I also worked in radio and wouldn't have been able to escape them even if I wanted to.

Cal's voice travels throughout the room and straight to my vagina. Has his voice always been this sexy? It's deep and smooth, like a set of warm, strong arms surrounding you. It's not just his voice, though. It's his whole presence. The confidence he exudes as he stands there and belts out the upbeat song. The way he sways behind the mic, his eyes pinched shut as he feels the lyrics and the music.

A finger under my chin snaps my mouth shut from where it was apparently hanging open. I peel my gaze away from Cal long enough to find Jo standing next to me, amusement dancing in her eyes.

"They're pretty good, right?" Jo asks, laughter in her voice. I know she's making fun of me right now, but I'm too shocked to care.

I knew I was attracted to Cal. You'd have to be blind not to be. Probably deaf too, because his voice is sexy by itself.

But this is a whole new level of attraction. And I live with the man.

Fuck.

The music fades as my brain wars with my heart. Or vagina. Both, probably.

"I think that man just sang your panties off," Jo jokes. I give her a halfhearted glare and turn to Jon.

"How are you doing anything without a producer?" I ask him, trying to distract myself, but actually curious.

"Oh, I'm not. I mean, I know enough that I could probably be of some help, but the space is already rented. So I'm just going to make them practice until lunch," Jon says, shrugging.

"Can I say something to them?" I ask, trying to smile innocently, but Jon shakes his head and sighs.

"Today is a bust anyway, so have at it." He shows me which button to press.

"You were kind of pitchy, VD," I say into the mic. I watch Cal's eyes go wide and then narrow in annoyance.

"VD? What does that stand for?" Mav asks him. Cal's eyes go wide again, and I'm laughing so hard that Cora is bouncing in front of me. She's laughing along with me.

"That's my girl," I tell her as I continue to laugh at her dad's attempts at dodging the question.

"Ew, Cal. Do you have a venereal disease?" Belle asks, looking horrified, which just makes me laugh harder.

"Harlow!" Cal yells, stomping towards the door that will bring him into this room.

"Oh, shit!" I yelp as I try to duck behind Jo. Cora is squealing and giggling. She's loving every moment of this. I'm glad because it's probably the last she's going to get with me as her nanny, judging by the murderous expression on her dad's face.

Willa runs past him and slips into the room first. "You *have* to tell us what VD stands for!"

"She does not!" Cal yells. His expression softens significantly when he sees how funny both Cora and I are finding this. Probably more so Cora than me. "Are you having fun, baby girl?" he asks Cora, cupping her cheek gently. He takes her from the carrier and hands her to Belle. Then his gaze turns to me and where I expected to find fury, there's something else entirely. Something a lot closer to lust.

"Oops," I whisper.

"Yeah, oops," Cal says, pushing a stray hair behind my ear. He leans closer, his cheek against mine and his palm on my lower back. "You're asking for me to take you over my knee."

My breath hitches in my throat. My cheeks are on fire.

"Tell me, Firecracker. Do you enjoy making me angry? I can hear the way your breathing changed when you thought about my palm on your sweet ass. Is that what you want? You want me to spank you?" His breath tickles my ear, his hand hot against my back. Every nerve in my body is acutely aware of this man.

"N-no," I say, but it sounds like a question.

Cal chuckles and it's low and full of sex. "I bet if I slid my hand in your panties right now, I would find evidence that says otherwise." He backs up then and turns to his friends like he just didn't melt my brain.

I touch my face and feel how warm my cheeks are. I look up to see Cal's dark brown eyes locked on me, a victorious smirk on his face.

Fine.

He wants to play. I can play too.

"VD stands for Vocal Daddy. Cal loves it when I call him that," I announce to the room. Cal's mouth drops open, and Willa laughs loudly. Kai and Belle look just as shocked. Mav is smiling but doesn't seem surprised. I glare at Jo, and she shrugs. She definitely told him. Traitor.

Cal's face is now just as red as mine, and he's glaring at me. I walk up to him and get close enough for him to hear me as I whisper, "I'm not wearing any panties." I watch him long enough to see his eyes dilate and his jaw clench.

Turning, I grab Cora. "Jo and I are going to lunch. She fired Geoff."

There are a lot of questions, but Jo directs them to Jon, who seems less than enthusiastic about having to answer them.

"See you at home, Vocal Daddy!" I throw over my shoulder, not bothering to see any reactions as I walk out the door.

Silently hoping I'll pay for it later, but terrified my heart will pay too.

nine

CAL

"HARLOW!" I yell, slamming the door behind me. I texted my dad and asked him to take Cora to hang out at Belle's. So I know it's just Harlow in the house right now.

I hear a small yelp coming from the kitchen. I smile and make my way to the fiery redhead that's been under my skin all day. After she left the studio, we decided to make use of the space since it was already paid for and practice the songs we haven't yet.

"Don't hide from me, Firecracker," I say, rounding the island and seeing her crouching behind it.

"Um, hi," she says as she pops up from the floor.

"That's all you have to say for yourself?" I ask, slowly stalking her as she tries to put space between us. She's always beautiful, but right now, with her flushed cheeks and wide eyes. Fuck, she's perfection and temptation rolled into one.

"I put panties on?" she says, still trying to keep the island between us.

"Did you? You don't seem too sure. Should I check?" I smile, knowing I look every ounce the predator I feel.

"Cal," she says, but then her eyes go impossibly wide as she trips over one of Cora's toys and falls backwards. I grab her right before she hits her head on the floor. Pulling her into my chest, I watch as her eyes trace my lips before coming to my eyes. I feel her chest heaving against mine, her heart beating so loudly I can hear it. Or maybe that's mine I hear.

I lean in, waiting for her to pull away. To tell me that this attraction is one-sided. Or hell, to be the logical one and tell me that it's a line we shouldn't cross.

But she doesn't do any of that.

She grabs the back of my neck and pulls me the rest of the way. Her soft lips meet mine hesitantly. I pull her into me until I can feel the warmth of her body everywhere.

"More," I whisper against her lips. The change is instant. The hesitancy is gone. Harlow wraps her arms around my neck and pulls herself up to wrap her legs around my waist. I turn so I can prop her on the counter. She gasps when the cool granite meets her hot skin.

Her tongue prods at the seam of my lips, demanding entrance. And fuck do I let her in. Her tongue tangles with mine in a dance for dominance that I never want to end.

I trace my hands up her smooth thighs until I get to the hem of her shorts. She changed out of the leggings she was in earlier into a pair of loose cotton shorts. I pause and pull away from her lips so I can meet her eyes. Those beautiful green eyes are unfocused, but she still sees the question in mine. She nods her head vigorously.

"Touch me. I need you to touch me, Cal. I'm so wet," she pleads, trying to rub herself against me, needing the friction.

"Fuck, baby. No panties," I groan as my fingers explore. "You're so fucking wet."

"Please," she mutters against my lips before kissing me again.

I slip a finger inside her and groan. She's so hot and so tight. I'm on the edge of my control. I've never lost it.

But I've never wanted anyone the way I want Harlow.

Being near her is intoxicating. Her laugh, her smile, the smell of her lavender shampoo in the air after she showers. I'm drunk on her.

I break away from her lips so I can kiss along her neck. I add another finger and rub her clit with my thumb once I find the pulse point on her neck.

"Oh god," she says as she throws her head back. Her pulse races under my lips, encouraging me to keep going. "Right there, Cal. God. Don't stop."

"There are no gods here, Firecracker. Just me and it will be *my* name you scream."

"Yes. Yes, Callahan," she gasps. "Make me come. Please let me come." Her hips grind against my hand, desperately seeking her release.

"That's it baby, fuck my hand." I curl my fingers inside her and put more pressure on her clit. I feel her walls contract around my fingers as she screams out her release. I keep my hand there as she slows her movements, letting her ride out the rest of her orgasm.

Once her breathing slows, I pull back, keeping eye contact as I slowly pull my hand out of her shorts and raise my fingers to my lips. Harlow gasps as I suck the evidence of her off my fingers.

"Why is that so hot?" she says and then laughs, still dazed from how hard she came.

"You taste so fucking sweet, Firecracker. Why don't you see for yourself?" I kiss her before she has time to respond, caressing my tongue against hers so she can taste herself. She moans into my mouth, making my impossibly hard cock twitch in my jeans.

"Cal! Why the hell is your kid at my house, and you aren't?" Kai's voice echoes throughout the front of my house.

Harlow jumps and pushes me away from her. I stumble back, startled. She jumps off the counter and quickly straightens up.

"Cal!" Kai yells, closer than before. I ignore him and reach for Harlow, but she steps out of my reach. The small movement is enough to make my heart constrict painfully. Does she not feel this? Can she not see the connection we have? The pull towards each other that I couldn't resist? I thought we were on the same page.

"I'm sorry," she whispers and then quickly darts up the stairs.

"Dude. Are you deaf?" I hear Kai as he comes to stand next to me, but my eyes are on the stairs. "Why does it smell like sex in here?"

"Fuck off," I tell him, but there's nothing behind the words. I still haven't bothered to look at him.

All I see are the stairs and the curtain of red curls as they ran away from me.

"SHIT! SHIT SHIT SHIT," I angrily whisper to myself. I just let my boss finger me on his kitchen counter. "Shit!"

Don't get me wrong. I wanted it. Wanted him.

I still want him. I can feel the ghost of his fingers on me, inside me, and it makes me want him even more. But I can't have him. I'm only here to save money and be the first one to break the news on Ezra. Whatever that turns out to be.

That's it. Just business.

"Business."

"Just business."

"Don't fuck your boss."

If I keep repeating it like a mantra, maybe I'll believe it.

A knock sounds on my door, and I know who it is before he even speaks. "Harlow? Let me in, Firecracker. We need to talk."

I sigh and drag my feet to my door. I open it just a crack. Cal stands right outside, eyes on me, a sad and pleading look in his eyes that almost breaks me.

"Can I come in?" he says softly. I nod, turning to take a

seat on the small sofa in my room. Maybe if my back is to him, this won't hurt as much.

That plan is shot to shit when he takes the seat next to me, his thigh firmly planted against mine. The woodsy smell of his cologne surrounds me, making me weak.

Business. Just business. Don't fuck your boss. I repeat it in my head as I wait for him to speak.

"Harlow, I —"

"I think we need to have a strictly professional working relationship," I blurt out before his words can sway me.

I can't look at him. My eyes are firmly locked on a very interesting spot on the wall.

"Professional working relationship?" The hurt in his voice cuts through me, but I stick to my resolve. "I care about Cora too much, and I need this job. I can't risk it just to be another place for you to stick your dick while you wait for someone new and hotter to come along."

I feel Cal stiffen beside me. He sucks in a shocked breath, and his eyes burn into the side of my head. I can't look at him. I'll take everything back if I do.

A tear slips down my face at the realization that there's truth in what I said. Cal isn't the serious type of guy. His friends joke about it constantly. But that's not who I am. I can't do casual and not get hurt.

"You think you're just a place to stick my dick?" he asks, anger seeping into his words.

"Aren't I?" I ask the wall, still refusing to look at him.

He doesn't speak right away. With every moment that passes without a sound, I get more terrified. Terrified that I'm going to lose this job.

Lose him.

I never really had him, but the thought that I might never be in his presence again is scary. Cal attracts people because he shines so brightly. I don't want to be without that light again, and I'll take it in whatever form he's willing to give.

As long as that form keeps my heart safe.

"Fine. Professional relationship it is." Cal stands and a moment later, my door slams shut.

I curl into a ball, inhaling the faint smell of him that was left in his wake, and cry until I fall asleep.

CAL HAS BEEN AVOIDING me for almost two weeks now. We speak enough to go over Cora's day, but that's it. I can't even blame him for it.

He's not being rude or mean. He's just distant, and I hate it. I'm the one who put the boundaries there, and he's respecting them.

But I miss him. Fuck, do I miss him. I miss the way he would tease me or sass me right back. The way he would smile when he saw how much fun Cora and I were having playing with him. I even missed the way his lips felt on mine. The heat his touch would leave hours after it was ever there.

"What do you say us girls have a nice day? Maybe go shopping and get cute new outfits?" I ask Cora as I feed her another spoonful of the gross smelling baby cereal. She claps her hands in response, making me laugh. She just learned to clap yesterday, and it's her new favorite thing to do.

I've had this job for almost two months, and I've absolutely fallen in love with this adorable little girl. It's that fact that I hold on to at night when I want to be held by her dad.

I pack Cora up in my car and head to the mall. There are usually one or two paparazzi at the gate to the community. Since Shattered Halo has been working on a new album, and Belle started dating Kai, they've been interested in getting a story. But for a rock band, they like to keep things pretty low-key.

It's nice that the jerks behind the cameras have no idea who I am or that Cal even has a daughter. It allows me to come and go as I please. They just assume I'm some rich housewife that lives here. It helps that Cora looks so much like me. If anyone sees me with her, they assume she's my daughter.

I mentally add lack of privacy to the list I have running of why being with Cal is a terrible idea. I just wish it was a longer list.

"What do you think of this one?" I hold up a pair of purple overalls. Cora claps, and I take that as her approval. Just like I did when she clapped at everything else I've held up in her size. "I agree. It's Daddy's treat, so you can get whatever you want."

Cal gave me the credit card for Cora's expenses. A shopping spree in this bougie kid's store isn't exactly what he meant. Maybe I'm hoping he'll see an astronomical charge and get angry enough to have a conversation with me.

Maybe I'm regretting pushing him away.

Maybe I hate seeing him every day and not being on the

receiving end of his warmth. It's damn cold where I am now, and I hate it.

"What do you think, Cora girl? Matching shoes and bows for every outfit?"

"Da!" she yells and claps. I look around, worried that Cal somehow found out about my shopping spree already, but we're the only ones in the store other than the bored-looking teenager behind the counter.

I sigh. "You miss Dada?"

"Da!" Cora says again with a small giggle.

"Me too, pretty girl."

After filling our cart, plus a special bonus cart that's waiting for us at the register, with everything in the girl's section, plus a few items from the boys' section, I'm ready to test out this credit card.

"You know, girls are allowed to like dinosaurs and foot-balls too," I say to the disinterested girl ringing up all the items as I place two pairs of 'boys' PJs on the counter. "They also like trucks and sharks and robots."

Cora claps in agreement. So I take that as encourage-ment and keep going. "And boys are allowed to like flowers and kittens and the color pink."

The girl finally makes eye contact. "Okay?"

"I'm just saying. It shouldn't be restricted by gender," I mumble.

"Didn't seem to stop you," she says, going back to scan-ning and bagging everything.

"Right. Well, I suppose it didn't," I admit.

It's awkward standing here for as long as I have been while she bags everything up. So long that I think about going on another rant about baby clothes.

"Your total is $6,342."

I snort and tap the card against the reader. "Your dad is going to be so pissed," I whisper to Cora.

"Da!"

"You're right, Cora girl. He can't be angry when he sees how cute you look in all of this."

The cashier seems surprised when it's approved. I catch my reflection in the mirrors behind the desk. Ah. That's probably why. I'm in leggings and an old, faded college sweatshirt that has a stain on it from Cora's breakfast. My hair is tied in a haphazard bun on the top of my head.

I've looked . . . better.

"Can I see your I.D.?"

I chuckle to myself but dig it out of my wallet and hand it over anyway. The card is in my name, and I'm thankful Cal thought of doing that instead of just handing me one with his name on it. The cashier studies it a lot longer than what's probably standard.

"I look like a hot pile of garbage today. I get it. You don't need to be so rude about it." Cora claps, and I shake my head. "That wasn't really a clapping occasion, Cora."

The cashier hands me my license, along with the receipt. I look at all the bags and flinch. "I don't suppose you'd be able to help me get these to the car?"

"Can't. Only one working." She picks up her phone and goes back to ignoring me.

"Alright. Just me and you, Cora girl."

"Cart stays in the store."

"Can't I use it to bring my bags out? I promise I'll bring it back."

She just points to a sign next to the exit. "The wheels lock if I push the cart past the threshold? Are you serious?"

I strap Cora to my chest, grateful that's how I decided to carry her in here in the first place and load my arms up with bags.

It works well enough. I'm sweaty, and I think some of the handles from the bags have cut into my arms, but I've made it back to my car.

I'm breathing heavily by the time I get Cora strapped in. Of course, now my phone is ringing. I pull it out of my purse to see Cal's face on the screen. It's a picture I took of him with Cora. They were playing with sticks and leaves in the backyard. They looked so happy that I snapped a picture and immediately set it as his contact picture.

Guess it's time to face the music.

"Beautiful daughter you have there."

I jump, my phone hitting the pavement.

I spin to see a man dressed in an expensive black suit. He has dark hair peppered with gray around his temples and eyes so dark they're almost black.

"Thank you," I stutter. I don't like the way he's looking at me, the way his eyes roam my body. He's a predator, but not in the predictable sense. This man wants nothing from my body. He's assessing, calculating. Hopefully finding me severely lacking.

"The smallest scandal can end a career these days. Sad, don't you think?" the man says, hands in his pockets, making no move to come closer. My key fob is still in my hand, and I quickly lock my car, keeping my eyes trained on the stranger.

He laughs. The sound is one of the scariest I've ever

heard. I move to the side, putting myself between the man and Cora's door. I don't think there's much I can do if he tries to get to her, but I will do anything I can to stop him.

"Do I know you?" I ask. Something about him is familiar, but I can't place it. I need to keep him talking. Maybe someone will walk out to this weirdly empty parking lot. That's what I get for having a breakdown over my employer in the middle of the day on a Wednesday. No one is here.

The man chuckles darkly. "Your generation doesn't pay attention to the world. Just yourselves, and your selfish desires."

My phone continues to vibrate on the pavement. Cal isn't giving up on his quest to yell at me for spending so much, but right now, I wish he was here to do it in person.

The stranger takes his eyes off me long enough to glance at my phone. Whatever he sees there makes him smile.

It's horrifying.

"Callahan always did have a type," he says, and I blanch. My phone must have landed face up, and I just gave this stranger proof that Cal's daughter is in my car.

"What do you want?" I ask him, willing to give him just about anything if he leaves Cora alone.

"Nothing you can give me."

He walks away then, leaving me shaking against my car. I grab my phone, which has stopped vibrating. Cal has given up and is probably getting ready to let me have it when he gets home. With a deep breath, I quickly make my way to the driver's side of my car and get in, locking it again as I do and starting it immediately. I call my dad and then start driving. I need to get Cora back behind the security of the gates and her house.

"Hi Harlow," my dad's happy voice comes through the phone.

"Dad! I was just confronted in the parking lot of the Southside Mall. I parked in front of 4-Ever Kidz. The man was tall, probably at least six feet, wearing an expensive black suit with dark hair. He looks like he has enough money to take care of any security footage, so I need you to get to it first."

"Did he touch you? Are you being followed?" My dad asks after a short pause.

"No to both. I'm heading back to Cal's. But Dad, he knows about Cora. I think he suspected, but then he saw the proof on my phone."

"Get back to Cal's, and I'll get that footage. Text me when you get there."

"I will. Love you."

"Love you too."

twelve

CAL

"SHE SPENT over six thousand dollars at some stupid kids' store and now she's not answering her fucking phone!"

Mav laughs from his spot in the passenger seat of my car.

"This isn't funny!"

"I disagree. You've been ignoring her for weeks and being a miserable bastard because of it. She should've spent more." He keeps laughing.

"I'm glad my life is so amusing to you," I grumble as I white knuckle steering wheel.

"Me too."

I roll my tinted window down enough for the guard at the gate to see my face as we approach.

"Hey Cal. Harlow just flew through here. She looked really shaken up," the guard, Dean, says once he sees me. He's already opened the gate.

"Thanks, Dean!" I yell, already pulling through and speeding towards my house.

Harlow's car comes into view, parked sideways in the driveway like she flew in at an angle and ran out. I throw my car in park in the middle of my lawn and jump out, running towards my front door. I don't even bother turning the car off.

"Harlow!" I call the moment I cross the threshold. "Cora!"

"Here! We're here!" Harlow's voice is strained as she comes rushing into the living room. She has Cora clutched to her chest. I run to them, anxiously checking them over, trying to figure out that terrified look in her eyes.

"What's going on? What happened? Why wouldn't you answer me?" I ask more harshly than I meant to, but she's freaking me out.

"I-I-I'm sorry about the money," she stutters out around the fat tears falling down her beautiful face.

"I don't give a fuck about the money, Harlow. Why are you so scared?" I ask, more gently. I want to take Cora from her, just to assure myself she's ok. But Harlow seems to need her more than I do right now, and Cora is asleep against her chest.

"Someone knows," she cries. Then proceeds to tell me about some man that cornered her in a parking lot.

All I see is red. Rage that someone would do that to her and rage that Cora was even there at all.

"You threw a hissy fit and put my daughter in danger! What the fuck were you thinking? What is wrong with you?" I scream at her. I can't contain it.

Harlow flinches back like I hit her, and Cora wakes up with a loud cry.

"I understand you're upset, Callahan, but if you ever speak to my daughter like that again, it will be the last thing you do."

I turn to see a furious Harrison Ray standing behind me with a disappointed Maverick.

"She put my daughter in danger!" I argue.

"My daughter was in danger! *My* daughter! She took your daughter to a store to get clothes. A very public store. Do not take this out on her!" The anger in his voice has me wanting to cower. Physically, I stand my ground, but mentally, I'm already trying to figure out how to apologize to Harlow.

"It was my fault, Dad," Harlow says meekly, and that tone alone is what breaks me. Harlow is anything but meek. I put that sound there, and I hate myself for it.

"I have the security footage. Everyone sit down so we can watch it and you," he says, looking directly at me, "you can find a way to beg for Harlow's forgiveness."

We all sit dutifully on the couch, Harlow choosing to sit on the opposite side of me, Cora still cuddled against her. Mav sits beside me, shaking his head.

Harrison pairs his phone to the TV and plays the footage. I watch as this man scares Harlow. I can see, even in the grainy picture, how scared she is. I watch as she puts herself between him and the door Cora is directly behind.

Harlow put herself directly between danger and Cora. I cover my mouth, but I can't help the sob that escapes.

"Firecracker," I say, looking over the woman I so poorly judged just minutes ago. She keeps her focus on the screen, and I can see the determination there.

Mav goes rigid next to me, causing my attention to swing back to the screen.

"Fuck," I mutter.

"You know who that is?" Harlow asks.

"It's my fucking dad," Maverick answers, standing abruptly and pacing the room.

"Why would your dad be in the parking lot of a mall? In Massachusetts? He's a Maine Senator." Harlow asks.

"He keeps sending me emails asking if I'm done with my 'little rebellion' as he puts it," Mav answers, running his hands through his hair. "He keeps saying I need to join the family business. He wants me in law school and in some political position. I'm an embarrassment to him as I am now."

"You're leaving out the part where he wants to arrange your marriage to one of his political allies' daughters," I add.

Mav snorts. "Yeah. There's that too."

"So you're not falling in line, so he went after me?" Harlow asks, trying to put together the pieces of a puzzle that I'm pretty sure aren't even from the same puzzle. "Wait," she says suddenly. "He said something about how even a small scandal ends careers. He's going to use Cora to try to bring negative attention to the band."

"Seems likely," Harrison says.

"What if he has something to do with Ezra and he's going to use Cora as a threat?" I ask, panicking and mentally making plans to move to another country and change our names. I will not let my daughter get caught up in this.

"I don't think that would make sense for him. He was threatening me out in the open, seemingly uncaring if anyone caught him," Harlow says, and Harrison nods. "If it was connected to Ezra, and we could connect the dots to him, that would end his career that he seems to love so much."

"I don't think this is related to Ezra, even if he is involved there. He wants me back in his orbit. And if it means protecting Cora, I'll go," Mav says, and I see the determination on his face. He'll give up everything and go back to the toxic family.

"No, Mav. We'll figure something out," I tell him immediately.

"I have an idea, but you might not like it," Harlow says, looking at me, and I see the spark back in her eyes.

"Lay it on me, Firecracker."

"You get out in front of it. Put out a press release telling the world about Cora."

I feel my body tense, but she puts her hand up before I say anything.

"I know it's not what you want. But plenty of celebrities have announced their surprise children and the news dies down within weeks. I can't even tell you what famous people have kids and which ones don't."

"I don't want Cora to have to deal with a public life," I tell her, even though she knows that.

"She won't. You don't need to release any pictures or even her name. Just tell the world you have a child, probably have your PR team put a better statement together than I could, and let it fizzle out. It takes away Wolfe's one piece of leverage."

"No. I won't let you do that," Mav says, making his way to the door, like he's planning on leaving for his parent's house right this minute. Knowing him, he probably is.

"I'm doing it, Mav. It makes sense. He won't stop at using her to get you back. He hates all of us. If he even smells you thinking about leaving him again, he'll threaten her. Harlow is right, Mav. We need to get ahead of this."

Mav nods, realizing I'm right, that Harlow is right. He makes his way over to her and puts his arms out for Cora. Harlow smiles sadly and hands her over. Cora immediately snuggles into him and continues to sleep. "I'm so sorry," he whispers into her hair.

"Don't blame yourself for the evil of another, Maverick. You didn't do this, and nothing is going to happen to Cora. If anything, she's just going to have to go to an expensive school with other rich kids to have the added security. Which Cal was probably going to send her to anyway," Harlow says.

I laugh, and that seems to ease some of the tension in Mav's shoulders.

"What the fuck is going on? Why is everyone parked like a bunch of drunks?" Willa yells, coming in to join the party with Kai, Belle, and Jo right behind her.

"We need you to get a press release together," I tell Jo.

Harlow fills them in, with Harrison adding how quickly she called him to get the footage, making sure whoever threatened my daughter wouldn't get away.

I look at the woman who willingly put her body between my daughter and a threat and wonder how the fuck I can make it up to her.

"Can we talk?" I ask Harlow. Everyone went home hours ago, and she's sitting alone on the couch watching an old 90s movie I've seen Belle and my cousin Millie watch. Her legs are curled underneath her, and she's snuggled into a knit blanket that's up to her chin.

She pats the seat next to her, not taking her eyes off the screen.

"I'm so fucking sorry for the way I reacted today, Harlow. I should never have jumped to conclusions. Not about you. I know you would never put Cora in harm's way."

"Are you sure that you know that? You seemed pretty sure that I would." The hurt in her voice is so obvious that it breaks my heart.

"The thought of something happening to Cora has been my biggest fear since she was born. It felt like my fear came to life, and I handled it with anger. I know I was wrong."

She just nods, still refusing to look at me.

"Look at me, Firecracker. Please."

She turns her head, and her broken eyes meet mine. "I'm sorry I spent so much money."

"I really don't care about that," I tell her. "But why did you?"

"I just wanted you to talk to me," she admits. "I figured if I made you mad, even if you were only speaking to me because I pissed you off, at least you were speaking to me."

If I wasn't sitting already, I would have collapsed to the floor.

"What? I thought that's what you wanted?" I know I've been more distant than I needed to be, but I didn't think I could stay away from her if I wasn't.

"I wanted to keep things professional, not turn into your enemy."

"You're not my enemy, Firecracker. You're the woman who was about to throw down your life for my daughter."

"That's a bit dramatic," she scoffs.

"If that man raised a gun and told you he would shoot you in the head if you didn't move, would you have moved?" I ask her my worst fear. The one that's been running through my head all day. I don't know when, but somehow the thought of losing Harlow has been added right next to losing Cora on the running list of nightmares I seem to be keeping.

"No," she says without an ounce of hesitation.

"Exactly."

"So, where does this leave us? Because I don't think I can take you avoiding me anymore," she says, looking down at her hands like she can escape the vulnerability she just showed.

"I'm sorry I made you feel that way. I never meant to hurt you. Can we go back to being friends?" I ask, hoping I can manage to give her that much. It's the least she deserves, even if it crushes me.

Her bright smile tosses aside every worry I have. Even if I have to want her in silence, I will, just to see her smile at me like that.

"We're really behind on Senseless Love," she says, grabbing the remote and changing it over.

"You didn't watch it without me?" I ask, surprised.

"It kind of felt like our thing, and I didn't want to watch it alone anymore."

"Are you making popcorn?" I ask her with a grin. She rolls her eyes and stands from the couch.

"Fine, but I'm making you your own bowl, and you're not allowed to eat out of mine when you inhale it like a vacuum cleaner."

"We'll see," I say, smiling as I follow her into the kitchen.

Yeah, protecting my heart from her is going to be super easy.

Fuck.

THE PRESS RELEASE went out this morning. The world knows Cal has a daughter.

"Cal, she needs to nap," I tell him, attempting to reach for Cora. He spins around, keeping her pinned to his chest and out of my reach.

"I can't," he pleads, his eyes wide. There are a ton of reporters at the gate, which we expected. They can't get in though, and they definitely can't see into the house. Not with all the curtains closed.

"Keeping her awake and cranky isn't going to help anyone."

"She can sleep in my arms," he counters. I look at Cora, who is currently smiling and gnawing on a teething toy.

"You know she won't sleep." I grab his arm gently, and he stops moving. "Jo and my dad will be her soon to meet with us. Cora needs to nap. We're not leaving the house."

"But . . ."

"It's going to be okay, Cal. No one in this house is going to hurt her. She's as safe as she'll ever be here with you."

"And you," he says, placing his hand over mine where it's still resting on his arm.

"Family meeting time!" Belle's voice calls from the bottom of the stairs.

Cal sighs and kisses the top of Cora's head. "I'll put her down for her nap and meet you in the living room." He turns and makes his way into Cora's room, not waiting for me to respond.

"Do you think you can talk Cal into making Midnight Macaroni?" Belle asks from where she's sitting at the kitchen island.

I look at the clock on the stove. "It's one in the afternoon."

"It's more of a stress thing than a time thing," Willa says from behind me, making me jump.

"Maybe we can watch Practical Magic. It's my comfort movie," Belle says.

"Mine too," Willa agrees.

"Where are Kai and Mav?" I ask, looking around and not seeing them.

"Kai went to get Mav. He's uh . . . not doing so hot after finding out what his dad did to you yesterday," Belle says, her shoulders slumped.

"I was just freaked out. He didn't touch me or anything." I don't know why I'm defending the asshole. Probably because I hate when people are upset.

"Doesn't really matter, considering the snowball he set in motion," Willa says with a shrug.

"What's Cal's comfort movie?" I ask, circling back to Belle's comment. For some reason, it bothers me more than it should.

"I don't think he has one. Never really needed one." Belle says, her face scrunched as she thinks.

"Yeah. Cal is never really stressed. He just lets things roll off his shoulders. Always admired that about him," Willa adds.

I just blink at the two of them. "What do you mean? Everyone needs comfort sometimes."

"Not Cal. Don't get me wrong, he gets frazzled when he's stressed, but that passes pretty quickly," Willa says.

Are they talking about the same person? The man I know has been in a constant state of stress since I met him. Kai and Mav arrive with my dad right behind them before I can open my mouth to argue.

"Do either of you know Cal's comfort movie?" I ask the guys. They both look at me, confused. I don't know if they're confused about why I'm asking or if they don't know. There's no way he doesn't have a comfort movie.

Apparently, this is a hill I'm willing to die on.

"Talladega Nights."

I smile but don't bother turning around. I can feel Cal's presence. I probably didn't even need him to speak to know he was in the room.

"Told you," I say to everyone in the room. They all just shrug.

"How come you didn't jump?" Willa asks.

"I knew he was there. I could smell him," I joke. Well, mostly. I can smell his clean, woodsy scent from where he's standing behind me. Is it weird that I kind of want to stick my face in his chest and just smell him?

Yeah. Definitely weird.

"I'm not sharing my popcorn with you tonight," Cal

huffs in mock outrage. I turn around to see him frowning at me, but then he winks. I know what he's doing. He's breaking the tension in the room. I've seen him do it a million times over the weeks I've been living here.

"You're the one who steals my popcorn! We went through a whole box last night! That's eight bags, Cal! You ate eight bags of popcorn!" I shout playfully, going along with him. I think he needs to break the heaviness in the room more than anyone else that's here right now.

He smiles at me appreciatively, knowing full well he only ate two bags.

"Have you guys watched the latest episode?" Jo asks, making me jump. Willa narrows her eyes, definitely noticing there was only one person in this room that didn't startle me by suddenly appearing behind me.

It's because he lives here.

That's definitely the reason.

"The date he took her on was —"

"Shh! No spoilers!" Cal screams, covering his ears and singing so he can't hear her.

Everyone laughs in a *that's classic Cal for you* way, and I hate it. I'm all for silly moments to break the tension, but that's not the looks he's getting. He can see it in my face and shakes his head, asking me to keep my thoughts to myself. I press my lips together and nod.

Only because today is about protecting Cora and figuring out Senator Wolfe's goal with all this. We're running with the assumption he needs Maverick, but it's not a good idea to put all our eggs in that basket.

But once this is all over, I am not keeping quiet. These

people are his family and as much as they love him, I don't think they even know him.

"The initial response is positive overall. Your fanbase was relatively unsurprised you have a child," Jo says, looking over analytics on her iPad.

"Really? Because it shocked the shit out of me," Cal says, making everyone laugh. I smile at the joke, but I'm watching Jo's eyebrows slowly draw closer and closer together. She's seeing something she doesn't like.

"What was the crowd at the gate like?" Kai asks my dad.

"As we expected, but the police are there keeping them in check," my dad answers. "And we're sure we're not worried about your neighbors selling pictures?"

"No. You don't live in gated communities unless you want to keep people away from you. There's no way they want reporters in here," Kai answers.

My dad nods in agreement, and I know that's because he already ran background checks on everyone that lives here.

"Where are we on connecting my dad to Ezra?" Mav asks.

My dad stills and looks at me. I tilt my head in confusion, waiting for whatever he has to say.

"I think I have a way to get Ezra's cell. From what my contact tells me, it's still in evidence. I'm working out a way for it to go 'missing.'"

"Dad!" I blurt, shocked. My dad has always been very strict about doing things by the book, so any case he helped with couldn't be thrown out.

"I know, Harlow. But it's becoming clearer the more I search and find absolutely nothing, that there is something to hide. The fact that the phone even still exists means someone forgot about it. Right now, it's the only lead we have."

"And you think there will be something on there to incriminate my dad?" Maverick asks.

My dad shakes his head. "Right now, I'm treating these as two separate cases. I'm hoping the phone will give us a lead on either where he went or why he ran. As for your dad," he looks at Maverick in a way that tells me he's trying to choose his words carefully. "Is there a way you could meet with your mom without alerting your dad? Maybe ask her some questions?"

Mav sighs, leaning back into the couch, his head tilted to the ceiling. "She asks me to meet her for lunch all the time. At least she did when I still lived in Maine. I'm sure I could arrange that." He sits forward and looks at my dad. "I have to be honest, though. She's become more of an accessory for my dad than anything. I doubt she knows much."

"You'd be surprised. Those are the people who usually know the most." All eyes swing my way. "What?"

"She watches a lot of true crime," Jo mutters, still glaring at her iPad as she scrolls furiously through something.

"You're one to talk," I scoff.

"Wait. So all this time we could've been watching murder documentaries and instead you have me waiting to see if the deaf man and the blind lady can figure out how to communicate and fall in love?" Cal asks, an affronted look on his face.

"Stop acting like you don't text me after every episode to talk about it," Mav says.

"Bro! That was our secret!" Cal complains.

He's playing it up again, but his hands are in fists in his lap like he's barely holding it together. And yet again, no one else notices. He catches me watching him and gives me a forced smile. I don't return it. The slightest shake of his head lets me know he doesn't want me saying anything right now.

"How did you not know? The girls want to start a podcast. That's their career goal."

Well shit.

I glare at my dad, who looks at me like he has no idea why I'm mad at him. And I guess it might be my fault. Anytime an end date is brought up, I brush it off since I don't have one to give. I know he's asking so he can plan for the future.

I risk a glance at Cal, and he is absolutely fuming. Great. Perfect. Our one day of friendship is over.

"The Internet is trying to figure out who Harlow is," Jo interrupts.

"What the hell for?" I yell, a little too loudly, judging by how Willa flinches. She's sitting directly next to me, and I definitely just screamed into her ear.

"Someone got a picture of you pushing a stroller. It's far away and grainy. Cora can't be seen at all, but your hair is hard to miss," Jo says.

"He did say Cal has a type," I mutter, patting down my hair like it's wronged me.

Kai snorts. "You're too smart to be his type."

"Cal isn't stupid," I defend immediately. I'm sick of

everyone implying he is. I'm getting a lot of startled and confused looks right now, and it's making my skin feel itchy.

"Can we get back to the matter at hand, people?" Jo phrases it as a question, but her voice is sharp.

"I'm heading up to Maine tonight to retrieve the phone," my dad says. "Maverick, let me know when you set up that meeting with your mom and we can go over questions." Mav nods. "Harlow, try to stay out of trouble until I'm back."

I scoff, actually offended. "Shopping and walking with a baby in a stroller are hardly things I should be in trouble for."

My dad ignores me, kissing the top of my head as he leaves.

"I'm going to keep monitoring this," Jo says. "Harlow, don't leave the house for now."

I don't have time to answer. She just turns on her heel and leaves, Mav getting up and following her immediately.

"Is there something going on there or am I crazy?" Willa asks what I was just thinking.

"Well, she ignores him most of the time. So I'm going to have to say no," Belle says.

"He might have some sort of mean woman kink because she is not nice to him," Kai says, shaking his head.

I snort. "You didn't hire her because she's nice."

Willa laughs and then stands. "Let's go, losers. I don't want to be here when Cal explodes."

I hear the three of them leave, but my eyes are on Cal. He's practically vibrating with rage.

"Uh. I think I'll just go to my room," I say quietly.

"Sit the fuck down, Harlow." Cal's voice is low, menacing.

I've never sat down faster.

"You're just going to leave m-Cora?" His voice is calm, but like that eerie calm before you're suddenly hit by a storm that pulls your house off its foundation. His reaction is confusing since I never promised to stay forever. But maybe he's feeling just as attached to me as I am to him and Cora.

"You want the truth, Callahan?" I fight back.

"Always," he growls.

"I don't fucking know!" I stand up and pace the length of the room. "Jo and I have had a dream of starting a true crime podcast. But not like the ones that are popular right now. We want to start one that only goes over cold cases and enlist the help of specialists, like my dad, to try to get closure to families. That's what I want at some point in my life." I stop and take a deep breath, deciding the full truth needs to be said. "I initially took this job because I thought our first case could be Ezra's. That maybe you guys had information we could use to find him or to help in some way while also bringing a lot of attention to the podcast."

Cal's frown deepens, and I know I'm just digging myself into a hole that I'll never find my way out of. So might as well keep digging.

"But the more time I spent with you, with all of you, I realized that approach might do more harm than good. You guys are already in the spotlight, which puts Ezra's case in the spotlight without any help." I bite my lip, nervous that he hasn't said anything. "And what if this just reopens old wounds for people instead of healing them, like what we intended?"

"Now that you can't profit off our pain, do you plan to quit?" he asks between clenched teeth.

Alright, we're going for broke here.

"No. I love Cora. I love being part of her life. I love being part of your life and being your friend." The word 'friend' feels wrong on my tongue, but that's all we'll ever be. Especially now. "I had no intention of deceiving you. Podcasts can take years to take off. I would never have left you high and dry."

"You love Cora?" he asks, only slightly less angry.

"How can you even ask me that? That little girl stole my heart the moment I walked into this house, and you know it." It's my turn to be pissed.

"Yeah. I know, Firecracker." His lips twitch with the hint of a smile.

"Since we're laying the cards on the table," I say, crossing my arms and glaring at him. "What the hell is with the dual personalities?"

Cal shakes his head. "You're the only person that's ever noticed."

"Not an answer, Cal."

He sighs, gesturing for me to sit next to him. I don't. I just keep my arms crossed and glare. But he waits.

"Goddammit," I mutter, taking the seat next to him.

"Has Belle ever said anything to you about how we grew up?"

I shake my head. "The only thing I know is what you told me that first day. Your mom doesn't know, and you want to keep it that way." My eyes go wide. "She knows now! Shit."

"Don't worry about that right now."

"Fine, but I'm going to worry about it later."

Cal chuckles.

"My mom was and is all about appearances. She married my dad because he made good money. She became friends with Kai and Ezra's mom because Adira was popular in social circles. She had kids because it was what you did to secure your husband."

I scrunched up my nose in disgust.

"Yeah. She was never really a mother. She didn't work and was somehow still less of a parent than my dad, who worked two jobs to keep up with her spending."

"I can see where you didn't want her in Cora's life. She would just use her for money or clout or something."

Cal nods. "She would."

"What does this have to do with your dumb man act?"

"My mom never really liked Belle for some reason. Willa's theory is that Belle is prettier than my mom, and my mom hates her for it. I don't know if that's true or not, but Belle would always be pushed on me. When we were small, I was resentful that I always had to take my baby sister everywhere, but as we got older and had the same group of friends, I became protective."

"You divert the attention and alleviate the stress by acting stupid and making jokes," I surmise what I already figured out weeks ago. I just didn't know the why behind it.

Cal's eyebrows shoot up. "I shouldn't be so surprised you figured that out."

I shrug.

"I've been doing it for so long, I don't think they know what my actual personality is."

"Do you?" I ask.

"I think you might be the only person who does," he admits softly.

"I'll help you figure it out."

He reaches for my hand and squeezes. "Tell me you're staying." His words are steady, but the worry in his eyes is clear.

"If you'll let me."

He lets out a breath. "Let you? I think Cora would leave with you."

We both laugh and then settle quietly into the silence that follows. I gave him until I figured out my next step when I interviewed, but I don't think that's what he's asking. I can read between the lines and see he wants me for much longer than that, but the lines are messy, and we're too confused to explore it.

"Cal?"

"Yeah?"

"I'm sorry."

"I know, Firecracker."

fourteen

CAL

"HOW COME you haven't released a statement about Cora's mom?" Harlow asks as soon as she steps into the kitchen. It's too early for serious conversations. Not that it stops her.

"I don't want them digging up any skeletons from Bailey's closet."

"She had skeletons?" Harlow asks, stealing the coffee I just poured myself. I glare at her, but she just grins.

"No idea. I didn't know her that well, but I kind of feel like I owe it to her since she's not alive to defend herself," I admit.

Harlow tilts her head as she mulls that over. "Makes sense," she agrees.

"Have you heard from your dad?" I ask, curious about Ezra's phone.

She sighs. "Yeah. He said he wants to talk with you guys in person later."

"Is that good or bad?"

Harlow shrugs. "Could be either. He didn't give anything away." She looks around the kitchen. "Where's Cora?"

"My dad had the day off, so he took her over to Belle's."

Which leaves me alone in my house with the woman I can barely resist. Even when I was angry with her yesterday, I still wanted her. I think that just infuriated me even more.

She has my balls in a vise, and I just want to thank her for it.

What the fuck is happening to me?

When she said she was staying last night, I almost crossed that line. Part of me really wishes I had. I still think about the way her lips felt against mine and the sound she made when she came all over my hand.

I clear my throat and sidestep so the island is hiding the tenting in my pants.

I watch as Harlow takes a sip of my coffee and spits it right back into the mug.

"Callahan Elizabeth Griffin! Is there rum in this coffee?"

I bark out a shocked laugh. "My middle name is not Elizabeth."

"Rum at eight in the morning?"

I shrug. "It's the first time I had an actual day off, and I was celebrating."

She dumps out the contents of the mug into the sink and places it in the dishwasher.

"I have a better idea," she says, grabbing my hand and pulling me along with her.

"Where are we going?"

"The basement."

"You want to use the gym? I already worked out this

morning." Although I could go for an entirely different type of workout right now.

"Not the gym," she says, pulling me down the stairs. I freeze in place.

"You want to go to the recording studio?" Those are the only two things down here, and I can't figure out why she'd need to use the studio. I've heard her sing.

Oh no. What if she thinks she can sing?

"I'm not going to sing."

"I said that out loud?"

Harlow laughs. "No, but the panic on your face wasn't hard to read."

"Sorry," I mumble.

"You know what your dad told me the other day?" she asks, continuing to pull me along.

"I didn't do whatever it was."

She laughs again and what I wouldn't give to hear that sound on repeat forever.

Harlow stops in front of the door to the small recording studio and turns to me. "He told me that you play guitar and used to write poetry."

"Guitar is Kai's thing and writing is Belle's," I say, backing away. She stops me with a look and a tug on my hand.

"Kai doesn't own all guitars and Belle isn't the only person alive that can write a song, Cal."

"What do you want from me?" I whisper.

"I want to sit with you as you write or sing or play off the feelings you have right now. The ones you're pushing down because you're putting everyone else's first."

I gape at her. "Uh . . ."

"Let's go," she says, pulling me into the room and shutting the door. She leaves me standing there as she takes a seat on the couch.

"I don't know what to do," I admit, pulling on my neck anxiously.

"Whatever feels right. Yell into the mic. Strum on the guitar. Write down how mad you were at me last night in that notebook over there," she gestures to a notebook that wasn't in here before.

"You don't have to stay in here," I tell her, watching as she puts headphones on and pulls up a book on her phone.

"Yes, I do. You'll just nap on the couch if I don't." She turns away from me and leaves me in shock to look around the room and figure out what to do.

I WAKE WITH A START. The leather cushion is stuck to my cheek. I peel my skin away and look over my shoulder. Cal is sitting on a stool, guitar in hand and a notebook filled with his scribbles in front of him. His brow is pinched in concentration. I smile. He looks sexy as hell right now.

Which is why I turn back around and grab my phone. My headphones are still on, keeping me from hearing what he's working on. I pick it up to pick a new song and see a text from Jo.

JO

We need to talk.

Are you breaking up with me?

JO

Kind of?

That was supposed to be a joke. You're stuck with me forever.

JO

I like this job. I don't want to quit. Maybe the podcast can be a part-time thing?

I already told Cal I wasn't leaving. So I guess we're on the same page.

JO

Thanks for telling me, jerk.

I don't think I want to do the podcast.

JO

Yeah, I'm having second thoughts too.

Hitting too close to home because you're banging Mav?

JO

I am NOT banging Maverick.

That's too bad. He's hot.

JO

So is Cal.

Fair point.

I peek over my shoulder again. Cal is scratching out something he wrote with an aggressive amount of frustration. I smile, hoping he's letting it all out.

JO

I'm working with Jon and the label to book the next tour. Are you coming? Are babies on the road a thing?

That seems like something I should know the answer to.

JO

Ya think?

I'm shrugging.

JO

Figure it out because I have an idea.

I can't know the fun idea until I know what the Cora plan is?

JO

Who said fun?

If it's not fun, I don't want to do it. I have had enough of serious and depressing things for now.

JO

It's fun.

Ha! Knew it.

JO

I have a meeting. Let me know when you talk to Cal.

"Talk to me about what?"

I gasp and clutch my phone to my chest. "You sneaky little shit." I pull my headphones off and glare at him.

Cal throws his head back and laughs. He seems lighter, and I'm glad. That was the whole point of bringing him down here.

"I promise you, Firecracker, nothing about me is little."

My face heats even as I try to glare. Cal just smiles in victory.

"So. What are we talking about?" he asks, patting my legs to move them so he can sit next to me. I go to sit up, but he just slides under my legs, keeping hold of them and putting them on his lap.

"The Cora plan," I tell him, trying not to concentrate on the little circles he's making on my legs with his thumbs.

"The Cora plan?" he asks, brows raised.

"Yeah. Jo's working on the tour schedule. She wanted to know what the plan for Cora was during that. I told her I'd ask you."

"Hmm," he drums his fingers lightly against my calf. "What do you think?"

"Me?" I ask. "You're her dad."

Cal smiles, and that twinkle is back in his eyes. "I am, but you're a huge part of her life too. I'd like to figure it out together."

It takes me a minute to overcome the shock, but then I really think about it. "Can you give me an idea of what a show day is like versus a travel day?"

Cal explains all their responsibilities. Apparently, it also includes a lot of television and radio appearances too. I knew there would be a few, but not the amount he's explaining right now.

"Can I go over the schedule with Jo and get back to you with what I think? I don't want to make any promises without having all the information," I tell him after mulling it over.

"That sounds fair to me," Cal says. "Let me make you lunch." He stands and holds his hand out to me. I take it and let him lead me upstairs.

I escape his grasp the moment we get upstairs, telling him I wanted to call Jo right away in case there's something she needs to account for on her end if we decide to take Cora on the whole tour.

I dart up the stairs and close myself in my bathroom.

I'm about four seconds away from a panic attack by the time Jo answers her phone.

"Harry, I told you I had a meeting," she huffs.

"Jo, I need help." I'm close to tears, and I know she can hear it.

"What the hell happened? You were texting me less than an hour ago."

"Cal wants my opinion on how much or little Cora travels with them."

There's silence and if I couldn't hear someone talking in the background, I would think she hung up on me.

"That's making you cry?" she asks. "Are you pregnant?" she whispers harshly.

"No! I haven't had sex in months."

"I need you to help me out here, Harlow."

"I can't go on tour with them and watch . . ." I pause and take a deep breath. "I can't watch him with other women, Jo. I can't do it."

"Oh, Harlow," she says, her voice sympathetic. "I don't think he would do that to you."

"I don't think what the nanny thinks about his sex life is something he even thinks about," I mutter.

"You're not just the nanny. I see the way you look at each other. You just won't let yourselves go there. And I get it, I really do."

"But?"

Jo laughs softly. "But you're both close to snapping and when you do, Harlow, it's going to be epic."

I snort. "You've been reading too many romance novels."

"I've been reading dragon smut. Get it right."

"My sincerest apologies," I say with a laugh.

"Better?"

"No idea."

"I need to get back to my meeting."

"Thanks, Joey."

"Anytime, Harry."

Lunch with Cal was nice. We just ate sandwiches and talked. I really liked it.

But I couldn't help the way my conversation with Jo was bouncing around my head the whole time. Could she be right? Are Cal and I epic? I still think that was a really dramatic word to use, but maybe it's not dramatic enough.

I like him. I really like him. He hasn't touched me, other than little caresses here and there, since that night in the kitchen. And I want him to. I want his hands all over me.

My phone vibrating interrupts my thoughts.

CALLAHAN ELIZABETH

Are you up?

I snort. I changed Cal's name in my phone this morning.

Really? Booty calling the nanny?

CALLAHAN ELIZABETH

No!

Never mind.

I'll talk to you tomorrow.

I'm just kidding. What's up?

CALLAHAN ELIZABETH
Meet me in the living room. Please.

Ooh! I like when you beg.

CALLAHAN ELIZABETH
Firecracker…

Will there be popcorn?

CALLAHAN ELIZABETH
I need you down here.

Okay. That's not playful Cal. Something's up.

Give me ten minutes. I'm in the tub.

I watch as the three little dots dance on the screen before disappearing completely. I can't help laughing. Cal is so easy to get riled up.

I get out of the tub and dry off quickly, throwing on the first thing I see. Well, the second thing. The first thing is my PJs, but they're pretty revealing.

Actually?

No. Cal sounded serious. Sexually frustrating both of us seems like a bad plan.

My phone vibrates again, and I'm about to ignore it and just head downstairs, but then I see it's from an unknown number.

Great. Did a reporter get my number somehow?

Oh. Threats. Cool.

I block the number. I'll bring it up with my dad later. It's probably nothing. Even if I was Cora's mom, where is the threat there? I'm not in the public eye and threatening me isn't going to do anything.

People are so annoying.

The living room is full when I make my way down there. I'm glad I opted for leggings and a sweatshirt instead of just going to see what Cal wanted in my PJs.

"Ten pm on a Thursday is a weird time for a party," I say as I sit down next to Jo. I look around and realize everyone looks somber. "What's going on?"

"Your dad figured out who was trying to hack into his system," Belle says, looking apologetic. I know I look as confused as I feel because she smiles sadly before explaining. "My ex, Brad. Apparently, he was released on parole."

"Which is bullshit for an attempted murder charge," Kai says, holding on to Belle, who is sitting in his lap.

"He's trying to get into my dad's system?" I ask, still very confused. I know who Brad is. I know he was stalking Belle and tried to hurt her. I also know he was found guilty of attempted murder only a few months ago. My dad was looking into him just in case he somehow had any connection to Ezra. He didn't, but this seems suspicious. "How did he get parole so early? It takes people with his charges years to even qualify."

"What are you thinking, Firecracker?" Cal asks, watching me from where he's leaning against the wall.

"Well, first of all, Brad clearly has some powerful connections, which we kind of already guessed, but this proves it. Second, my dad doesn't believe in coincidences, which I'm sure he's told you." Cal nods. "He didn't find any connections between Ezra and Brad before, but he also said that whoever is behind everything is powerful enough to erase records."

"So Brad could be working for this person, and we would never know because a record wouldn't exist," Willa states from her seat on the couch next to Mav. I glance at him and debate how to phrase my next question.

"Maverick, your dad. He's pretty powerful, right?" I ask as gently as I can. Senator Wolfe is on the list of suspects. He has been for a while, which is why Mav is setting up a meeting with his mom. But there is some sort of connection here I'm missing. It's right on the edge of my brain.

"Now he is. Your dad asked the same question. He was a judge at the time Ezra went missing. He didn't have the power he does now as a senator. Definitely not the record erasing type of power."

"But he's not a good guy, right?" Jo asks.

Mav looks at her with annoyance and affection. Which is honestly kind of how I look at her most days and if the topic wasn't serious, I would probably be laughing.

"No. He's not a good guy, but I don't see why he would want Ezra gone," Mav says, looking down at his hands. He's sick of this conversation, and I think we're honestly all sick of having it. Everyone in this room wants Ezra found and this all to be over and done with.

"He runs a very conservative campaign, and his son was dating another man," Jo says. I elbow her. "What?"

"There's no way my dad hasn't asked these questions, and you don't need to upset everyone by asking them again," I tell her.

"I'm not trying to. I'm just hoping there's something your dad missed that can help. Especially if there's a crazy person who tried to murder Belle out there."

Mav sighs and leans forward, grabbing Jo's hand and squeezing. My eyes are locked on the action, and I wouldn't be surprised if everyone else's were too. Jo isn't a physical affection type of person. I think we've hugged maybe twice in all our years of friendship. The fact that she's not only letting Mav touch her, but also squeezing his hand back is alarming.

"It's ok. Really," Mav says. "My dad wasn't thrilled about me dating Ezra, but he also hadn't started his campaign to run for senator. He never asked me to break things off or anything, so I don't see why he would go to extremes. He could've easily threatened me." Mav scratches his jaw. "If he threatened Ezra, I would have left. If it was his safety at risk because of me," Mav says, choking up. "I would have put Ezra first. I will always put Ezra first."

I watch Jo's eyes dim as she slowly pulls her hand back from Mav. Definitely asking her about what's going on there later.

"Do we know where Brad is now?" I ask Belle.

"Yeah, uh," she stutters, fidgeting with the hem of her shirt. "He asked to see me."

"Fuck no. Absolutely not. Not happening." Kai exclaims, standing and then pacing the room.

"I'm going with you," Cal says, then turns to me. "Are you okay staying with Cora for a few days? I refuse to bring her anywhere near that psycho, but I can't let my sister go without me either."

"Of course," I say immediately.

"No one is going!" Kai yells.

"Oh yeah? Try telling her that," Cal says, gesturing to his sister.

"I'm going," Belle tells Kai gently.

"Mo chridhe," he pleads, his hand over his heart.

"I have to, Kai. He's in a jail cell in Bangor right now for breaking his parole. He can't hurt me from there, but maybe he'll give me some answers. Answers that can help us find Ez."

"We can leave in the morning. Just the three of us. Willa and Mav can stay here in case Harlow needs help with Cora. Dad will be here too," Cal says, seemingly ending the meeting since everyone nods and stands to leave.

"Are you okay?" I whisper to Jo while everyone says their goodbyes.

"Yeah, just tired."

I accept her answer, but I'll be keeping a closer eye on her. Something is going on with her and Mav, and I don't want her to get hurt.

I shut the door behind Jo, but when I turn around, I step face first into a solid chest.

"Cal?" I ask, looking up into those soft brown eyes and seeing fire behind them.

He walks closer as I back up into the door, but he doesn't stop until he's pressed against me, and I can feel every hard line of his body.

"Cal?" I ask again, but this time it sounds more like a squeak.

He places his hand around my throat. His grip is gentle, barely there, but the heat from his palm sets my body on fire. Cal leans close, his breath hot against my ear.

"I don't beg, Firecracker. I lick and nip and suck and kiss until you're the one on your knees begging for me. Begging for me to touch you, to fuck you." My breath hitches in my throat as my pulse races. I know he can feel how fast my heart is beating at his words. "Be careful, baby. You have no idea who you're playing with."

With that, he lets me go and heads for the stairs, taking two at a time. I watch him go, trying to calm my heart rate and wrap my mind around what had just happened. I was questioning sending that text to him, but not anymore. He's right though. I had no idea who I was playing with.

But I'd be lying if I said I didn't want to find out.

sixteen

CAL

THAT WAS STUPID. So fucking stupid.

Having Harlow against the wall like that? Her soft body pressed into mine and her pulse beating beneath my hand? Fuck. I could come in my pants right now just thinking about it. I thought the memory of her begging me to let her come was hot. But I think my dick could cut glass right now.

I can't fuck the nanny, right? That's taboo. Or cliche. Or something.

I'm fucking thinking about it though. Nonstop. Every time my dick has been in my hand for two months, it's been Harlow I've pictured.

I'm so fucking screwed.

Because I know her being the nanny isn't the problem. It's because she's Harlow. She takes my breath away while making my heart beat. I can blame my position as her boss, or how taboo the situation would be all I want, but I would be lying.

I'm barely controlling myself around her now as it is. Her sassy mouth makes me want to kiss it. Her curves make me want to grab them. And if I'm honest, she's really fucking interesting to talk to. She's fun and smart and observant in a way that's bordering on creepy. I like being around her. I like talking to her. Fuck, I even like the stupid reality shows she makes me watch. And if all that wasn't enough, she's amazing with Cora. My daughter fucking adores the woman. She loves her. And Harlow loves her right back.

As if she was summoned, Cora lets out a wail, and I'm rushing to her room. I see Harlow peek out of hers when I'm at Cora's door.

"I've got her," I whisper and Harlow nods, then shuts her door.

I scoop my baby girl up from her crib and bring her to the rocking chair to snuggle her. She still wakes up at night sometimes, but it isn't from hunger. She just wants comfort. So I spend a lot of nights rocking her while she's curled up against my chest.

I don't mind it. I know I'll miss these small moments.

Cora smiles up at me as her eyes slowly close. This is why nothing can happen between Harlow and me. This perfect little girl right here. She needs Harlow in her life right now, and I will not be the one to take that away from her. And it would be my fault. I'm not good with relationships. I don't know how to be in one. I don't know that I could ever be. Harlow deserves better than that, and so does Cora.

For Cora, I would do anything.

Give up anything.

"I REALLY THINK one of us should've gone with him."

Cora blows a raspberry in agreement.

"See? Cora thinks so too." I point out. Jo and Willa both roll their eyes at me, but Jason laughs. At least Cal's dad is on my side.

"Maverick will be fine. He's meeting her at a restaurant. In public," Willa says.

"I know. I just don't like it. Cal, Kai, Belle, and my dad are all in Maine. Now we're sending Maverick to New Hampshire alone," I groan into my hands. Mav's mom offered to meet him halfway between here and her house for lunch and she could only do today. So he went.

"The guys aren't going to be happy he went while they're gone," Willa admits.

"It'll be fine. He promised to go with our plan," Jo says, picking at her nails. It's the only tell she has that shows how nervous she is. It's not that we think he's in danger. Physically, anyway.

Mav's hair has grown out to his chin. The plan is, he's

going to wear an AirPod in one ear and make sure his hair is covering it. He'll call Willa's phone once he gets to the restaurant. She'll put him on speaker and mute the call. Jo is going to record everything on her phone. Jason and I are on Cora duty. She just started crawling, so it involves a lot of chasing and making sure nothing ends up in her mouth.

"What if someone recognizes him?" Jason asks.

"He'll be polite, but short, and they'll lose interest. It's what he always does," Willa says.

"Phone's ringing!" I yell the moment Willa's phone lights up. "Sorry," I say in a normal tone. "I'm anxious."

"It's just lunch, Harry. Jeez," Jo says, laughing at me.

"Cal is in a prison, and we just sent his best friend into the lion's den!" I whisper-shout at her while Willa answers and gets her phone set up.

"Cal isn't in prison. You need to relax, or I'm sending you to your room," Willa whispers, shutting me up with a terrifying glare.

"He's in *a* prison," I hiss, earning myself a glare from Willa in the process.

Jo gets her phone set up to record and we wait.

"I've got Cora. We'll go play in her room. Focus on one thing at a time," Jason says, squeezing my shoulder. I thank him with a smile.

"Maverick! I'm so glad we could finally get together," a soft voice says.

"Hi, Mom." Mav sounds exhausted already.

They make small talk and discuss the menu. You'd think they were strangers.

Then his mother makes her first mistake.

"Governor Daley, you remember him. His daughter is

your age. She agreed to a date with you on Saturday. She's staying in our guest house, so you'll need to pick her up there. I suggest —"

"No."

"Excuse me?" that voice that was soft before is harsh now. It made my spine straighten, and I'm not even there.

"I'm not taking anyone on a date. Especially someone that you will then expect me to marry to form a political alliance for Dad. It's not happening." Mav's voice is firm and brokers no argument.

"It is your responsibility to this family."

"What happened to Ezra, Mom?"

The silence on both ends of the line is tense. We're all staring at each other in shock. That wasn't on the list of more subtle questions Maverick was supposed to be asking. He went right for her throat.

"He died. You know that," his mom says eventually.

"He's not dead!" We hear something slam and gasps filter through the phone. "What did Dad do to him?"

"What reason would your father have to do something to some child?" his mother scoffs.

"What reason does he have to do anything he does? Because he wants to and fuck what it costs anyone else."

Another scoff.

"Why did he corner Cal's nanny in a parking lot?" The press hasn't figured out my name yet, and I'm grateful to Mav for not giving it to his mother.

She scoffs for a third time. It's her tell. She makes that noise when she's about to lie or avoid the truth. At least it seems to be from what I've heard from her so far.

"He was trying to help the girl with her bags. Don't twist it."

I had to hold my breath, so I didn't say something and mess up the recording Jo was taking of all this.

"The security footage shows otherwise," Mav says. "What's wrong, Mother? You look pale."

"I have no knowledge of any security footage."

"I've seen it."

"Your father wouldn't have to go to extremes if you would just get in line!" she hisses. "You've had your rebellious stage. Now it's time to come back home."

"Tell me what Dad did to Ezra, and I'll do it. I'll quit the band today and move back into my old room."

There's another pause. I look at Jo and Willa. Their eyes are just as wide as mine and we're all holding our breaths.

"Ezra is dead. Ask the police. Stop blaming your father because your little friend died." I flinch at the coldness in her voice.

"Why? Why do you protect him? He hits you, Mom," Mav pleads with her.

Of course, she scoffs.

"We argue. That's it."

"We're done." Mav says, and there's the sound of a chair being pushed back. "Did you guys get that?" he asks us a few moments later.

Willa quickly takes her phone off mute. "We got it, Mav."

"I'll be home in an hour."

The line goes dead and we're all standing around, staring at Willa's phone.

"Do we think she was saying Ezra is dead because that's

the official ruling or because she knows her husband killed him?" Jo asks. I wince at her direct words. She really needs to work on that.

"She didn't scoff," I say.

"What?" Willa asks.

"She made a scoffing noise whenever she lied or tried to redirect. She didn't when she said Ezra was dead."

"So he's dead?" Willa asks, tears forming in her eyes.

"She believes he is, at least. I don't think that's proof he is." I bite my lip to keep from speaking more. The person closest to the man we think did something to Ezra thinks he's dead. It's more information than we've had in months and it's not good.

"What are you thinking?" Jo asks.

"Gavin Irons," I answer.

"What about him?" Willa asks, wiping under her eyes.

"If he loved Ezra enough to either find him or maybe eventually avenge him, he has to love Kai that much too."

"Breadcrumbs," Jo says, reading my mind.

"You think Gavin left breadcrumbs for Kai to follow?" Willa asks, and I'm happy she's following. "But he called Kai and told him to stop looking."

"He called Kai on an unsecure line."

"I didn't know that," Willa says.

"My dad found the number but couldn't find where it came from since the call was so short and the number disconnected so quickly."

"And Gavin covers his tracks too well to make that mistake. He did it on purpose," Jo adds.

"We find Gavin, we find Ezra," Willa says, eyes dry and hopeful.

I just hope I'm right.

I just hope I'm right.

eighteen

CAL

"NO PUNCHING HIM," Kai says. I'm not sure if he's talking to me or himself, but I nod anyway.

"Do you really think he's going to tell you anything?" I ask Belle. She glares at me. I may have asked her the same question a few times on the drive up here. "Right. Can't hurt to try."

We're in my car outside the correctional facility where Brad is currently being held. Hacking is obviously illegal and when Harrison traced it back to Brad, he was sent back to prison for breaking his parole. Once Harrison is here, we'll all be going in to speak to Brad.

I tap on the steering wheel impatiently, earning another glare from my sister. "And everyone thinks you're the nice one," I mutter under my breath. I pull my phone out to have something to do before she sets me on fire with her eyeballs.

How's it going?

HARLOW

Good.

I bite the inside of my cheek. *Shit.* Harlow and I both pretended nothing happened last night when we saw each other this morning. Maybe that was the wrong call.

> About last night…

I bite my lip waiting for her response. I crossed a line, and I know it, but I don't want to go back. Having her pinned against me, her pulse fluttering beneath my fingertips, is all I've been able to think about.

HARLOW

> Nothing happened last night. So there's nothing to talk about.

> Right.

HARLOW

> Don't worry so much, Vocal Daddy.

I snort.

HARLOW

> Do you have a sixth sense about when I'm in the bath?

> If you're in the tub, then where is Cora?

I look at the time, trying to stop picturing Harlow wet and naked. The last thing I need is to get an erection with my damn sister in the car with me. It's too early for Cora's bedtime. Maybe my dad has her. I hate not being home and knowing what's going on.

HARLOW

> She's with me. I think she's getting another
> tooth. Poor girl has been clingy today.

She sends a picture of her in a one-piece pale green swimsuit in a shallow bath with Cora sitting between her legs smiling up at her, bath toys floating in the bubbles all around them. Harlow is smiling at the camera, bubbles sticking to her red curls. That fucking smile is going to stop my heart one of these days. I set the picture as the background image on my phone.

> You're killing me.

Shit. Shouldn't have sent that. I know I shouldn't have. Yet here I am, anxiously waiting to see what Harlow has to say. I've never been like this before. Felt like this before. I don't know how to handle anything right now.

HARLOW

> Are you ready to beg yet?

I smile. I fucking smile even though I try like fuck to fight it. There's no way Belle isn't watching me right now. I can feel her eyes on the side of my head. Having siblings is annoying.

> I don't beg, Firecracker. I thought we went
> over this last night.

HARLOW

> Hmm. I think I need a reminder. I hear
> better when you're on your knees.

I gulp. Fuck. *This girl*. She's like the forbidden fruit, and I'm powerless to resist her.

> We'll see who's going to be on their knees.

HARLOW

> Promises promises.

"Are you growling?" Belle asks, looking slightly horrified. I look up and see Kai looking amused in the mirror.

"No," I say immediately. Was I? I have no idea.

"You growled, dude," Kai says, laughing like the asshole he is.

"I'm not a fucking dog," I argue. Not really sure I can actually make that claim. It's getting to the point where if Harlow asked me to bark, I'd fucking bark.

Kai holds his hands up. "I get it, man. I'm feral for your sister."

I turn around and try to punch him. "Quit reminding me you're hooking up with my sister!"

"It's a little more than hooking up," Belle says.

"Not you too," I groan.

"Was it Harlow you were texting?" she asks.

"Yeah," I admit. She knows when I'm lying, so I don't bother.

"Do you think that's a good idea?" I look at my sister. I know she's asking out of concern for me and Cora, and not because she doesn't like Harlow. They actually get along really well.

"I don't know what I think anymore. It's like the moment I see her, my brain stops working."

"Like it ever started," Kai says, still laughing by himself in the backseat.

"Harlow is good with Cora. I don't think you should risk it by sleeping with her. Cora adores her, and she would be devastated."

My sister's words cut. Of course, she thinks I just want to sleep with Harlow. That's what everyone thinks. That I'm only capable of casual sex and breaking hearts. Hell, even I think that most days.

So maybe she's right.

"Yeah. You're right. I'll keep my distance."

And this time, I will.

CORA and I are playing on the floor of the living room while Jason is cooking dinner in the kitchen. She has new bath toys she loves, so we took a bath. I even went in with her in a swimsuit. She loves it when I play in the bubbles with her.

It's been a pretty normal night for us. Except it's the first time Cal won't be home, and Mav came home from lunch with his mom in the angriest state I've ever seen him in. Which seems to be really stressing Willa and Jo out. So maybe not the most normal night.

Willa and Jo come bursting through the front door, Maverick sauntering in behind them. Their eyes are practically bugging out of their heads.

"What is it?" I ask, worried they found Ezra. Or more specifically, his body. It's what's been running through my mind all day. The only time Mav's mother didn't lie was when she said Ezra was dead. I knew it would destroy them all if she was right.

Jo doesn't answer. She just walks over to the TV and puts

on the evening news. I gasp at what I see. The Bangor Correctional Facility is in lockdown. There's video of the alarms blaring and lights flashing.

"Early reports state witnesses heard two gun shots within a few seconds of each other. No report on Shattered Halo members Callahan and Bellamy Griffin and Malikai Irons or the man they entered with."

My heart stops, my stomach clenches, my ears are ringing, and I don't think I'm breathing. Cora grabs onto my pant leg and tries to pull herself up. I grab her into my arms and hug her to my chest, burying my nose in her hair.

"I have you, Cora girl," I whisper.

Jo and Willa are on either side of me. Mav is on the floor in front of us with his head in his hands, waiting for news like the rest of the world. Jason came into the room at some point. I can see him pacing out of the corner of my eyes, but I can't tear my gaze away from the news long enough to check on him.

My dad is in that building. Cal is in that building. Kai and Belle are in that building. Was there a shooter? Did the guards have to pull a gun? How bad would things have to be if they had to shoot?

Willa is furiously texting next to me. "Come on, Belle," she cries.

I grab my phone to try calling Cal. He told me they wouldn't be allowed to have their phones on them, but I try anyway. Call after call goes to voicemail. I switch to trying my dad, but that has the same result.

"Answer the phone, Kai!" Mav screams. It makes Cora cry. "I'm sorry, sweet girl. Uncle Mav didn't mean to scare you," he says softly, rubbing her back. She calms quickly and snuggles back into my chest.

I catch Jason looking at us. His phone is in his hand, trying to get in touch with his kids. Fuck. Both of his children are in there. I can't imagine the panic he's feeling. I gesture to Cora with my chin. He comes over and scoops her into his arms.

"Thank you," he whispers, a tear falling from his eye onto Cora's head.

"Look!" Jo shouts, jumping up from the couch. We all turn and watch as Cal's SUV leaves the prison. The windows are all tinted, so it's hard to see who's in it. My dad's car follows shortly behind.

"Why are they still not answering?" Willa asks, frustrated.

I try Cal a few more times. She's right. They're not.

I pull on my hair. We just need one of them to answer us and tell us they're okay.

"No," Jason whispers, sounding broken.

I look up and gasp. A van just entered through the prison gate. The word printed in black, stark against the white of the van, was clear as day.

Coroner.

CAL

THE GUARD LEADS us into a room set up with a bunch of round metal tables. Round seats are attached to them. It seems like everything in this place is bolted to the floor. Which is good. It means Kai can't throw anything at Brad.

"Remember, let myself or Belle do the talking. I'm not even sure the two of you should be in here," Harrison says, giving a stern look to both Kai and me. I scoff while Kai glares. Like we'd let Belle in here without us. "Yeah, yeah. Overprotective macho men. Got it."

Brad is led into the room by a female corrections officer. His blond hair is slicked back, and he's smiling like the shit-head he is.

"Are you allowed to have hair gel in prison?" I whisper to Kai.

"Seems like it," he whispers back. Harrison hears us and shoots us a warning look.

"Thank you so much, Nikki," Brad says, winking at the officer. She blushes and fucking giggles. I look at Kai and

154

widen my eyes, making sure he saw the same thing I did. From the way he seems to be trying to make Brad explode with his eyes, I think he did.

"We have some questions, Mr. Foley," Harrison says to the arrogant asshole that's currently smirking at my sister. If I didn't have my girls waiting for me at home, I'd wipe that smirk off his face.

My girls. Shit. I'll need to figure out that thought later.

"You look really good, Bellamy. Fame is working for you." The creep licks his lips as he looks directly at my sister's chest.

Harlow can bring Cora to visit me in prison. She'll understand.

"Funny, I was just thinking how good you look in orange," Belle counters, not affected by his comments. Brad, however, suddenly looks murderous.

"Listen, you stupid bi—"

"We're here because you said you'd only speak to Belle. So speak," Harrison says, controlling the situation. Sometimes I forget he used to be a cop.

Brad glares at him, still completely ignoring that Kai and I are sitting here too. Which is fine with me.

"My boss has a message for you," Brad says, his cocky mask back in place.

"Oh? Which boss is that? Your mom? Or Senator Wolfe?" Belle asks. My head whips to her. We have no proof of that. I'm the only shocked one because Harrison and Kai haven't reacted at all. Brad, though? Brad looks really pale suddenly.

Oh damn. Maybe he is involved.

"My boss," Brad continues, like Belle didn't speak, not confirming or denying what she said. I guess he doesn't really need to. His reaction was enough for Harrison to want to keep digging into the senator, "wants you to know that as long as you keep digging up old dirt, they will end your career." He's smiling again, and it's the most unsettling thing I've ever seen. "They will end your pathetic life."

"So about Senator Wolfe," Belle says. "How do you get in touch with him? What did he do to Ezra?" Brad keeps the smile on his face, but I can see how hard it is for him to keep it there.

"I don't know what you're talking about," Brad says.

"What's it going to take? Money? I know your mom needs a care team. I could pay for that in exchange for information. I doubt the senator will continue to pay her bills now that you're no use to him." I watch my sister in awe. I've always said that she was the strongest person I know, but apparently, she's also a badass.

I'll high five her later when I'm not risking Harrison's wrath. Fucker is scary when he wants to be.

Brad's smile falters, like he's just realizing he's at the end of his usefulness. He opens his mouth to speak, but something whizzes past my ear. I watch in slow motion as a bullet pierces his forehead and the contents of his skull spray on the wall behind him.

"Under the table!" I barely register Harrison's voice as the alarms sound and lights flash. I'm dragged under the table, but I make the mistake of looking up. The guard that brought Brad in puts her gun in her mouth and pulls the trigger.

I hear screaming, and I don't know who it's coming from. Might be me. I snap out of the shock long enough to see that my sister and Kai are under the table with me and seem unharmed. I look around and find Harrison a few feet away from us, banging on the locked door we came through to get here.

My ears are ringing. Something hot is dripping down my face. There's a horrible smell that's making my stomach turn. I crawl out from under the table and move away, where I immediately lose my lunch.

The muscles in my stomach ache from how violently I'm heaving. My face is sweaty, and I can't catch my breath.

"Cal! Cal, look at me!" I barely hear a voice over the ringing in my ears and the alarms in the room.

I blink. Something is in my eyes. I swipe at it, trying to see who's screaming at me.

Red. I see red in my vision. Red on my hands.

It's blood. I heave again, but there's nothing left to come up.

"It's okay, Cal. It's a graze. We'll get you some stitches. Heads just bleed like a bitch."

I look and see Harrison. I register the feel of his hands on my shoulders, keeping me standing. Looking over his shoulder, I see Belle cuddled into Kai. They're both standing and I think my sister is crying, but no blood. I take a deep breath and then another.

"Sit down. They're sending in the prison nurse to help you," Harrison says. I nod and let him lead me to a seat close to the exit. He faces me away so I can't see the bodies I know are behind me.

There's a million people in this room. Some try to ask me questions, but Harrison is able to get them to talk to him instead.

Belle holds my hand as the nurse stitches my head. I

barely notice the small pricks of the needle she used to numb it. There's a weird pulling sensation as she stitches my skin back together. I try to focus on that.

I know I'm in shock. I know that's what this weird state where I feel awake and asleep, in my body and not. Maybe if I focus on the sensation, I can snap out of it.

I somehow end up in the back of my car. I don't remember walking there. I don't remember getting in.

Turning my head, I see the base for Cora's car seat. That's what does it. It's like someone suddenly took the world off mute. I can hear the music playing, Belle speaking, the GPS giving Kai directions to the hotel. I gasp and my body starts shaking.

Belle swings her head around at the sound. "Kai. Pull over," she says. Once we're on the side of the road, Belle scrambles into the back seat and pulls me into her arms. I have a full foot on her, and I'm much broader, but she holds me like I'm a small child.

And I don't give a fuck.

I fall apart in my sister's arms.

"Are you sure you don't want me to stay in here with you?" Belle asks.

I smile as much as I can. "I'm good now, Belle. I promise."

She nods. "We're just in the next room."

That makes me snort. "Belle. I'm good. I swear."

"You should call Harlow. She's probably freaking out."

"What?" I jump up from the bed and fish my phone out

of my pocket. I didn't even feel it ringing in the state I was in. "Twenty-eight missed calls! Did you tell her what happened?"

"Uh, no. Someone saw us going into the prison and called the paps. They were there when the sirens went off. It's all over social media and the news."

"Belle! Did you tell her we're fine?"

"Honestly, I just realized she's probably freaking out because Willa has been calling me, and Mav has been blowing up Kai's phone."

"Go call them. I need to make sure my nanny isn't on her way her with my daughter."

She sighs but takes Kai's hand and leaves the room.

Harlow answers on the first ring.

"Cal! What the fuck happened? Are you okay?"

"I'm fine," I tell her.

"Fuck this. I'm FaceTiming you."

I sigh, knowing I don't have a choice and accept the call.

"What happened to your head?" Harlow yells, her eyes are wide with panic.

"I'm okay, Firecracker."

"Like fuck you are. Don't you lie to me, Callahan Elizabeth Griffin! You gave me a heart attack."

I smile. It feels almost foreign on my face right now, but the way she clearly cares about me makes me happy.

"Stop smiling! This isn't funny! I thought . . . I thought," her voice cracks.

"I know. I'm so sorry. I just got back to the hotel. We weren't allowed to have our phones in the room."

"Cal! What happened? All I know is that you went into that prison and the fucking emergency sirens went off.

That's all anyone is reporting. My dad won't tell me anything."

I sigh and go to rub my face. Luckily, I stop in time. That would've fucking hurt.

"I'll tell you when I get home tomorrow. I don't think it should be discussed over the phone," I tell her. She examines my face and gives me a quick nod.

"Your head, Cal," she says. I can see how panicked she is. It makes me feel terrible.

"I'm sorry I made you worry, Firecracker," I say softly. I can't tell her what happened to my head without telling her everything else. She seems to pick up on that because she doesn't push.

"Cal," she says my name, and I can see she's about to cry. My heart breaks right there. We're past the point of no return already. There are too many feelings. We mean too much to each other. I can try to avoid her all I want, but it won't amount to anything. Harlow has wormed her way in somehow.

"Tell me about your day. How is Cora?"

Harlow's smile is watery, but she goes with my change of subject. "It was good. Cora really loves to stack things." That makes me chuckle. Her favorite game is to stack her blocks and knock them back down. I wouldn't be surprised if that's what Harlow did all day.

"Is she sleeping?"

"Yeah. Once my dad called me and told me that you were all okay, your dad took her to rock her to sleep."

"Fuck. My dad. I'm such an asshole. I should call him."

Harlow laughs. "Well, considering he's probably still rocking your daughter, I wouldn't."

"Right."

"Cal?"

"Yeah?"

"I'm really glad you're okay." Harlow's voice is a whisper.

"Me too, Firecracker."

"When will you be home?"

"Early afternoon. Earlier if I can get Kai up in the morning."

Harlow nods. She's biting her lip like she's nervous. "Make sure you shower before you come home."

"Why?" I ask, confused.

"Your face is covered in blood, Cal," she says, looking like she wants to cry again.

"I'll go shower right now. You get some sleep. I promise we'll head straight home."

"Okay," she says softly. If I could hug her right now, I would, and I don't think I could let go.

"Goodnight, Firecracker."

"Goodnight, Vocal Daddy."

I laugh as she hangs up.

Only she could make me laugh after watching two brains splatter on walls. The reminder makes me nauseous again.

I carefully clean up in the bathroom and then lay on the bed. I know I won't be able to sleep tonight.

So instead, I stare at the ceiling and think about the beautiful woman waiting for me at home.

twenty-one

HARLOW

THE MOMENT I see Cal's black SUV pull into the driveway; I'm running out the door. The cold pavement bites into the soles of my bare feet, but I don't care. I need to see for myself that he's okay. Feel for myself that he's still here.

"Firecracker," Cal grunts as I leap into his arms, knocking him back into the car door. He laughs as he catches me, and I can feel the vibrations from it in my own chest. That's how close I'm holding him. "I'm okay, baby," he murmurs in my ear.

I burst into tears, clutching him impossibly closer. His arms tighten around me as he continues to whisper reassurances in my ear. He's warm, and he's safe and he's home. Cal feels like home.

I thought something had happened to him. I thought I had lost him without ever being able to tell him what he means to me.

"Cal," I croak over my tears.

"I know," he whispers and then his lips are on mine,

meeting me in a shared desperation. Then he's moving with me still in his arms and his lips on mine. "Cora?" he asks breathlessly.

"Napping," I tell him, going back in for more. I can't get enough of him; of the way he kisses me.

"My dad?" I hear him shut the front door.

"Belle's. Didn't want them coming home to an empty house."

I kiss my way along his jaw and under his ear, down his neck and nip the spot where it meets his shoulder. He practically runs up the stairs, long legs taking two steps at a time, even with me in his arms.

Placing me down on his bed gently, Cal looks at me with a hunger that has me clenching my thighs together. His arms are on either side of my head, and one of his legs is between mine, making the clenching not only impossible, but obvious. His mouth twists into a sexy smirk. He knows exactly what he's doing to me.

"Tell me I can have you," he says, chest rising and falling rapidly. "Tell me you're mine, Harlow, because I can't stay away from you anymore."

Using my name tells me how serious he is. He's been struggling to stay away from me, just like I've been struggling to stay away from him.

"I'm yours."

The moment the words leave my lips, he pounces. He's kissing me like he won't survive another moment if he doesn't. I lift my hips, trying to find the friction I need against his thigh. Cal chuckles against my mouth, then knocks my legs open and settles himself there.

"Take what you need, baby," he says before kissing me

again. I grind myself against his hard length. I grind and moan and pant like a dog in heat, but I don't care. I'm surrounded by Cal, his smell, his mouth as it traces a path down my neck, his weight on my body.

"Cal," I moan his name just as the coil that's wound itself tight inside my body snaps. White spots take over my vision as every nerve ending in my body screams.

I open my eyes as I come down from an orgasm that was way too intense for having come from dry humping. Cal's eyes are on me, his smile so bright it's blinding.

"I love when you say my name like that, Firecracker. Let's see if I can get you to do it again."

I pull at the hem of my shirt, trying to get it over my head as quickly as possible. I've never wanted anyone the way I want Callahan Griffin. Just being near him is like getting too close to a fire. My whole body burns for him. My world feels incomplete without him. And I think . . . I think my heart might beat just for him.

Cal chuckles at my attempt at breaking the speed undressing record. He doesn't stop me though, instead he removes his own clothes while I remove mine, then settles himself back between my thighs within seconds. He reaches for his nightstand, and I take a moment to admire the way his muscles flex with the movement. He really is beautiful.

"Wait," I say, grabbing his arm. Cal freezes and looks down at me. "I'm on birth control. I'm clean." Cal stays frozen for another second. "But we can use a condom if you're uncomfortable."

I bite my lip and look away, feeling uncomfortable and annoyed with myself. He's a famous rock star. He's probably heard those words a million times. And who knows how many times they were lies? Protecting himself is smart.

"Look at me, Firecracker," Cal whispers. I meet his eyes, and he smiles. "I've never gone bare before."

I frown and look in the direction of Cora's room. Cal laughs and kisses my temple.

"The condom must have broken," he answers my unasked question. "But I want that with you. I don't want anything between us. I was tested at my last physical, and I'm clean. Haven't had sex since Cora was born."

I feel my eyebrows raise at that admission and Cal just laughs again.

"You're laughing a lot for someone whose dick is less than an inch from my vagina," I gruff.

"What can I say? You make me happy, Harlow. Happier than I've ever been," he admits, kissing me sweetly.

That sweet kiss soon turns hot, and he's nudging my entrance. I moan as he pushes inside me.

"Fuck, baby. You're so tight," he groans through clenched teeth. "Hold on."

I grab his biceps as he grips my hips and slams forward. He pauses there, letting me adjust and kissing every inch of my face.

"You're perfect. So fucking perfect, Firecracker."

"Move, Cal," I demand, trying to move my hips to get what I want.

"Be careful what you wish for," he whispers in my ear and then does exactly what I wished for. He moves. He pulls all the way out, causing me to whimper from the loss of him, but then he snaps his hips forward, filling me completely once again. "You make the prettiest noises, baby."

Cal starts moving in earnest. His hands are everywhere. My hands are everywhere. Our lips never leave each other, my mouth capturing his sounds while his captures mine. His arms hold me tightly to him, our chests pressed together. It's like he can't get close enough to me.

"Yes, Callahan. Right there. Don't stop," I moan. He groans and tightens his grip.

"Never," he growls.

I feel him everywhere, inside me, surrounding me. And I never want to be without that feeling again.

Cal nips at my lip and meets my eyes. "Come for me, Firecracker."

I nod quickly, more than willing to obey. And boy do I obey. He sets me off like, well, a firecracker. Cal's mouth covers mine, swallowing my screams and giving me his as he finds his release with me.

We kiss slowly, lazily, as we come down from the high of our release.

"Don't move," Cal says, getting up and making his way to his bathroom.

I look around. I haven't been in his room before. The sheets are navy blue, the comforter matches. The walls are light gray, but the ceiling is the same navy blue as his sheets. Belle might be onto something with the unconventional ceilings because it really makes the room. I think it's around the same size as mine, maybe a little bigger. Where the sitting area in my room is, his has a play area set up for Cora. It's very Cal. Masculine, clean, and a spot for his daughter.

"Spread those legs for me, baby," Cal says, nudging my thighs. He has a wet cloth in his hand, so I move my legs for him. Although, I probably would've let him between my legs no matter what.

I watch him as he gently cleans the mess we made between my legs and spot the bandage that's partially hidden under his dark hair.

"We need to talk," I say, running my fingers through his hair, making sure to keep my distance from his injury. He turns his head so that his cheek nestles into my palm. Closing his eyes, he nods.

After tossing the cloth into the hamper, he lays down next to me, pulling me into his arms and holding me like I'll float away if he lets go. My grip on him becomes just as tight as he speaks, telling me about the conversation with Brad and then the chaos that followed. How he got the injury on his head and why it took him so long to call me back.

By the time he finishes, I'm sobbing, and he's clinging to me, reminding me he's here and he's okay.

"You were millimeters away from death!" I try to shout, but it comes out closer to a sob.

"I know," Cal says, kissing each tear that falls from my eyes. "I'm sorry."

"Why are you apologizing?" I ask.

"Because I scared you. I never want to scare you. I never want to hurt you." His eyes are pleading.

"I'm not mad at you," I tell him honestly. "I'm angry at the entire situation, but not you."

The tension in Cal's shoulders releases, and he kisses me. "There's one more thing we need to talk about."

Now it's my turn to tense. "I swear if you're about to tell me you're going to do something else dangerous, I will actually be mad at you. You need to stay here with me and Cora. No more almost getting shot in the head. I can't take it."

Cal shuts me up by kissing me intensely. I almost forget what we're talking about by the time he pulls away.

"We need to talk about us," he says, causing my heart to jump and a million horrible thoughts run through my head.

"Uh," I stutter. Cal laughs at my panic and kisses the line between my brows.

"This isn't just sex for me. You are so much more. I want us to be so much more. You brought me to life, Firecracker. I want to explore that."

My mouth is hanging open with that admission. I know how much he means to me, but I don't think I ever thought I could mean much more than a friend to him.

"Tell me you want this too. Tell me you want to be with me." the vulnerability I see on Cal's face floors me.

"I want to be with you," I tell him honestly.

"Thank fuck," he says, kissing me soundly.

We're about to go for round two when a sharp "da!" comes through the baby monitor. Cal sighs into my neck, but I just laugh.

"Time to go see your baby girl," I say, patting Cal's tight butt as he stands. The man has a glorious ass.

We get dressed quickly. Cora doesn't like to stay in her crib after naps. I watch Cal try to get his hair to cover the bandage on his head.

"Let me," I say softly as I walk up to him. He has to bend a little so I can reach. Cal's eyes close when my fingers brush against his skin, like he's memorizing the feeling.

"I don't want her to see me hurt," Cal whispers. "She won't understand."

I nod and then laugh as a louder and more demanding "da!" echoes through the room.

"Come on," Cal says, grabbing my hand and lacing our fingers together. "Let's go get our girl."

I'm smiling like a fool as he leads me out the door.

twenty-two

CAL

"WILL YOU STOP BEING SUCH A BABY?" Harlow sighs, taking my outstretched hand.

"It hurts, Firecracker. I need you to hold me through the pain," I say, smirking at my girl. The doctor tries to hide her smile as she continues removing the stitches from my head.

"This might scar. I can give you a recommendation for a plastic surgeon, or you could try scar cream."

"No thanks, Doc. The scar is going to make me look like a badass," I give my best *everything is fine* smile to the doctor, but it falls when I see Harlow. The haunted look in her eyes every time she stares at my head too long guts me. I know she's seeing what she could have lost, and I don't know how to help her. I squeeze her hand, her green eyes snapping back to mine.

"Your fan base is going to have a lot of questions." Harlow fights a smile. Fans have been rabid for information. We've been asked not to say anything publicly until the investigation is complete. Which we're fine with since we don't know what to say anyway.

I shrug and smile up at my firecracker. "I'll just tell them I hit my head falling for you."

Harlow snorts and rolls her eyes, but she's smiling. I will do anything to keep that smile on her beautiful face. I'm half gone for her as it is, but when she smiles at me like that, fuck, I might already be there.

"Alright Mr. Griffin," the doctor says, snapping her latex gloves off. "You're all set."

I stand, pulling Harlow to me as the doctor leaves the room. "Thanks for helping me through the pain, Firecracker."

Harlow laughs and buries herself in my chest. I hold her tightly and kiss the top of her head. We stay like that for a moment, but Cora's giggle breaks us out of the moment. She's in her stroller, chewing on a giraffe teething toy. Her teeth are coming in hard now. She has two that just broke through and another four that we can feel pushing on her gums.

"Da-mmm!"

Harlow's head swings around, causing her hair to hit me in the face. "Did she just say damn?"

"I don't know. I was busy being assaulted by a red monster," I say, making exaggerated spitting noises.

"You liked that red monster when you were pulling on it and fucking me from behind this morning," Harlow mutters under her breath.

I groan and pull her back into my chest. "Don't make me hard in the doctor's office with my daughter right there, baby."

A knock sounds on the door and a nurse pops her head in, looking frazzled and wide-eyed. "I'm sorry, Mr. Griffin, but there're reporters gathered at the front of the building. We've been denying that you're here, but they must have spotted you. Dr. Green is keeping them from entering, but I don't think you can get to your car in the parking lot without having to go through them."

"Shit," I mutter. "Thank you. I'll figure it out," I say to the nurse.

"Give me your phone," Harlow says, holding her hand out. I hand it over without question. She pauses when she sees the picture of her and Cora in the tub on the lock screen.

"I can't go too long without seeing my girls, even when I know I'm coming home to them," I tell her. She kisses me quickly before going back to whatever she is doing.

"Da-mmm!" Cora says, giggling when she gets the reaction she wants. Meaning me with wide eyes and an open mouth.

"Dada, baby girl. I'm Da-da," I say, pronouncing it slowly for her.

"Da-mmm!" is her reply. I just sigh and rub my chin. Maybe if I don't react, she won't keep saying it.

"Here you go. We should be good to go in a couple of minutes." Harlow hands me my phone.

"What did you do?" I ask her, squinting my eyes in suspicion.

"Quit looking at me like that. I just posted a picture on your socials and had the rest of the band comment on it."

I keep squinting at her before turning to my phone and finding the post. I bark out a laugh when I see what she's done. It's a selfie I took of us a couple of days ago. I'm smiling like an absolute goon and only Harlow's forehead is visible. It was funny then, and it's even funnier now that she posted it for the world to see.

Until I see the caption.

"Major announcement happening today! First to find where this was taken gets to break the story." I read out loud. Willa and Belle have both commented, saying how excited they are. Kai only commented a thumbs up and Mav said he's so happy. "Uh, Harlow?"

The nurse pops her head back into the room. "They're gone. I don't know what happened, but they literally ran away."

Harlow laughs and thanks her.

We make our way to my car, my eyes darting everywhere just in case there was a straggler. But the parking lot is deserted of anyone with a camera.

Once Cora is strapped into her seat and Harlow and I are settled in the front, I turn towards her. "What's the plan exactly? That picture was taken at a rest stop in Maine." I had to go back to make a full statement to the police on what happened that day with Brad. Harlow refused to let me go alone.

Harlow laughs. "I know. It's going to take them forever to figure it out."

"And when they do? What's the big announcement?" I ask, trying to ignore the notifications piling up on my phone.

Harlow shrugs. "You should probably figure that out."

I glare at her, but she just smiles sweetly. "The picture makes it seem like I'm announcing you as my girlfriend," I tell her, holding my breath to see how she responds to that.

She is my girlfriend if we're using labels, but she honestly feels like so much more than that.

Harlow turns her head to look at me, that happy smile still on her face. "I'm not worried about the media, Cal. We can keep this for us, or we can tell the world. Whatever you want to do."

"What do you want?" I ask. I'll do whatever she wants. I'll keep her hidden from the scrutinizing eyes of the world, or I'll go shout that she's mine from the tops of mountains.

"You, Callahan."

I grab her and press my lips to hers in a chaste kiss. "I want to tell the world, Firecracker. You're mine, and I want everyone to know."

"Then tell them," she says, not worried at all.

"Some people won't be nice. They won't like that you tamed the untamable."

Harlow laughs so hard she doubles over in her seat.

"Okay, that reaction is a little much," I grumble.

"Tamed," she laughs and has to take a deep breath as tears stream down her face. "The untamable," she continues. Her laugh is so loud and contagious that Cora is laughing now too.

"Okay. Both of you can stop laughing at me now." I frown and cross my arms, which just makes Harlow laugh harder.

"Okay, okay. I'm done," she says a few minutes later, wiping under her eyes. "Your dad is a funny guy, Cora girl."

"Dammm!" Cora exclaims, feet kicking the mirror in front of her.

"Da. Da," I tell her.

"Da-dammm," Cora says and then claps.

"Closer I guess," I grumble, starting up the car.

Both mine and Harlow's phones start pinging with texts.

KAI

Harrison's guy finally broke into Ezra's phone.

Harlow gasps next to me. Her dad was able to obtain the phone with relative ease, but getting into it has been another story. It looked like it had been erased, but Harrison said he had a guy that worked miracles. So we've been playing the waiting game ever since.

Did he find anything?

KAI

Don't know yet.

JO

I'm out getting Maverick a new coffee table. I'll pick lunch up on the way back and we can have a meeting. I'll let Harrison know to meet us at Cal's.

Why my house?

JO

Cora's naptime is in a little over an hour.

"Wow. She really knows our schedules," I say.

"It's kind of her job," Harlow laughs.

FIRECRACKER

Thanks, Jo! I picked up your favorite wine yesterday.

JO

You're my soulmate, Harry.

"I don't think so," I grumble under my breath. Harlow snorts next to me. We haven't said those words to each other yet, but it's clear we're moving quickly in that direction.

BELLE

Is no one going to ask about what happened to Mav's other coffee table?

WILLA

I just thought he finally realized it was ugly.

MAV

It was not ugly!

JO

You really don't want to know what happened to it.

Well, now I do.

KAI

I kind of want to know too.

MAV

My naked ass went through it.

WILLA

You were right, Jo. We didn't want to know.

I laugh and toss my phone in a cup holder.

"Is it weird that I still want more details on what happened to that coffee table?" Harlow asks. I grab her hand and kiss her knuckles, keeping my eyes on the road as we head home.

"Da-dammm!" Cora says from the backseat.

"You're right, Cora girl. Curiosity killed the cat."

"Da!" Cora replies, sounding serious.

"Don't worry. Your dad doesn't want to know either."

I smile to myself. These two have some sort of language all to themselves. I admit, I was jealous when I first noticed it, but now it fills me with a warmth I wasn't expecting. I love how much they love each other.

I suddenly have this little family that I never expected, but I'm so grateful for it.

twenty-three

HARLOW

"DID SHE JUST SAY DAMN?" Willa asks, breaking the silence we've been sitting in while we wait for my dad. Cora is supposed to be napping, but all her favorite people got here before we could put her down. Now there's no way she's going to go to sleep.

"Da-da," Cal says, trying to get Cora to stop saying her new favorite word.

"Da-dammm," Cora responds, giggling and clapping when Kai barks out a laugh he was trying to contain.

"Not helping, Uncle Kai," Cal says sternly, which just causes everyone else to laugh.

"Alright, let's make this quick because you're about to have bigger problems," my dad says, coming into the room followed closely by Jason. I do a double take. I've never seen Cal's dad look so distraught.

"What do you mean?" Cal asks, sending a questioning look to his dad, who just shakes his head. Jason heads straight for the kitchen, not even greeting anyone.

My dad takes a seat next to me on the couch. Cal is on

my other side with Belle and Kai taking up the loveseat. Willa is on the floor with Cora and Mav is pacing. Jo quietly watches him from where she's leaning on the wall. I know she feels like she's intruding on private moments with these meetings, just like I do. But they've all assured us that they want us here. Cal's hand on my thigh reassures me.

"As I've mentioned," my dad says, getting right into it and not telling us what the bigger problem is. We all focus on him without speaking up, wanting to know what information he has just as much. "Ezra's phone was erased, but that's not as permanent as people think. I have a guy that's able to get the information back."

"You have a guy?" I ask before I can stop myself. I'm barely able to contain my snort. My dad is making himself seem like some sort of mob boss.

My dad shoots me a look telling me to shut up, but he answers anyway. "He was a kid I brought in when I was still a cop. He was hacking into his school's system to change his grades and the grades of all his friends. I talked the school out of pressing charges since he was only sixteen and it would've ruined his life." My dad shrugs. "Now he helps me out."

"He got Ezra's phone restored?" Kai asks, looking both scared and hopeful. He reaches out to Mav who grabs his hand and holds on.

My dad nods and hands them a piece of paper. I watch their eyes fly back and forth, a single tear falling from Mav's eye. Kai's face loses all color. Belle gently takes the paper and reads it over, with Willa and Jo behind her. By the time it gets to us, our friends are either pale or crying. Cal takes

the paper gently from Belle and holds it out so I can see it
too. It's a printout of a text conversation.

UNKNOWN

I know what you saw. Meet me at the river
at 10.

EZRA

I already told you no.

UNKNOWN

Meet me at the river at 10 and no harm will
come to Maverick.

EZRA

What are you talking about? I don't know
anything!

UNKNOWN

I know what he means to you. I know you
saw what I can do to people. Turn yourself
over to me, and I'll spare him.

EZRA

He has nothing to do with anything. Leave
him alone!

UNKNOWN

Whether or not I leave him alone is up
to you.

EZRA

I have your word that if I meet with you,
nothing will happen to Maverick?

UNKNOWN

Nothing will happen to Maverick. 10pm.
The small bend in the river.

EZRA

I'll be there.

My eyes fly to Maverick. That single tear is the only one that fell, but his gaze is unfocused, and he isn't moving. Kai is next to him, his gaze just as unfocused, but their hands are still joined in a white-knuckle grip. Like they're holding on to each other for dear life.

"I heard him arguing on the phone with someone that night," Cal says. "He was mad at someone. I thought it was Kai all this time until now."

"What did he say?" my dad asks.

"Just that he couldn't do something and that whoever he was talking to couldn't be serious. Nothing helpful," Cal says, sighing into his hands. "I should've checked on him."

"If you thought it was me and I was pissed, I would've punched you," Kai offers.

"Why do you think I turned in the other direction instead?" Cal says, trying to smile, but it's more of a lip twitch.

"I've tried tracing the number, but it was from a cheap burner that was purchased at a gas station that no longer exists. So I have no way of looking into who purchased it," my dad says, sympathy on his face. "The number that texted him was also in his call log from that night, so we can assume it was the same person. The call came first."

"No. This is not where this ends!" Willa exclaims, making everyone jump. "I'm so sick of all these dead ends! Did you look at his call logs? Search history?"

"Of course I did," my dad says calmly.

"Dad?" I ask, getting that itch that tells me we're missing something.

"You know I wouldn't have shown up here if I didn't go

over that phone with a fine-tooth comb, Harlow," he says, sounding disappointed.

"I know. That's not it." I chew on my bottom lip, thinking. "What's in place of the gas station?"

"A garden or something. I drove by it to check. It's just grass and flowers now. There's nothing there that can help us," he says.

"Can you send me the address?" I ask.

"You're not going," Cal says immediately.

I glare at him and cross my arms.

"Uh, I mean. Please don't put yourself in danger. I don't think I could handle it if something happened to you," Cal says, looking a little guilty.

"That's what I thought. And I'm not going. I was just going to look it up," I explain. My dad looks at me with curiosity and sends me the address. I immediately look it up on my phone. "It's a community garden," I explain, looking over the town page that the address pulled up.

"What does that mean?" Jo asks.

"It looks like you can rent space and plant things," I say, continuing to read. "They also offer classes on gardening and field trips where kids can plant something themselves."

"Not sure how any of this pertains to the case," my dad says carefully. He knows better than anyone that I can be like a dog with a bone when I think I'm onto something.

I open my mouth to agree that nothing is here, but then I get to the bottom of the page. I gasp and almost drop my phone. I look up to see everyone's eyes on me, even Cora's.

"What is it, Firecracker?" Cal asks, squeezing my thigh gently.

I show him my phone, at a loss for words. He takes it

from me and reads it out loud. "Community Garden was generously donated by the Wolfe Family to the community of Summer Bay."

I watch as Mav stomps out the front door and slams it behind him.

"I've got him," Kai says, following him.

"Is he taunting us?" Cal asks my dad.

My dad runs his hand through his hair, which is becoming more white than red these days.

"That gas station was bought and demolished within a month of Ezra going missing. If anything, I think it was meant as a warning," my dad says, considering the new evidence.

"He'll claim ignorance if you confront him," Willa says, cuddling Cora to her.

"Covering his tracks by donating land for community use. It's smart. Really smart," I admit.

Cal's phone rings, the guard station number coming up. He picks it up and immediately looks angry.

"So tell her to leave," he says. We're all watching him as he listens. "Fine. Let her through."

"I'll get out of your way," my dad says, looking like he's in a hurry to leave.

"What's going on?" I ask.

"Paula's here," Jason says, coming in from the kitchen and taking Cora from Willa. He gives her a quick kiss on the head and hands her back.

My eyes fly to Cal. He looks just as angry as his dad. "Willa, can you take Cora to your house?"

"Of course," Willa says immediately. "I'll take her through the backyard."

I quickly get up and put a bag together for Willa to take with her. She grabs it and squeezes my arm. Jo follows them out.

"I'm staying," I hear behind me and sigh.

"Belle, come on. She's here to yell at me, not you. There's no reason you need to deal with her. You don't either, Dad," Cal says, looking suddenly exhausted.

The doorbell echoes through the room. Cal sighs again, knowing he isn't going to win. He looks at me, his eyes pleading for something. I don't have time to figure out what before he's turning and heading to the door. The three of us follow him, silently offering our support.

It's ridiculous that this is happening for one woman. But I guess that's what happens when it's a parent. I can't imagine what it's like being raised by someone who uses you more than they love you.

The moment the door opens, Paula storms in like she owns the place. She looks around the foyer and then spots everyone else.

"Of course you're all here. You always love to gang up on me," she sneers, storming past everyone, not even acknowledging I exist. Which I'm honestly not that mad about.

"What are you doing here?" Belle asks her. She looks just like her mother. They have the same shade of dark brown hair and blue eyes. But where Belle likes to leave her curls free, Paula's are pulled tightly into a bun at the back of her neck.

"I came to meet the granddaughter you were hiding from me," she says, glaring at Cal. I want to punch this woman in the face. I've never punched anyone before, but I think she might be the exception.

"You're not welcome here, and you will not be in my daughter's life," Cal says, much more calmly than I think I would've managed in his place.

"Of course I am! You are my son, and she is my granddaughter. I will be in her life, and you will let me see her this instant!" Paula stomps her foot. I snort at the action before I can stop it. It was such a childish move coming from a grown adult.

"Oops," I say under my breath as Paula turns her hateful gaze to me.

"And who are you? The help? My bags are in my car. Go get them and take them to the biggest guest room." The woman tosses her keys to me. I keep my hands down and let them fall to the floor at my feet.

Cal moves in front of me, forcing his mother to look at him instead. "That is my future wife you're speaking to, and you will show her respect."

Paula laughs humorlessly. "Oh, is that how this all came about? She tricked you with her magic cunt and now you have a baby with her? She trapped you, Callahan. Don't be such a fool."

"Magic cunt?" I say, baffled by her language.

"You should have listened when I warned you," Paula sneers.

"You're the one who texted me? I wouldn't call it a warning. I thought some tabloid got my number. I blocked it and haven't heard a peep since."

"What texts?" Cal asks, eyes narrowing on me, but I shrug.

"It was literally two texts that told me to watch my back

and then nothing. It was a while ago, and I honestly forgot about it."

"I have to take out the trash, as usual!" Paula yells, reaching out like she might grab me. Cal pulls me behind him again.

"Enough, Paula!" Jason yells, shocking us all. Apparently, his ex-wife brings out the anger in him. "How dare you come into this house and be so disrespectful!"

Paula looks shocked. So do Belle and Cal. I don't think Jason has ever raised his voice to her. I'm kind of loving it.

"That woman has been more of a mother to my granddaughter than you ever were to our children, and you will not speak to her like that," Jason continues. "Callahan has made the choice to remove you from his life. Maybe instead of coming in here and embarrassing yourself by pointing fingers, you should go do some self-reflection."

"You're not welcome here," Cal says. I move to his side, taking his hand. He squeezes it, letting me know he appreciates it, but he keeps his eyes on his mother.

"I'm your mother!" Paula screams. "I raised you! You have no right to push me away like this!"

"I was done with you the day you accused Belle of ruining her relationship with her abuser," Cal says, standing his ground.

Paula scoffs, sounding a lot like Mav's mom. Maybe there's something in the water up there. "You know how dramatic your sister is. How was I supposed to know he'd get a little too obsessed with her?"

"He tried to kill her!" Jason shouts. There's a vein pulsing in his forehead that has me a little concerned for his health.

"She's not even the dramatic one," I mutter. Everyone's eyes turn to me. I really need to work on saying things more quietly. "What? It's not my fault she doesn't know her kids."

"She's right," Cal says. "You don't know us. I'm sure you're here for money or clout or something just as selfish, so please see yourself out."

"I am not selfish!" Paula argues. "I raised you two on my own!"

"Because Dad was working two jobs to support your spending habits. And if we're really being honest, Cal raised me more than you did," Belle says.

Jason looks defeated, and I hate that Paula can come in here and disrupt everything like this.

"Leave. Now. And if you ever try to come back here, you will be arrested on the spot for trespassing," Cal says, turning his back to his mother, who is sputtering, trying to come up with something to say. Belle ushers her out the door and locks it.

"I'm guessing she was the bigger problem?" I ask Jason. He nods sadly, plopping down onto the couch and resting his face in his hands. Belle sits next to him and hugs him. I tug on Cal's arm to get his attention and gesture to his dad. Cal looks up from his phone and nods, taking the seat on the other side of Jason.

"I notified the guard house. She's on the no entry list, and they've been informed they can call the police to remove her if they need to," Cal says.

"I'm so sorry. I failed you both," Jason says.

"You didn't, Dad," Belle says, hugging him.

"I did."

"You tried your best to make your family happy. You can't do better than that," Cal says.

I feel like I'm intruding on a family moment and try to back out of the room.

"Harlow." I look up and see Jason watching me. "I'm sorry for what she said about you."

"You're not responsible for her actions, Jason. I would never have blamed you for what she said." It hurts my heart that he blames himself.

"I should've divorced her much sooner. I should've been around more to make sure my children were being taken care of. I just assumed she was being a mother. I should never have assumed."

"We're both happy and healthy, Dad. What else can you ask for? That's all I want for Cora." Cal bumps his dad's shoulder, and Jason gives him a small smile.

"I guess that's true," he admits.

I sit on the coffee table in front of Jason. "You're here now. You love Cora, and she loves you. You're a huge part of her life, and you see your kids almost every day. You show up and prove that you want to be in their lives for no other reason than you love them. Everything you do just shows how amazing of a father and grandfather you are. Don't let the dragon-woman plant doubts in your head."

Jason stands and pulls me up into a hug. "I'm so glad Cal found you," he whispers into my hair.

"Not as glad as I am," I whisper back.

"Secrets don't make friends!" Cal whines, breaking the tension and making everyone laugh.

"I need to go check on Mav and Kai," Belle says, giving her dad a quick hug.

"I'm going to go and get some Cora time in," Jason says.

Once they're both gone, I turn to Cal. "Future wife?" I raise an eyebrow and watch him turn pink.

"You caught that, huh?" he says, smiling as he grabs me by the waist, pulling me into him.

"You didn't exactly whisper it."

Cal shrugs. "It wasn't a lie. One day, you'll have my ring on your finger and my last name."

"You're pretty confident," I say, staying calm on the outside, but on the inside, I'm squealing and kicking my feet.

"I don't need to be, Firecracker. When I think of my future, I see you. I see Cora playing with as many siblings as we'll give her. I see us in rockers on a porch in some country house we retire to, old and gray, watching our grandkids. I see your hand in mine as we take our last breaths together and become stars in the sky, watching over everyone we love." He kisses the top of my head while my jaw hangs open, and I try to get my body to move. "You're not ready for that yet. But when you are, Firecracker, I will be asking. And you will say yes."

"Stars?" is all I'm able to say in my shocked state.

Cal shrugs. "I always kind of liked the idea of becoming stars after we die. Belle and I used to lie in the grass at night and point to where we thought our grandparents were in the sky. It's an idea that planted itself in our heads after she made me watch The Princess and the Frog."

"I think I like that."

"Come on. Let's go get our girl," Cal says, pulling on my hand. I follow him, still in shock.

I might not be ready yet, but I could really get used to his idea of our future.

Later that night, Cal and I are snuggled on the couch watching Talladega Nights and eating popcorn. He pauses it and looks at me like he has a question but doesn't want to actually ask it out loud.

"What's the deal with your mom?" he finally asks slowly.

I snort. "Were you afraid to ask that question?"

"You saw my mom. You've never mentioned yours. So, honestly, yeah. What if she's worse?" Cal says, throwing his hands up defensively.

I just laugh and shake my head. "She very well could be. I have no idea. I've never met her."

Cal looks puzzled for a moment. "But you're so good with Cora."

Now it's my turn to be confused. "Yes. And?"

He shakes his head. "I guess I just thought people learned to be maternal from their mom."

"A lot of people do, I guess. Is that where you learned to be good with Cora?" I ask, knowing the answer definitively after today.

Cal just laughs. "Touché."

"My dad has always been enough for me. My mom got pregnant right after my parents got married. She didn't want me, but my dad begged her to have me. Said he would take full responsibility and never come after her for anything. I think he even paid her off, but he won't admit that to me." I shrug. "But my dad never made me feel like I was missing something. There were definitely moments when I was a kid, seeing other little girls with their moms, that I would get sad. As an adult, though? I can never thank him enough for the way he loved me and made sure I was always his priority."

Cal's eyes are glassy from tears he hasn't let fall. "I worry about that. With Cora."

I move myself into his lap and wrap my arms around his neck. "You are more than enough for her, Cal. Plus, look at the support system she has around her. She has so much love around her that she won't know what to do with it." I kiss him on his cheek. "Cora's going to be fine."

A look passes over his face that I can't identify. His lips are on mine, quickly making me forget about it.

"I talked to the guys," Cal says, pulling away from the kiss. I pout, that's not where I thought this was going. He just laughs. "I know. I just wanted to mention this to you before Mav talks to Jo."

I pull back even more so I can see his face. He has my attention, and judging by the smirk on his face, he knows it.

"We want you and Jo to do the podcast, and we want you to start with Ezra."

I almost fall off his lap. He has to grab my waist to keep me there. "What?" I ask, making sure I heard him.

Cal's smile is sad. "With it looking a lot more likely that Ezra is actually dead," I watch his Adam's apple bob as he swallows, "we need all the help we can get. Your dad already agreed to sorting through all the tips that are bound to come in."

"But . . ." I say. But what? I have no words.

"And it has to be you, Firecracker. You're close enough to this case to do Ezra justice and removed just enough to keep a logical head when people start sending you their opinions." Cal makes sure my eyes are on his before he continues. "You see things others don't, baby. You knew you had to look into that garden when even your dad had dismissed it. You might be the only one we would ever trust with this."

I mull it over for a minute. "How is that going to work? You're going on tour soon. Won't that bring the kind of attention to your shows that you wanted to avoid? What about the podcast? We don't even have a name for it since we shelved the idea. Can I even do that from the road? I'm not leaving you and Cora, so don't even suggest that." Cal kisses me to stop my rambling.

"The tour starts in August, baby."

I count on my fingers, not trusting my brain not to fail me right now. "That's two months away."

"The album comes out in July," Cal offers.

"Right. It's June right now. So we have time to figure this out before all the chaos of the album and then not much time between the album and the tour. So really, Jo and I need to figure this out now."

"The tour is three months long, and we'll be on the road for all of it," Cal says, searching my face for my thoughts.

"I knew that. I've been planning with Jo on what to do with Cora the whole time. She got us our own bus so she can sleep without her noisy aunts and uncles bothering her. Oh, and I found a bunch of children's activities I can take her to in each city. Since her first birthday is going to be on the road, I was thinking we could rent out this water park I found and have a party for her there." I was excited to show

Cal the whole schedule Jo and I have inked out so that Cora has fun on the tour. I know that was a big hangup for him.

Cal smiles and kisses me. "Cora is so lucky to have you, Firecracker."

"What about Cora's dad?" I ask him, wiggling closer.

"Oh, her dad is the luckiest bastard there ever was," Cal says, nuzzling into my neck.

"Stop being in love. We don't have time for that right now."

I yelp and practically fly out of Cal's lap. He laughs and shakes his head at me.

"What the hell, Jo?" I stand, putting my hands on my hips and glare at my best friend.

"We need to get to work on the podcast and rework the tour schedule we have for you to add in time for it. You can make out with your unfairly pretty boyfriend later," she says, grabbing my hand. Cal is grinning, and I know it's because she called him pretty.

"It really is annoying how attractive he is," I say, letting Jo tug me into the kitchen.

"No one compares to you, baby!" he yells after us.

I'm smiling like an idiot as I watch Jo pull out her notebook and iPad.

MY FINGERS ARE SORE. They're not used to playing the guitar anymore. Ever since Harlow dragged me down here, I've been playing on my own. It feels good to play again, but I won't do it on stage. I'm not that good, and honestly, I don't want to.

But here in my own home? Here I can sit and play and write songs that no one will ever hear. If I even mentioned I wrote I song, I would be laughed at. Which I guess is my own fault. I started cultivating this jokester personality almost by instinct when I was a kid. Now I play into it. Everything around us is so heavy, it has been for years. So I let them laugh at me, call me dumb, think of me as the nice guy with only air in his head. If they need to laugh at me, let them. I can handle it.

Harlow noticed, though. My firecracker. She doesn't miss anything. And she hates it. She might be the only person who really knows me inside and out. But she stays quiet while everyone laughs. Because I asked her to. Because she knows why I asked her to.

I close my eyes and bring my tired fingers to the strings, playing the notes to the song I wrote that day. That first day, Harlow brought me here and fell asleep on the couch.

I sing about the fire that's just out of my reach. The fire I want to consume and burn with. The one I know will incinerate me and help me rise from the ashes.

I let the last note fade and see Harlow standing in the doorway with tears in her eyes. "What's that song called?" she asks.

I swallow the lump in my throat. No one was supposed to hear that. I know I'm not a good songwriter, but I don't think I can handle Harlow telling me that. And she's not the type to sugarcoat her opinions.

"Firecracker," I admit.

She walks into the small studio and takes a seat on the couch. "Play it again."

I shift uncomfortably in my seat. "It's late. We should probably go to bed."

"Play it again, Callahan," she demands. "Please," she adds softly.

I nod and take a deep breath. I close my eyes and play the song again. Even as the last notes fade, I keep my eyes closed. The vulnerable part of me that I keep pushed down is terrified of her reaction.

I smell her sweet perfume, and I know she's right there. Gently, she removes the guitar from my hands and replaces it with her own body. Her lips trace a line along my jaw and up to my lips.

"Did you write that about me?" she asks before kissing each one of my closed eyelids.

"Yes," I admit in a whisper.

"Why did you say you were bad at writing songs? I'd bet my left boob that would be a Top 40."

My eyes fly open and search hers. I can't tell if she's making fun of me or not. "But the left one is my favorite," I joke.

"Mine too. That's how you know how serious I am." And she is serious. I can see it in her face.

"You really think it's okay?" I ask anyway.

"Okay? Cal, it's amazing! And I'm not saying that because my super-hot rock star boyfriend wrote me a song."

"Super-hot, huh?"

Harlow rolls her eyes. "Of course, that's what you focus on."

I smile and kiss her fiercely. The relief that she isn't laughing at me almost makes me want to cry. I should've known better. Harlow never laughs *at me*, only ever *with me*.

"Your super-hot rock star future husband," I correct her.

She laughs. "You're not going to let that one go, are you?"

"Only when I'm your super-hot rock star husband."

Harlow shakes her head, but she's smiling. She kisses me sweetly before standing and holding out her hand.

"We actually do need to go to bed. Cora is going to be up in a few hours."

I groan playfully but follow my firecracker to bed.

"Absolutely not." I'm pacing back and forth in the kitchen as Cora claps in her highchair, where Harlow is helping her with breakfast. I don't know if she's clapping for me or for the French toast I made. Probably the French toast.

"Absolutely yes," Harlow counters.

Apparently, Harlow recorded me singing last night and wants to show the band and have it added to the album. I think she's biased and thinks I'm better than I actually am.

"I can't," I plead with her. Harlow smiles sadly and walks over to where I'm standing. She takes my face in her hands, forcing me to meet her gaze.

"You, Callahan Elizabeth Griffin, are so much more amazing than you give yourself credit for."

I laugh. "My middle name is Jason."

"That makes a lot of sense, but I like Elizabeth better."

I laugh again, feeling like a thousand pound weight has been lifted off my chest even though we're still in the middle of a disagreement. That's just how perfect Harlow is. She makes me laugh in the middle of an argument.

"I don't think I can handle the rejection. Not with something that personal," I admit.

"I'll be right there with you. And if you think I won't get into a fistfight with each and every one of them, well, you'd be right because Willa is terrifying," Harlow says, making me laugh once again. "But the rest are fair game."

I pull her into me, holding her close and basking in her warmth. Just being near her makes me feel like I can do anything.

I sigh, and I can feel her smile against me. She knows she won. "You're willing to die on this hill, aren't you?"

"You bet your tight ass I am."

I bark out a laugh and shake my head. "Fine. If my dad

can watch Cora, we can do it today." I'm not going to embarrass myself in front of my daughter.

"He should be here any minute," Harlow says. I drop my cheek to her head and sigh again. She knew. Of course, she knew I wouldn't want to do this in front of Cora. Even though Cora won't know what's going on or even remember.

"What did I do to deserve you?" I ask Harlow.

"You just had to be you, Callahan. Stop thinking you have to be anyone other than yourself to deserve love." She kisses me quickly and moves to clean the syrup off Cora, leaving me standing there dumbstruck by her words.

I knew Harlow had firmly planted herself in my heart, but I think maybe she's in my bones too.

I suddenly know what Eminem was rapping about when he said his palms were sweaty and his knees were weak. My arms feel like uselessly heavy stumps by my side. Arms heavy, check.

"Why do you look like you're trying not to shit your pants?" Kai asks from where he's sitting with everyone else on the couch. Harlow made all the band members, other than me, squish together on the one couch. Belle is in Kai's lap so that they would all fit.

I just glare at him and continue pacing.

Harlow is connecting her phone to the TV since, according to her, it's not enough for them just to hear my song, they need to see it too. I might actually shit my pants. Or throw up. Or shit my pants while throwing up.

"Don't distract him, he'll trip," Mav says, causing everyone except Harlow to laugh.

"I swear if you have another surprise baby," Willa says, looking completely serious.

"Even Cal wouldn't be that stupid," Kai says, laughing. Harlow's expression is tight, but she keeps her thoughts to herself.

"What are we here to watch, Harlow?" Belle asks. "We know Cal can sing."

Harlow turns to face them. "Yes, we know Cal can sing. But he can write too. You're here to watch a video of him singing a song he wrote."

Belle's eyes light with interest, but everyone else laughs.

"Cal can't write," Mav says laughing so hard he almost doubles over.

"Can he even spell?" Kai says.

I wince. Normally, I don't care about being the butt of a joke, but I'm feeling really vulnerable right now.

Harlow picks up one of Cora's toy cars and throws it against the wall behind the couch, startling everyone into silence.

"Callahan is not stupid. He is not illiterate. He lets you use him as a joke because your lives have a lot of darkness in them, and he is the fucking sun! That man sacrifices so much for you, and you're too busy making fun of him to see it." Her face is red with anger, and I want to reach out and pull her to me, but even I'm frozen in place. "You wrote a song about a purple dildo and put that on an album," Harlow says, pointing at Mav, who looks embarrassed.

Harlow walks over to me and grabs my hand. I grip hers

so hard, I might be hurting her, but if I am, she isn't letting it show.

"All of you are going to sit down and shut the fuck up. You will watch the entirety of the video I'm about to play. Then you will give your honest opinions." With that, she hits play on her phone and pulls me along with her to the loveseat. Pushing me down, she puts herself in my lap and watches the video with everyone else.

I tighten my arms around her. "Thank you," I whisper. She leans into me, her focus still on the image of me singing her song. I didn't know how much I needed someone to stand up for me like that. Those three little words are on the tip of my tongue, but I don't say them. This isn't the time or place for that.

"HOLY SHIT," Belle says the moment the video ends.

Cal stiffens against me, a small tremor going through his body. I hate how nervous he is. He shouldn't be nervous about sharing something with the people he considers family. I hold him tighter.

"Why didn't you tell us songwriting ran in the family?" Willa asks, looking genuinely confused by what she just saw.

"Dude," is all Kai says, his jaw hanging open.

"Can you play it again?" Mav asks me. I nod and play the video again.

"Is your guitar in the basement?" Kai asks.

Cal nods slowly. Kai picks Belle up and puts her where he was sitting before running to the basement.

"What's happening?" Cal whispers.

"Something good," I tell him. At least I'm pretty sure that's what's happening.

"Okay, what if we change the key and did something like this?" Kai says, coming back and propping himself on the edge of the couch and playing a few notes. "Cal, you need to sing, buddy," he says when Cal misses his spot.

I try to get off his lap to make it easier, but he holds me to him as he picks up on the change easily and sings the song he wrote for me.

It only takes them an hour to tweak the song. I loved the way Cal sang it, but I have to admit, the version they created together will be perfect on their album. The entire time, Cal kept me on his lap, singing to me. I've been smiling so hard my face hurts.

"I'm going to call Isla and get this on the album," Jon says. Willa called him on the third or fourth attempt, and he's been listening over the phone ever since.

Everyone gets up to leave, but Mav loudly clears his throat. "I'm sorry, Cal. I really am. You're right that you were the joke, and we let you be. Because we needed to laugh, and you let us laugh at you. It wasn't right."

I look up at Cal. He's shaking his head. "I let you."

"That doesn't matter. We're adults. We know better," Kai says.

"I knew what you were doing, and I let you. It was easier to laugh at you than cry with you. There's no excuse, but we are all so sorry, and we'll do better," Willa promises.

Cal nods, acknowledging their words, but not saying anything. I watch them all leave, but Belle lingers. She walks up to me and hugs me.

"Thank you for watching out for my brother. He's always been the one to watch out for everyone else." She turns to Cal. "I'm sorry for my part. We have each other's backs, Cal. You don't have to hold everyone up on your own."

Cal hugs his sister. "Love you."

"Love you," Belle says before turning and leaving.

"Do you have any idea what you did for me today?"

I turn to see Cal with a look of reverence in his eyes.

"I only did what I thought was right," I tell him, trying to shrug off the weight of his gaze. There are so many emotions swirling in his eyes, and I think I could drown from the weight of them.

Cal grabs my face and kisses me, letting me feel everything he can't vocalize. "You are everything, Harlow Ray. Everything." The awe in his voice floors me.

"Cal, *you* are everything. You deserve everything," I tell him, letting the emotion in my voice show. "Never accept less."

"Never again," he says against my lips, claiming them in the next breath.

I laugh as he sweeps me into his arms, bridal style.

"Where are we going?" I ask him, laughing into his neck.

"Our bedroom," he says, climbing the stairs. I haven't been back to my bedroom since the first night we were together. Cal declared his room as ours and there really was no going back from there. Especially after he moved all my stuff into his closet.

I kiss his neck, making him moan.

When he sets me down on my feet in front of our bed and smiles at me, it suddenly hits me.

I love him.

I'm in love with him.

His hands are under my shirt, thumbs rubbing small circles on the bare skin of my stomach. Cal dips his head to kiss me, and I pull back.

"I love you," I blurt as he frowns. That frown quickly turns into a dazzling smile.

"You beat me to it," he says, one of his hands moving to cup my cheek. "I love you too, Firecracker. I think I've loved you since you told me I sucked at singing and shouldn't quit my day job."

"I did not say that!" I exclaim and then laugh at the goofy look on his face.

"That's what I heard," he shrugs. I just shake my head at how ridiculous this man is.

Cal pulls me back to him. We undress each other slowly, savoring each moment, each touch, every kiss.

We're laying chest to chest on the bed, Cal on top of me, careful not to put his full weight on me. He's kissing his way along my neck and down my body. My hands are in his hair, grabbing the silky strands, trying to get him where I want him.

He laughs against me, his hot breath hitting my clit. "Please, Cal. Stop teasing me," I beg.

"I'm not teasing you, baby. I'm worshipping you. You're just impatient."

I cross my arms and blow my hair out of my face, refusing to acknowledge what he said. Mostly because it's true. My hands fly back to Cal's hair with the first swipe of his tongue against my sex.

"You're so good at that," I tell him, back arching off the bed as he goes in for more. Cal eats pussy like it's his last meal. He sucks and nips my clit with precision before pressing two fingers inside me.

"I'll never get over how wet you get for me, Firecracker."

"Only you," I pant. He seems to like that because he

picks up speed. One of his hands reaches up and grabs mine, interlacing our fingers. I come with the next swipe of his talented tongue, squeezing the fingers in his hair and holding his hand to my chest.

Cal kisses his way back up my body until he's settled between my legs, the head of his erection at my entrance.

"Tell me again," he says against my lips before kissing me. I can taste myself on him. It's hot.

"I love you," I say, knowing exactly what he's asking for. He smiles against my mouth and slowly presses into me. I don't think there's any way to get used to the size of him.

"I love you too," he tells me, pushing into the hilt.

The way Cal moves this time is different. It's a slow worship. The only time his eyes leave mine is when he's kissing me. Neither of us is racing towards the finish line. We're walking hand in hand toward an explosion.

Cal takes my hand and holds it against his heart as he pumps in and out of me. "It's yours," he says. "It beats for you."

I nod. "Mine," I agree. "Oh god, Cal."

My orgasm is building slowly, but I'm right there, and I can tell it'll break me when it hits.

"It's okay, baby. Come for me," Cal says against my ear. His words are what it takes to tip me over the edge. I scream, my vision blacks out, and I'm vaguely aware of the way I'm clawing at Cal's ass as I lose all sense and pulse around him.

Cal's grunts and moans pull me back to the surface. I open my eyes just in time to see his face as he comes. It's one of my favorite things to witness in the entire world. It's the only time Cal completely lets himself feel.

He collapses on top of me, rolling slightly so not all his

weight is on me. We're both panting and sweaty, but clinging to each other, refusing to let go.

"I've never come that hard in my life," Cal says, then kisses my sweaty temple.

"Me either. Let's do it again."

"I'm going to make love to my future wife every day, twice a day until I'm dead," Cal declares. I laugh and push at his chest. "What?"

"How are we going to find time to do that twice a day? You have a tour coming up, and I have a podcast to figure out and that's on top of taking care of the most perfect little girl to ever exist."

Cal is grinning at me like he just won a bet. I'm racking my brain trying to figure out if we actually did make a bet that I forgot about. "Why are you looking at me like that?" I ask, coming up empty.

"You didn't argue the future wife part," he says, same giant grin on his face.

I roll my eyes, but I'm smiling too.

"I love you so much, Firecracker," Cal says, nuzzling into my neck.

"I love you too."

We stay snuggled together. I don't know how much time passed. The sun was slowly sinking before we moved and that was only because Jason texted that he was on his way back with Cora.

If I had known this was the last peaceful moment Cal and I would have together, I would have held on tighter.

twenty-six

HARLOW

"IT JUST DOESN'T FEEL RIGHT," I tell Jo, again. She sighs up at the ceiling in frustration. Not a single platinum blonde strand is out of place in her tight bun. Meanwhile, I've been pulling on my hair so much, I don't think all the detangler in the world is going to fix it.

We've been trying to figure out the format for our podcast for weeks. The album comes out in five days, and we don't even have the formatting down yet. We did come up with a name though. Melt the Ice. Because they're cold cases that we're looking into specifically. Ezra's is the exception, but only by technicality. If he wasn't declared dead without evidence, his case would be considered a cold case right now.

"You keep saying that, but you're not offering up any ideas either."

"We need something that stands out. That makes us different." It's the same argument I've made this entire time. We have a rough outline of what we want to do, but it just doesn't feel like enough. For one, I want this to be a success.

But even more than that, I want to bring some justice to these families that would potentially be seeking our help. Starting with Ezra.

Jo studies our calendar again. Everything is color coded. Red for band specific events. Blue for the podcast. Pink for anything Cora. Green for anything we have planned for everyone as a group, like Cora's first birthday.

"What if we put feelers out now?" I ask. I feel like something is at the edge of my mind, trying to break through. "Cal announced our relationship on his socials last week," I say. I made him wait a little bit so we could enjoy each other. No one ever found that rest stop from the picture I posted, so it gave as time. But since the album is coming out soon, and the tour starts close behind it, I figured it was the end of our quiet time together anyway.

"Oh, I'm very aware. Who do you think is fielding all the calls asking for information?" Jo snorts. I shake my head. She loves telling people off, so it's not as much of a hardship for her as she's pretending it is.

"There's a lot of attention on me right now, so let's use it," I offer.

Jo taps her pen on the table as she thinks about it. "People are going to accuse you of using Cal for publicity if you do that."

"Let them. Everyone important knows that's not true."

Jo sighs. "I don't know how you can be so blasé about people attacking your character."

"I'm not a feral cat like you," I tell her and flinch a little at her glare. "But if we get one legitimate person reaching out for every one hundred negative comments, then it would be worth it."

"Sometimes I don't think I could love you more, and then you go and say something like that." Cal comes into the dining room where Jo and I have set up our workspace. The table fits twelve people, and it's covered in paper. He kisses me quickly and then takes the seat next to me, pulling mine closer to his so that our thighs are touching.

"Can you not show off in front of the chronically single person?" Jo complains, but I see the small smile she's trying to hide.

"Sorry, Jo. I need to be near her at all times. If I could be in her —" he starts, but I cover his mouth. He smiles against my hand as I squint my eyes at him in warning.

Jo rolls her eyes at Cal and then turns back to me. "So, what's your plan? Advertise our podcast and hope we get some leads in the middle of a bunch of trolls?"

"Kind of. We advertise and then list the cities we're stopping at on the tour." We already chose the cases we want to feature and have spoken to the families to make sure they're also okay with us using the cases in an episode. "We know the cases. The families have all signed waivers. So if we publish our episode topics now, we can maybe look into each case while we're in that city." The idea unfolds as I speak. "Then when we're back home, we sort through the tips coming in. Spend a couple of months trying to help with those cases and use the podcast to give updates and explain our process. Go over what evidence comes in. People value transparency and they won't get it with law enforcement trent."

"But they can with us," Jo nods. "Short term, that works. They're playing fifty shows in forty-two different cities. We only chose twelve. Aren't people in other cities going to be upset?"

"Well, we definitely can't do one per show," I say. "We can end the show asking for cold cases in other areas. Make sure people are aware that this is just the first season, and we aren't skipping over them."

"My girl is a genius," Cal says, kissing my temple. I smile at him even when I hear Jo complain under her breath.

"We can create a whole platform for amateur Internet detectives to use to help the case," I say. "We'll have to have someone moderating that though. It can get out of control quickly if we don't."

Jo nods, making a list of our ideas and what we need.

"That gives us," I sigh, thinking about it, "a lot more than we can handle."

"Maybe not. We can easily hire someone to create the platform in the way we want it. Look," she says, turning the notepad she was writing on, "moderators will be easy to come by as well. We just really need to figure out exactly how we want the platform to be set up. Do we have forums where people can discuss cases live? That would be great but need moderating at all times. Do we just have a submission section and post the appropriate comments we get?"

"Both. Forums for discussion and submissions for any evidence or insights," I say. "But we need to make sure whoever we hire to oversee it is as organized as you are. If they're like me, it'll be a mess."

"I think we need a website and an app. I can get to work on that today."

I smile. "That's perfect. The platform, combined with the interviews, will give us something no other podcast has."

"You two are going to kill it and change people's lives at the same time. Makes me question my job."

I look at Cal and shake my head. "You're only saying that because I threatened to strangle anyone who throws their underwear at you."

That makes Jo cackle. I look at her and frown. "It concerns me how much violence amuses you."

Jo shrugs. "So, what do you think? This could really work."

"I like it."

"Me too. Which is why I got you presents." Cal says, standing and strutting out of the room.

"You didn't even know what the plan was until a minute ago!" I yell, following him anyway.

"Ta-da!" he says, arms wide in front of a ton of boxes.

"You're giving me your recycling?" Jo asks.

Cal rolls his eyes. "Open them, demon Barbie."

I choke on my spit at that nickname, which she's never going to get rid of now.

Jo glares at Cal, and I swear I see her lip twitch. Is she trying not to smile?

Jo and I open box after box. It's top of the line podcasting equipment. Expensive podcasting equipment.

"Cal," I whisper, at a loss for words.

"Don't even try saying you can't accept it. You can and you will," he says, taking my face in his hands. "Please accept it, baby."

I pull him to me and kiss him. "Thank you."

"You can thank me by getting naked," he says, wiggling his eyebrows. I laugh and shake my head against his chest.

"Thanks, Cal, but I don't need to see that," Jo says,

putting her shoes on by the door. "We can iron out the finer details tomorrow and then map out the first episode."

She leaves before I can respond.

I smile up at Cal, and he returns it with the sweetest affection in his eyes. Then I drop to my knees and take pleasure in the way his eyes widen.

"Firecracker. Get up. I was joking." He tries grabbing for me, but I bat his hand away and pull down his sweatpants.

"I think you deserve to be thanked," I tell him. "Don't you think?"

"Yeah," he says, nodding frantically.

I laugh at his desperate, wide-eyed expression.

"Baby, it doesn't make me feel great when you're on your knees laughing with my cock in your hand," he says while trying to pull back, but I lick the underside of his cock from his balls all the way to the tip. "Never mind," he moans. "You can do whatever you want."

I take him into my mouth, sucking gently and then taking him as far back as I can.

"Shit. Do that again. Please do that again," he begs. Hearing Cal desperate under my touch might turn me on more than anything else he does.

I do as he asks, and then I take his hand, putting it on my head. "Fuck my mouth."

"Fuck, Firecracker," he breathes. "You sure?"

I nod as I lick the pre-cum from his tip.

"Tap my legs if you need me to stop, okay?" His eyes are on me, and I nod. "Words, baby."

"Yes. I understand."

That's all he needed. Cal fucks my mouth just like he fucks my pussy, with a beautiful mixture of passion and aggression. I gag more than once, but that just encourages him. He keeps his eyes locked with mine as he takes what he wants from me.

"Jesus, Firecracker. There is nothing more beautiful than you on your knees for me," he says breathlessly. His hand tightens in my hair at the same time I feel him swell in my mouth. "I'm going to come, baby. Swallow everything. Take everything."

He comes on a shout, and I swallow every salty drop.

"You are perfection," Cal says, pulling me directly from the floor into his arms. "I should buy you things more often."

I laugh and snuggle into him. "That wasn't for the equipment. That was for believing in me the way you do."

"You believe in me the same way, Firecracker."

"Da-dammm!"

Cal sighs, and I barely contain my laugh. There is no getting Cora to stop calling him that weird version of dad and damn she's created.

"Better go get our girl before she learns a more creative word to call you," I say, giggling. Cal puts me down and smacks my butt.

"Wait until she starts trying to say your name," he says like a threat, but we both know the moment she says anything like my name, I'll be sobbing like a baby.

Cora may not be genetically mine, but she's become mine in every way that matters.

twenty-seven

CAL

"NOTHING HAS COME from the shooting. Nothing has come from the texts on Ezra's phone. It's like we just keep banging our heads against the same wall over and over again."

Kai has been pacing and ranting for at least ten minutes now. Which I guess isn't a lot, but considering we were supposed to be having a fun guys' night before heading out on the tour, it's too much.

"Yeah, except that wall is a person, and that person is my father," Mav grumbles, hugging a black velvety throw pillow to his chest. We decided to gather at his house since the girls are at mine so Cora can be involved in their night too.

"That still doesn't make sense to me," I admit. Kai opens his mouth, probably to make a joke about nothing making sense to me, but then he closes it. Old habits die hard, but they're all trying.

Mav shrugs and hugs the pillow tighter. "He's made it

very clear he doesn't approve of my career, my choice in partner, or really my entire existence in general."

"He hurt Ezra because you like dick and to play bass and then went to borderline psychotic lengths to cover it up?" I chew the inside of my cheek. "It just doesn't make sense."

"Isn't this supposed to be Ray's thing? Why are we sitting around speculating instead of having fun?" Kai asks, although he doesn't offer an alternative. He's also the one who started this topic of conversation, but I don't think pointing that out will help.

"My dad has emailed me once a week since I joined the band. Every time, it's about forming an alliance and helping the family. Apparently, I'm a disappointment and need to get my head on straight, marry the girl he wants, take over the family business, and run for public office."

"Cal can be your campaign manager. He could convince a penguin to buy ice from a polar bear," Kai says.

I ignore him and grab my phone, calling Harlow on FaceTime. The guys roll their eyes at me, but keep their mouths shut.

"Miss me already?" Harlow's beautiful smile and glittering green eyes light up the screen.

"You know I do, Firecracker."

"Da-dammm!" Cora squeals. Harlow turns the phone so I can see my little girl. She's in Willa's arms and claps when she sees me.

"Hi baby girl! Do you miss Daddy?" I coo into my phone, ignoring the eye rolls from Mav and Kai.

"Why are you talking to the guys? We're supposed to be having a girl's night." Belle says from somewhere in my house.

"Why are you calling me?" Harlow asks, turning the phone back to her perfect face.

"I just thought of something, and I wanted to run it by you before I talked to your dad."

"Lay it on me, Vocal Daddy," she says with a mischievous smile.

"Firecracker," I growl.

"I'm just kidding. Tell me what you're thinking."

"Did your dad look into how Senator Wolfe funded his campaign?"

Harlow raises an eyebrow, and I can see her eyes sparkle with interest. "Yeah. He used old family money."

Mav shoots up from his seat on the couch and comes to stand next to me, pushing in so he can see Harlow too. I glare at him until I see the look on his face. He looks angry.

"We don't have old family money. My grandparents on my dad's side were dirt poor and lived off the system. The ones on my mom's side were middle class and died with debt," he tells Harlow.

"It was part of his entire campaign. He's from an old family with old money, and he's putting that money back into the state of Maine," Harlow says, watching Maverick's reaction carefully.

"I didn't pay attention to his campaign. I wanted nothing to do with him and made sure I didn't have to hear about it."

Harlow nods at his words. "What are you thinking, Cal?" she asks me.

"The senator has emailed Mav a lot."

"How often?" she asks him.

"Once a week since Kai talked me into joining Shattered Halo."

"Yeah, and he mentions things like the family business and forming alliances and things that sound a lot like old mafia movies." Anyone else would tell me I need to lay off the movie watching, but Harlow takes me seriously. She mumbles something to Willa and then runs upstairs to our room, grabbing her computer and propping her phone up on the bedside table so I can see the side of her face as she frantically types.

"I think you might be onto something," she says, not taking her eyes from the computer screen. "Maine has a drug problem. It isn't a secret. It's been all over the news for years. Especially since it's causing a huge uptick in deaths because of overdose in the 18-24 and an even bigger one in the 25-36 age range."

"He's a drug dealer?" That's not exactly where my brain was going, but it could fit.

"The first reports of an increase in overdoses and the start of his bid for senator started within months of each other," Harlow says, turning towards me. "I'm going to call my dad and see what he can find."

I nod, Mav still next to me, looking pale. Kai is in Mav's spot on the couch with his head in his hands.

"Thanks, baby."

"Callahan," she says, making sure she has my full attention. "Do you understand what you may have done? You may have found not only the motive, but the person who's been smuggling in all the drugs."

"Yeah, but none of that matters if it doesn't lead to Ez," I say, not feeling the same excitement she is.

"Not yet, but if this all checks out, we could be a lot closer than we have been in months."

I nod. "Let me know what your dad says, and I'll see you in a few hours."

"I love you, Cal," she says, beaming at me, and I wish I could reach through the phone and kiss her.

"I love you too, Firecracker."

I put my phone in my pocket and watch Maverick unravel. He drops to the floor at my feet, and I quickly sit next to him, pulling him into my arms as he cries. Kai is on his other side in an instant. We let him cry, holding our best friend between us like our combined strength can keep him from completely falling apart.

It may have been minutes or hours later, but Mav eventually runs out of tears.

"My dad is responsible for hundreds of deaths," he croaks. "My dad hurt the love of my life."

We've all been saying Ezra is hurt instead of dead. We don't have proof that he is, and we all silently agreed not to use the d-word until we have absolute proof. No one is giving up on him.

"Ezra must have seen something related to the drug stuff," Mav continues, his voice hoarse. "We're going on tour tomorrow."

"We have time for Harrison to make sense of all this. The girls are saving our interview for last anyway. So maybe we'll have more information for them. Then they'll release the episode . . ." I'm just rambling now. I don't know what will happen. Our tour starts and ends in Boston. We wanted to bookend it with home shows. It was Jo's idea so that they would have more time to work on Ezra's episode, but we all agreed because we liked the idea of starting and ending at home.

"There's still a lot we don't know, but we're getting there," Kai says. "This is the first time since Ezra went missing that I feel like we're actually making progress."

Mav nods and starts to stand. Kai and I move away so he can actually get up off the floor.

"Alright," he declares after taking a deep breath. "Let's order pizza and watch a movie with lots of explosions."

Kai and I watch from where we're still sitting on the floor as Mav walks into the kitchen.

"You alright?" I ask Kai. Mav has the bigger, more emotional reactions. So everyone's instinct is to help Mav first. But Kai is Ezra's twin and has to be taking this information just as hard as Mav is right now.

Kai sighs and scratches the back of his head. "It feels like the closer we get, the deeper Ezra's grave is, you know? Like we get closer to finding the truth, but the truth seems to lean towards his demise."

"Do you feel like he's dead? You with that weird twin magic thing?" There are so many articles talking about twin connections that science and logic can't explain. I would know. I looked it up.

Kai holds my stare for a beat and then shakes his head. "I would have to feel it, right? Like part of my soul was gone or something. But I don't feel that way. I never have."

I nod. "He's out there masquerading as a diner cook or a bartender in some remote town that's not even on a map. But we're going to find him, and we're going to bring him home."

Kai stands and offers his hand, helping me up. "Might

need to take down a crime lord pretending to be your friendly local politician while embarking on a national tour and selling albums."

"Easy."

twenty-eight

HARLOW

MY LEG IS BOUNCING UNCONTROLLABLY as I sit in Belle and Willa's dressing room. It's the first show of Shattered Halo's tour and it's in Boston. Jason is with Cora so that I could support Cal. I was excited when he offered, but now I'm so nervous I could throw up everywhere. I look around the room to distract myself. Cal doesn't know I'm here. It's going to be a surprise. I just have to hold it together.

The room is painted a light blue with one wall a darker shade. The couch I'm sitting on is the same darker blue, and the leather is sticking to my sweaty thighs. Willa and Bella are sitting on stools in front of a large vanity with a mirror.

"Why do you look so pale?" Belle asks, worry creasing her face.

"I think it just now hit me that Cal is a rock star," I admit. "We've kind of been in our own bubble."

Belle nods. "I get that. The first time I saw Kai out on that stage, I swooned. But on the inside because he was kind of being a dick at that point."

Willa laughs. "He's still just Cal. Fame has never gone to his head. He's always just Cal."

I want to tell her that Callahan Griffin isn't "just" anything, but I hold my tongue. I like the idea that there's a part of him that's only mine. Selfishly, I want to keep it that way.

The behind the scenes I'm getting right now would make entertainment industry reporters so jealous. Willa and Belle go over the set order while Belle drinks tea and Willa does both of their make-up.

"You guys don't have hair and make-up people?" I ask.

Willa shrugs. "We did at one point, but I get so sweaty from drumming that my hair never stays, and my make-up will run down my face. It just makes more sense to do it ourselves."

"Why lilac?" I ask her. I've always wondered why she picked that hair color and stuck with it. Willa hitches a brow, and I laugh. "I ask a lot of questions when I'm nervous."

"It was my mom's favorite color," Willa says eventually. "It's my way of keeping her with me."

I nod. Willa's mom died when she was young. It was sudden and the town gossips couldn't stop talking about it.

The conversation turns into my plans with Cora for the tour and the podcast. I give them a condensed version of the cases we have lined up and the interviews we have set up so far.

"Our interviews are last?" Belle asks.

"Yeah. We want to give my dad as much time as we can to dig into the drug theory. It's still going to be the first episode, though."

"How's the website coming along?" Willa asks as she wiggles into a black lace bodysuit. It's low cut with long sleeves. She pulls a deep red leather skirt on and then black combat boots. Her outfit combined with her dark and smoky make-up makes her look like a badass.

"Great actually. We hired a woman who's going to not only design a website but also an app. We still need moderators, but we'll deal with that once we have a better timeline on the platform." Cal funded the platform creation. He's refusing to let me pay him back. He says it's an investment in our future. I can't argue with him when he says things like that, and he knows it.

A knock sounds on the door before a bald head pokes in. "Fifteen minutes, ladies."

"You got it, Nate." Willa says. "This is Harlow. She's Cal's girlfriend. He doesn't know she's here, but she has free rein of whatever she needs."

"Nice to meet you, Harlow," Nate says before closing the door.

"Nice to meet you too?" I tell the worn wood.

Belle snorts. "Nate is straight to the point. I don't think he's capable of small talk." She's wearing a matching body suit to Willa's, but in dark blue and instead of a skirt she has black jeans on.

"Are the guys wearing lace too?" I ask, jokingly.

"I think Mav might be. He has a few lace shirts he bought when we got these," Willa says.

"Kai won't be. He wears these silk shirts you'd see on a pimp from the 70s. Says it feels nice on his nipples," Belle says, laughing so hard she snorts.

I open my mouth to ask about Cal. I didn't think to ask

him about his tour wardrobe. "Five minutes!" Nate yells without knocking or opening the door.

"The opener must be on time if he's yelling like that," Willa says, checking her look in the floor-length mirror on the back of the door. "Stay in here for now. I'll have Nate grab you once we're on stage."

I agree as Willa and Belle leave the room. The reason for most of my nerves, that I didn't share with them, is the amount of women that are going to be throwing themselves at Cal. The guys were joking about it all week leading up to this show.

I'm a jealous person. I didn't know that about myself until recently. Until Cal. But the idea of another woman trying to get his attention makes me see red. I'm hoping I'll get used to it. It's not like I think Cal will entertain any advances. I know he won't. I know that man is mine. But the urge to tackle him on stage and mark my territory is new and getting hard to ignore.

"Alright, Harlow. They're starting the show. Follow me," Nate says from the door. I stand and follow him. He's a lot shorter than I realized. Not that there's anything wrong with being short, but the lights are bouncing right off his shiny head and into my eyes.

"Can he see me from here?" I ask, standing on the side of the stage where Nate pointed.

"If you stay there, he won't. You're kind of in the shadows. He might notice someone there, but he'll just assume it's one of the many people working backstage right now."

I thank him and turn my attention to the stage. Cal is front and center, welcoming the crowd. Mav is to his left and Kai to his right. Belle and Willa are behind them on the keyboard and drums, respectively.

I think my mouth hangs open the whole show. I've seen Cal sing at the studio and at home. I've seen him sing in the woods and in videos of their concerts. But Callahan Griffin live and on stage is a whole different experience. He's wearing a tight white shirt, jeans, and brown boots. His brown hair has grown out in the past few months and it's floppy as he moves with the music. He said he let it grow because he noticed how much I like to run my hands through it.

The set is a mixture of their old songs with mostly the new album. Kai and Belle sing two of them alone, but other than that, it's Cal's show. The lights beat down on them, the fans scream with love and adoration, and . . . is that a tattoo? I inch forward, trying to get a better look. Cal's white shirt is almost see-through with the amount he's sweating, and I swear I can see a tattoo on his chest. He doesn't have any tattoos. I saw him shirtless last night, but he was out of bed before I woke up this morning.

I must have inched too close because Cal's head whips in my direction and the larger-than-life smile that he reserves just for me crosses his face.

"Oh shit," I mutter, trying to back into the shadows.

"We have a special guest, Boston!" Cal yells into the mic.

Oh no. No no no.

"The love of my life and the inspiration behind Firecracker!"

Oh fuck.

"Come out here, Harlow!"

I shake my head and look at Willa for help. She just shrugs and gestures for me to come on stage with her sticks.

Cal jogs over, leaving his mic. "Firecracker," he says, his voice low and full of wonder. "Please come on stage with me. Let me show every single person out there that I'm yours."

Dammit. The man knows me too well.

I take his hand and let him lead me out into the spotlight. The lights are hot. I can see why they're all so sweaty. Cal's grip on my hand tightens. I'm sure he can feel how my whole body is shaking with nerves right now.

Cal looks at Willa and nods. She bangs her sticks together and then they start playing Firecracker. Cal keeps his eyes on mine and my hand in his for the entire song. He's singing into a mic, and I know everyone else in this stadium can hear him, but it feels like he's just singing to me. Every word he sings is done with intent and emotion. I feel every moment of the song in my soul.

When the last note fades, the crowd erupts into enthusiastic cheers. My breath catches, my mind remembering where I'm standing right now. I look out into the sea of people. The lights make it so I can't make out their faces, but I still know they're there. And I know I'm not wearing make-up, and I have no idea what my hair looks like.

Cal grabs my face, forcing me to look at him. He conveys so much with a look that most people would have trouble doing with words. He's telling me he's here, he's mine, and he loves me. Then he kisses me deeply.

He keeps my hand in his when he turns back to the mic. "Thank you, Boston! We love starting our tours off in this city! You've been the best, as always! Goodnight!" Then he leads me off the stage.

I take a deep breath. Did I breathe at all the entire time I was out there? I must have if I didn't pass out, right? I close my eyes tightly, focusing on slowing my breathing. When I open them, I see Cal's sweaty shirt.

"When the hell did you get a tattoo?"

He just laughs. Probably not surprised that was the first thing I said to him. He takes his shirt off, pulling it over his head with one hand. Why is that so hot?

"This morning. I won't be able to spend as much time with my girls as I want to while we're on tour. I wanted to keep you with me at all times."

I look at the tattoo directly over his heart. "Cal," I breathe. There are two brightly colored fireworks exploding, one into my name and one into Cora's.

"What if we have more kids?" I blurt, my eyes going wide when I realize what I just said. I slap my hand over my mouth, but the words have already escaped.

Cal's smile brightens even more. "You want to have my babies, Firecracker?"

"Uh, maybe? I just meant, you know, in the future. If we want more kids, that is. Not that we have kids right now. You have a kid. Not me. But I think we're headed in that direction. Do you? We should have talked about this sooner. . ."

Cal kisses me to get me to stop talking. "We have a child. I want more children with you when the time is right. Make no mistake, Harlow. I want everything with you. Marriage, children, pets, arguments, and make up sex. Everything," he says, kissing me again. "And you are Cora's mother in all the most important ways, and I hope that she's your daughter too."

I smile through watery eyes. "Cora is my girl. I was just too scared to let myself believe she's mine."

"She's yours, baby. We both are."

I kiss him then. I kiss him, trying to show him everything I'm feeling. Everything he makes me feel. Cal pulls away and smiles, telling me he knows exactly what I'm doing.

"I got small ones too," Cal says softly, showing me the inside of his wrist. There sits an unlit firecracker and a pomegranate with the seeds spilling out to spell "family."

"A pomegranate?" I ask. The firecracker I understand, obviously.

"Did you know that Cora is another name for Persephone? I thought that was cool. It was part of the reason I chose that name," Cal says, his voice taking on that almost embarrassed tone.

"I didn't know that, but I love it," I tell him honestly, pushing up on my toes so I can kiss him. He picks me up by my thighs, wrapping my legs around him. His kiss deepens and turns more demanding. I grip his shoulders and pull myself as close to him as I can get, not caring about how sweaty he is.

"Can you at least wait until we get on the buses? You have your own now," Mav says, laughing as he passes us. He did end up wearing a lace shirt. His is black like Willa's, and he wore it with black jeans and black boots. Combine that with his black hair, and he almost looks threatening.

I pull back from Cal and look around. There are people everywhere, packing up the equipment and breaking down the stage. A few fans that scored backstage passes are getting autographs from Willa and Kai. Belle is kneeling on the floor, speaking with a young fan and his parents.

"Go talk to your fans. I'll meet you on the bus. I need to relieve your dad anyway." Jason is going to be with us on part of the tour, but he can't join us for another couple of weeks.

Cal grumbles into my neck, making me laugh. "I'm going to be with you for three months with no break. I think you'll be okay for an hour or so."

"Fine, but I get you to myself tonight," Cal says. I nod and untangle myself from him. Neither of us has any idea how Cora is going to adjust to sleeping on a bus. I don't want to jinx it by saying something, though.

I should've said something.

"Firecracker?" Cal's voice is thick with sleep.

"I'm here," I whisper from the end of the bed.

"What's going on?" Cal asks, scooting forward to sit next to me.

"Cora girl isn't happy," I tell him. Cora is snuggled in my arms, sucking on her thumb, but wide awake. She has been for hours. I got to her before she woke Cal so that I could let him sleep.

"What's wrong, baby girl?" he asks her, stroking her cheek with his knuckle. She reaches for him, and he takes her. I watch as she snuggles into his chest.

"I think the bus moving is bothering her."

"It's okay, sweet girl. Mommy and Daddy are here with

you. We'll get used to this together," Cal tells her. I don't think I'm breathing. Cal has said I'm like a mother to Cora, and Jason has pretty much said the same thing to me on more than one occasion, but it's different from hearing Cal use that title so freely.

Cal is so focused on Cora that he misses the hot tears streaming down my cheeks, but the loud gasp I make when I finally get my chest to expand and let in air has him turning. He looks alarmed when he sees my face. Then his sleepy brain catches up and he smiles, grabbing my hand and gently squeezing.

"There are very few things in my life I've ever been sure of. I always knew I was going to be singing in a band with my sister and best friends. I knew Cora was mine the moment I laid eyes on her. I knew you were meant to be mine the first time you told me I sucked at singing." I snort, but I don't argue. He was pitchy, and he knows it. "And I know you were meant to be the mother Cora needs."

"I just don't think I ever expected to hear the title." It still felt like something I wasn't allowed to say. It almost feels like I'm taking a spot that isn't mine. Cora's mom isn't here. She never got to be her mom, and that's making me feel guilt I don't know how to handle.

"Firecracker. Look at me."

I lift my head and see the understanding in Cal's eyes. "Bailey isn't here. Even if she was, you would still be in Cora's life. There isn't a single version of life I want to live that doesn't have you in it. If it's the title that scares you, we'll wait. But the life we're living, the hand we were dealt, it took Bailey from Cora. But it gave her you."

I take one of Cora's soft, red curls between my fingers. I

love this little girl just like she was my own. She owns half of my heart, and her daddy has the other.

Cora looks up at me with her big eyes. "Dada," she says.

"Finally," Cal says, making me laugh.

"Mama," Cora says. I gasp at the same time Cal chokes. "Dadamama," Cora says, turning it into a single word.

Cal's eyes are wide, looking between me and Cora. "Right, baby girl. I'm Dada and that's . . ." he stops. He just said we could wait on the title, but Cora seems to have made that choice for us.

"Mama," I fill in. Cora reaches for me, and I take her back into my arms. She settles into my chest, and I drop kisses to the top of her head. "I love you," I tell her.

"Mama," she sighs and closes her eyes. She's asleep within minutes.

"I guess she needed you to know what you mean to her before she went to sleep," Cal says, kissing my temple. I lean into him, snuggling Cora tight to me. "I love our family."

His words have me choking up again. "I love our family too," I croak. Cal puts his arm around me.

We sit like this, Cora in my arms and both of us in Cal's, until streaks of sunlight break through the gaps in the curtains.

twenty-nine

CAL

"I JUST GOT AN EMAIL," Jo announces, walking onto my bus.

"You get emails all day. Are you going to announce them all?" Harlow says, not even looking up from the book she's reading to Cora. They're both on the floor of the bus with Cora's stuff spread out everywhere. We've only been on tour for a week and Cora has already overtaken every square inch in here.

"I'm going to ignore that, Harry. I can't use the language required in front of young ears."

Willa, Belle, Mav, and Kai pile in behind Jo. They take Cora's toys off the couches that line both sides of the bus and sit down.

"Is this a bad email?" I ask, since she apparently needed everyone before telling us.

"No. I got an email from Asher Cross," Jo says. Everyone perks up. Even Harlow turns her head to pay attention. "He wants you to play a private show at his hotel in Vegas."

"You mean the most eligible bachelor in America? The

billionaire that no one knows anything about other than he's hot and single?" Harlow asks.

"You're not single," I gruff, crossing my arms.

Harlow laughs. "I'm very aware and happy about my relationship status," she reassures me.

"Yeah, him. He's throwing a private party for his younger sister and wants you guys to be the entertainment. He was willing to line the dates up so we will already be in Vegas. Well, we need to get there a day early, but that was an easy adjustment to make."

"Aw man. That means we have to skip that interactive museum," Harlow says.

"I found one close to Vegas that you and I can go to with Cora while they're at the party making three million dollars for a two-hour show," Jo says.

"Can you say that again?" Mav says, looking just as shocked as the rest of us.

"You heard me just fine."

"Where do we sign?" I say, laughing, but not really joking.

"The contract is with Frank. As long as it looks fine, you can sign on the dotted line by the end of the show tonight," Jo says, typing something out on her phone. She's always busy. I'm not sure how we handled it before hiring her.

Actually, yes I do.

We didn't. We were a mess.

"So we leave for Vegas in two days instead of three?" Harlow asks, confirming the plan. I know she has a schedule with Cora she likes to stick to. It seems to be helping to keep Cora happy with all the traveling.

"Correct. They have the show tonight, then one more

tomorrow. We need to get on the road right after the last show."

We're in San Diego for two shows. Harlow and Jo are taking Cora to the zoo tomorrow. I've been pouting about not being able to go. As much as I love my girls getting to spend time together, I can't help but feel jealous. My dad might even be going with them, depending on when his flight gets in tonight.

Harlow keeps reminding me that Cora isn't going to remember any of this and that we can make memories with her together when she's older.

"Jo has security set up to meet us there. We'll be back in time for you to see us before you need to be back for sound check," Harlow says, having noticed where my thoughts were already going.

"I know," I mutter.

"I will take tons of pictures and add it to places to take Cora when she's older."

I lean down and kiss the top of Harlow's head. "Thank you, baby."

"Alright, we need to get going," Jo says, ushering everyone out the door.

"Mama!" Cora says, clapping her hands. Harlow beams at her. My heart squeezes every time I see them together. I never thought it was possible to love anyone the way I love these two.

"Thank you, San Diego! Good night!"

I quickly make my way off the stage with the intent of

meeting with the fans that paid for backstage passes and then getting back to my girls. I know I rush this part, but I can't find it in me to feel bad. My whole world is back on that bus and that's where I want to be.

"Cal," Jo says, grabbing my arm to stop me. I look at her. The blonde hair that's usually neatly pulled back during the shows is sticking up all over the place and her face is pale.

"What's wrong? Is it Cora or Harlow?" I ask, panicking as I start to make my way to the dressing room to get my phone.

"No. They're both fine. It's an email I got on the Melt the Ice email."

"Here," she says, pushing her iPad into my hands.

`If your first episode airs, it will be your last. Make the smart choice.`

Below the threatening message are pictures. Pictures of Jo, Harlow, and Cora out on all the adventures they've been having on tour. Harlow holding Cora while they finger paint pottery. Cora pulling Jo's hair while a rare smile graces the woman's face. Harlow ordering food at a food truck while Jo holds Cora. The three of them at a water park.

"These are from everywhere we've been," I say angrily. "Someone is following us."

"It's not hard with a public tour schedule," Jo says.

"Did you send this to Harrison?" I ask.

Jo nods. "But Cal, they said the first episode specifically."

"Ezra's episode."

Jo nods again. "We didn't advertise that. We didn't even mention Ezra's case would be in any of the episodes."

"It could be a lucky guess," I say. Jo frowns. "Yeah, I don't believe that either."

"Double the security when you need to go anywhere. Get someone on Cora and Harlow at all times. Let me know what Harrison thinks."

"I will," Jo says, turning to go make sure everything is as it should be after the show.

I walk up to where everyone is waiting for me to talk to the fans. "I have to go. Jo will update you," I tell Kai.

"Everything okay?" he asks.

"No," I say and run for where the exit is. The buses are parked right behind the arena in a closed off area, but it feels like my girls aren't close enough.

I practically slam into the metal bar, pushing it open and running to my bus.

"Firecracker?" I say, panting as I make my way onto the bus.

"What's wrong?" Harlow asks the moment she sees me. I pull her into my sweaty chest and hold her as tightly as I can while still letting her breathe. "Cal? You're scaring me."

I tell her everything about the email without loosening my hold on her.

"You need to shower," she says after a few minutes of silence. I pull away just enough to see her face.

"What are you going to do?"

"Get ahead of it." She tries to get out of my arms, but I don't let her go.

"Are you sure that's a good idea?" I ask.

"Do you trust me?" she asks.

"With everything I am," I answer honestly.

She leans up and kisses the side of my jaw. "Go shower. Cora is sleeping. I won't leave the bus."

I sigh and let her go. "I don't like this, Firecracker."

"I don't either, but I won't let someone threaten me or my daughter."

A smile breaks through all my worry with the fierce way she just claimed Cora.

"What about Jo?"

Harlow snorts. "If they're dumb enough to threaten Jo, then it's their funeral."

I kiss her, but she pulls away too soon.

"Don't get any ideas. You smell."

"Can I get ideas after I shower?" I ask, wagging my eyebrows.

Harlow laughs. "We'll see."

And see we did.

"I CAN'T TELL if that was genius or idiotic," Jo says. We're almost in Vegas. Jo rode with us on our bus so we could do podcast stuff.

"I think that describes most of my ideas."

Jo laughs and shakes her head. She's reading through podcast emails. They're mostly tips on Ezra we'll have to sort through.

I may have announced the topic of the first episode, and I also may have mentioned Shattered Halo being a part of the first episode.

And there's a chance I made Cal repost it on his socials.

"We have hundreds of emails coming in and so many of them are bullshit," Jo grumbles.

"Yeah, but are any of them from the weird stalker person?" I ask.

Jo sighs. "Not yet."

"It's hard to threaten people with secrets when they're no longer secrets." I just used the exact same strategy we used when Mav's dad was trying to use Cora to break up the band.

"I'm sure they'll find something else to threaten you with," Jo says.

"Do not put that out into the universe!" Cal yells. He's at the other end of the bus with his dad playing with Cora. It's not as far as he seems to think it is with how loud he is when he talks to us.

"Crazy people don't need my help to be crazy," Jo shoots back.

"What if we just really pissed him off?" I whisper.

"Then we'll deal with it," Jo says, shrugging.

"How about I stay with Cora tonight, and you and Cal can have a night to yourselves? I'm sure you can get a hotel room somewhere in the city," Jason offers. My eyes go straight to Cora, then up to Cal's and back down to Cora.

Jo snorts and types something on her phone. "It's not funny," I mutter. Someone has been stalking us, and I don't love the idea of letting Cora out of my sight. I do love the idea of some alone time with Cal, though.

"Belle and Kai said they'll take the bunks tonight," Jo says, causing Jason to laugh.

I meet Cal's eyes and smile. "Parents' night out?" he asks me.

"Let's see how much trouble we can get into," I wag my eyebrows at him, trying to copy the way he does it. Cal and Jason laugh, but Jo groans.

"Don't make more work for me, please," Jo says, scowling at me.

"No promises," I say, laughing as I dodge her attempt to smack me with the back of her hand.

thirty-one

CAL

"THANK you for doing this on such short notice," Asher Cross says, shaking each of our hands. "My sister loves you guys."

"I'm just glad we could fit you into the tour schedule," I tell him.

Asher laughs, and it's that deep kind of chuckle that real men have. Not that I'm not a real man, but my laugh definitely doesn't sound like that. The man is huge. He matches me in height, which few people do. His hair is light brown with that messy on purpose look to it. His eyes are gray and always seem to be assessing.

Everything about him looks expensive. He's in jeans and a white button down that he's rolled at the sleeves, but I'd bet my house that he didn't buy any of it from Target. I can see why Harlow thinks he's attractive.

I'm telling her he looks like a troll in person. Smells like one too.

"My assistant confirmed the set with yours. Once that's done, you're free to stay for the rest of the party or you can leave. It's up to you," Asher says, putting his hands in his pockets, making him look like a model. That's annoying.

"I'm taking my girl out after. My dad has our daughter for the night," I tell him. No idea why. Maybe I wanted him to know I have a girl and he can't have her?

Belle snorts next to me. "Smooth," she says under her breath.

Asher raises his brow. "I'd love to comp a room here for you."

"Oh. That would be great, actually," I say, feeling bad for acting like a jealous idiot.

Asher nods. "Stop at the desk on your way out. I'll have everything set for you."

"Thanks, man."

Asher says his goodbyes. Something in his demeanor seems . . . sad?

Goes to show money doesn't buy happiness, I guess.

"Nate, you good?" I ask our tour manager. He's busy directing the crew that's getting our equipment back on the truck. The show went well. It was really easy for what we made doing it. The ballroom of the hotel was packed with college-age kids in short dresses and tight shirts.

"I'm good, Cal," Nate responds, not even bothering to look my way as he directs the guy holding an armful of cords.

I rush out of the room, which luckily had a stage and a small area behind it with a door that leads directly to the hallway. I didn't want to fight my way through the crowd.

"Cal."

I stop in my tracks. "Firecracker," I say, running to her and scooping her into my arms. She laughs as she snuggles into my neck. "What are you doing here?"

"Jo texted me and told me to meet you in the lobby," she says, pointing to the front desk.

"Remind me to thank her later," I say against Harlow's lips. A throat clears, and we break apart. I look over my shoulder to see the front desk attendant waiting for us.

"Sorry," I say, not the least bit sorry. "Asher said he has a room reserved for me. Callahan Griffin."

"Of course." He types something into the computer and then grabs a set of key cards. "Here are the keys to the Honeymoon Suite."

I give him a questioning look just as Asher walks by, winking at me.

Okay, maybe I actually like this guy.

"Take the elevator to the thirtieth floor. Your room is the last one on the left. Congratulations, Mr. and Mrs. Griffin."

"Thanks, uh," I look at the man's name tag. "Simon."

Harlow is looking at me with confusion. I just shrug and pull her along, following the directions Simon gave me. Her laugh is infectious as she tries to keep up with me.

The elevator ride is the longest of my life. "Why the fuck are there so many floors?"

Harlow laughs and pushes her back into my front. We're huddled into a corner waiting for the bachelorette party to get off. Of course, they're on the twenty-first floor.

I watch the red numbers climb. We're in the teens now. Almost there.

Harlow pushes back into me, her ass grinding against my semi-hard dick.

"Don't tease me," I whisper into her ear, giving it a little nip.

"It's not teasing, it's foreplay," she says with a smile so blinding I almost drop to my knees.

Fuck. I love her. I love every single thing about her. I love the way she teases me, the way she looks at me, the way she loves me.

The elevator door opens, letting the party off and leaving us alone.

"Do something wild with me?" I ask Harlow.

She looks at me, her head cocked to the side. "Okay."

I hit the button for the lobby and wait patiently to take Harlow on the adventure of her life.

thirty-two

HARLOW

"I THINK this one has a lot of potential."

Jo and I have been sorting through the emails and sending ones we think might lead somewhere to my dad. This one in particular is standing out to me.

Hello,

My name is Joseph Pitts III, and I live in Green Peak, New Hampshire. We're a small town that borders Vermont. I'm writing to you today because I believe I have seen the man you are looking for. I own the general store in town. It's been in my family for over a hundred years. I took over from my father when he retired in 1976.

A young man came through here almost seven years ago. He looks similar to that man in the band from Maine. The one that plays the guitar. Blue eyes, not brown. He was very scared and asked about a job. I gave him a job in my store. He even became friends with a local boy before they both moved somewhere together. The gossip around town was that they were an item, but I have it on good authority that the local boy, I can't remember his name, likes women almost too much if you get my meaning.

But that boy, I will never forget his scared face. I do believe he is your guitar friend. From the gossip rags the ladies' group loves to chat about, I see you are dating the young man that is the singer. If you might pass on my message and ask him to get in touch with me, I would much appreciate it. I have wondered how he is doing, and I do hope he is happy and well.

Warm Regards,

Joseph Pitts III

"That was a lot," Jo says after she reads it. "I can almost picture an old man typing this with one finger."

I laugh because I was picturing the same thing as I read it. "I think we should check it out."

Jo nods. "We have six weeks left on the road. Think it can wait until we're done?"

"I think it will have to," I tell her. I don't want to leave Cal or Cora, and I don't think he's going to want to be away from her if I take her with me.

"He left his number at the end of the email. Maybe we

can call first and see what we can get from him before we head to the woods of New Hampshire to talk to the town."

"Good idea." I forward the email to my dad as Jo dials Joseph Pitts III.

"Thank you for calling Green Peak General Store, home of Peaky Buns."

Peaky Buns? Jo mouths and I just shrug.

"Hi, could I speak with Joseph, please?" I ask the girl on the phone.

"Can I ask who is calling?" she asks, her voice switching from sweet to something that sounds almost like she's about to fight us.

"My name is Harlow. Joseph sent us an email regarding my podcast. I was hoping to speak to him about it," I tell her.

She lets out a breath. "I'm sorry about that. My grandfather isn't in his right mind. Whatever he sent you isn't true. I'm sorry he wasted your time."

"If I could just —" I start to ask, but she hangs up on me.

"Well, that was suspicious," Jo says.

"His email was kind of rambling, but he didn't seem confused or crazy," I say, reading the email again.

"It just seemed like an email from a lonely old man," Jo says, crossing her arms and frowning.

"Lonely?"

She shrugs. "It kind of has the vibes of someone who wants to talk because he doesn't get a chance to very often."

"Huh. Yeah, I can see that, but Ezra and Kai are identical. Maybe he knew Ezra but didn't realize he was a twin."

"Or he just knew someone with dark hair and blue eyes," Jo points out. My dad has sifted through so many emails claiming to be someone that knew Ezra that I can see where she's coming from. The number of sightings might rival Elvis at this point.

"Alright," she says, standing. "I need to go get the cake and then head to the water park to set everything up. Jason has Cora, Cal is with Mav and Kai doing whatever it is that they do, and you need to relax."

I glare at her. "I'm supposed to help you with her party." Cora's first birthday is next week, but it's in the middle of a long string of shows. So Jo and I planned her first birthday at an indoor water park. Jo booked the entire place so we would have privacy. Cora loves playing in the water, so I'm really hoping she loves it.

"Willa and Belle are helping me. You've been in full mom mode for weeks now. We want you to relax. Please let me handle this."

I look at my best friend and see the sincerity in her eyes. "Fine," I relent. "But I'm only allowing this because the water park handled most of it, and I picked out everything else."

Jo snorts.

"Mom's plan their daughter's parties," I say defensively.

Jo's face softens. "You're an amazing mom, Harry. You don't have anything to prove. Cora loves you. You don't need to plan some elaborate party to show her you care. She sees it every single day."

My shoulders relax. I didn't even realize how tense I was. "Thanks, Joey."

Jo glares at me. "I'm only allowing that because you're stressed."

I laugh and shake my head. Jo hugs me quickly and leaves me alone on the bus.

"Right. What do I do now?"

I have almost three hours before I need to be there. I just stand in the middle of the bus and look around. Apparently, I no longer know what to do without Cal or Cora.

"What did I do before?" I ask myself.

I grab my phone to look up nail salons. I could go for a good pedicure.

After a few calls to salons in the area, I find one that can do not only a manicure and pedicure but can fit me in for a massage too. I smile to myself as I pull up the Uber app.

I feel like I have a sunburn everywhere. When I said I was going to get everything waxed, I meant it. My fingers and toes are a cute shade of purple that matches the swimsuit I'm wearing to the party. I wiggle my fingers and let the sun catch the glitter in the nail polish. Cora is going to love it.

I bought her a swimsuit that matches mine, and Cal has a pair of trunks in the same shade.

"Harlow Ray?"

I look up to see a man standing in front of a black town car. He's wearing a worn blue cap and jeans with a dirty shirt that probably was white at one point. He looks very out of place, standing in front of the shiny black car.

"Yes?" I ask, already backing up. I ordered an Uber, but it's a yellow Prius driven by a woman named Barbara. I look at my phone and pull up my recent calls to see if Cal sent the car, knowing he wouldn't have sent that man as the driver. I hit his name to call him, but then my back hits a wall.

I try to turn to see what I've backed into, but a strong arm holds me in place and places something else over my mouth. I scream and try to get out of his grip. The moment I inhale, I know I've made a mistake.

My phone slips from my hand as my world goes black.

thirty-three

CAL

"YOUR MAMA IS CALLING," I tell Cora. I got her in her swimsuit before we left and she knows that means water, so she's been pretty excited for the entire ride to the water park.

"Hey, Firecracker," I say with a smile. I love how much effort she's put into our girl's birthday. "We're on our way."

A muffled scream comes through the speakers of the rental car I'm driving, and I almost drive right off the road. I pull over more carefully and throw it into park.

"Harlow?" my dad says, worry creasing his face.

"Harlow!" I say more urgently.

The line goes dead, and I immediately try calling back. It goes straight to voicemail, but I try over and over again. My dad puts his hand over mine before I can tell the car to redial.

"Where was she? We need to start there."

"I don't know. A nail salon?" I desperately try to force air into my lungs.

"Look at me, Callahan!"

I startle at the sharp edge of my dad's tone, but I do what he says.

"Who would know where she is?" he asks more calmly.

"Jo," I answer and immediately call her.

"Hey, are you —"

"Where is Harlow?" I ask, cutting her off.

"Getting her nails done. What happened?" Jo asks, hearing the panic in my voice.

"She called me and there was a scream and now her phone is off. Where is she, Jo?" My question comes out more like a demand, but I don't have the time to care.

"Sparkle Toes on West Sixth Street."

I look it up on my phone. It's less than three minutes on foot. I look at my dad. He nods before I get out of the car and run. Taking the car would be faster, but I can't put Cora in danger too.

My phone is still in my hand and disconnects from the Bluetooth as I move away from the car.

"Call Harrison and the police. Fuck, call the National Guard. Something is wrong, Jo. I can feel it."

"On it," she says and then hangs up.

I run as fast as I can, every muscle in my body straining to get to the woman I love. A little over a minute later, I come to a skidding halt in front of a strip mall. The police are already there and a small middle-aged woman with black hair and thick red glasses is speaking to one of the officers.

"Where is she? Where is Harlow?"

"I'm sorry sir, but this is a crime scene, and I'm going to need you to back up," the officer says, trying to get me to move back from them.

"Are you Cal?" the small woman asks me.

"Yes. Please. Where is she?" I plead.

"I don't know," she says, her eyes welling up with tears. "She walked out of the store to go to her little girl's birthday party. She was so excited. But then a man pulled up in a black car. He tried to get her to go in, but she was heading back in here. Then some other man grabbed her."

"Why didn't you stop him?" I scream, some part of me understanding how unfair that is, but the other part is too worried about Harlow to care.

"I tried!" she yells and turns to fully face me. One side of her face is red and swollen. "I called the police the moment I saw how uncomfortable she looked when the car pulled up. I went out to try to stop the man from taking her, but he knocked me down and drove off with the first man. Harlow was unconscious."

"Thank you," I choke out. It's the most I can manage right now, and she seems to understand.

"Where is she?" I ask, turning to the officer. "It's been what? Maybe ten minutes? Have you found the car yet?"

"An APB went out for a black town car, but so far, nothing. My partner is getting the plate off the cameras right now."

"Fuck!" I yell. I pace and pull at my hair. "What do I do? How do I find her?"

"Who are you to her?" the officer asks.

"That's her man," the small woman says. "She was telling me all about him and their daughter."

The officer seems only slightly more sympathetic with the new information. He hands me his card, and I give him my number. The best he can tell me is he'll give me a call when they have more information.

A red sports car comes flying into the parking lot, almost hitting the police cruiser. Jo jumps out of the passenger seat and runs for me.

"Do they know where she is?" Jo asks with the most emotion I've ever seen from her. Mav parks the car and runs up behind her.

I shake my head and let out a sob. Maverick quickly pulls me into him and holds me as I try to keep it together.

"I can't lose her. I won't survive losing her," I whisper between sobs.

"You won't lose her. We won't let you," he says.

"I have an email that might be of interest to you," Jo says, having pulled on her business mask and turned to the officer. She shows him a threatening email they received about the podcast. Specifically, Ezra's episode. I knew about it. She had me post something on my socials for her.

"She said there had been no more emails," I say, walking over to see what Jo is showing the officer.

"There wasn't. Until right after your phone call."

I warned you. Now face the consequences.

"Can we trace that?" I ask. Can you trace emails? I have no fucking idea. This is Harlow's thing.

"It will take a while," the officer says.

"Harrison is on his way. Belle called your cousin Millie, who is loaning us their jet to get him here," Jo says, ignoring the officer.

I look between her and the officer. I peek at his card to check his name. Officer Lionel Smith. Harlow and Jo have a theory that Senator Wolfe has the police in his pocket. Now I'm wondering how much we should be saying to them.

"We're in fucking Nebraska. If the police here are in the pocket of a Maine senator, then we have bigger problems," Jo says, staring down Officer Smith. The man looks baffled by the entire conversation.

"How the fuck do we find Harlow?" I say, anger and frustration taking over the soul-crushing fear.

"We're going to put out an APB for Harlow with the picture this woman just sent me and the plates my partner just ran. Unfortunately, they're for a rental company."

"They've dumped the fucking car, haven't they?" Jo says, her face turning red with anger.

"It's likely, but not confirmed," Officer Smith says, rubbing the back of his neck. "All you can do now is wait while my officers —"

"That is not all we can do. We'll let you know when we find our girl," Jo says, turning her back on the open-mouthed officer and stomping to the car. "Let's go!"

"Thank you, again," I tell the woman, making a mental note to send her concert tickets for life.

I run after Jo and cram myself into the back seat of the car.

"Harrison lands in four hours. We need to go through every email and make sure we didn't miss any. Maverick, you're going to pick Harrison up from the airport. Cal, you and I are going to go through every note and file we have on Ezra to find the connection," Jo says.

"Did you find her?" Willa's voice comes through on speakerphone.

"Not yet. We're headed back to you. I'm sending you the

login information for the podcast email. I need you three to go through every single one and see if we missed something. Jason is booking us a hotel suite right now to make it easier for everyone to be together. Belle should be getting that information from him soon."

"On it," Willa says.

The woman is a drill sergeant, and I've never been more thankful for it.

"We're going to find her. This will not happen again," Mav says through clenched teeth.

I don't know how Maverick lives every day without Ezra, because I know I won't be able to do it without Harlow.

I'd give up almost anything to find her.

thirty-four

HARLOW

"STOP," I mumble, trying to swat away whoever is tickling my face. My hand connects with something with too many legs. Screaming, I jump up, arms flailing. I try to run, but slam face first into a metal wall.

"What the hell?"

It's pitch black as I wipe my face and fling whatever was crawling on it. Once I check the rest of my body with my hands to assure nothing else is touching me, I put my hands out to feel around the room. My head and face are pounding, but I can't sit still in the dark.

"Cal?" I say, softly. No response.

"Where am I?" Still nothing.

Everything comes rushing back to me. The strange man trying to get me into his car and then . . . nothing. I inhaled chloroform or something similar. Fuck.

I keep my hand on the wall and walk around, figuring out the size of the room I'm in. I almost fall into an opening. Walking forward, I keep my hands out, but my toe immediately hits something. Feeling around with my hands, I realize what it is.

"Stairs!" I hurry up them on my hands and feet, hoping I don't fall back down them.

"Seven," I say to myself, counting the number of stairs. They're very narrow and there's a scratchy material covering them. "Ouch!" I yell as I hit my head on something before I can take the last step. Raising my hands over my head, I feel around.

Shit.

"Is that a door?" I keep feeling around gently until I find a curved metal handle. I try to turn it in both directions, pull it towards me, push it away. Nothing. It won't budge.

"Fuck me," I mutter.

Kidnapping 101: Don't let them take you to a second location.

Well, too fucking late for that.

Putting my hands on the walls, I slowly make my way back down the stairs. My hand hits something halfway down. It feels like a switch. I flip it on and am momentarily blinded by the light.

Blinking slowly, my eyes eventually adjust. I look around, taking in where I am.

"Storm shelter," I guess. I've never seen one in person, but the space is small with a bench along the walls and nothing else. White walls, white bench, white stairs with black grips.

Looking down at myself, I don't see anything alarming. My jean shorts are on and still clean. My yellow tank is wrinkled, but that's probably from the ball I was in on the floor. I'm barefoot. My flip-flops didn't make the trip.

I'm trying to look at the situation like I wasn't the one in it. What would I be telling myself to do if I was just watching? I walk around the small room. Then I walk around again. And again. And again. It's so small I wouldn't be able to lay down fully.

Sitting on the bench, I prop my elbows on my thighs and rest my face in my hands. I can't cry because if I cry, I won't be able to figure out how to get myself out of this situation.

"Think, Harlow," I tell myself. "What do I know?"

There's no way for me to get out of here until someone lets me out.

Someone put me here, but they didn't hurt me.

I was targeted. They knew my name.

They knew where to find me.

"But who?" I ask out loud to the bugs.

"Senator Wolfe? Unlikely. It's Mav he wants, not me."

I think about that for a moment.

"I supposed it could be him, but all the way out here seems like a stretch."

I guess it could be whoever sent that email.

"But who else would be angry about us doing an episode on Ezra?"

I don't want to say it out loud and make it true, but it would make more sense for my dad to be targeted over me. He's doing a lot more digging than I am, and he's close to getting dirt on the senator.

"Unless I am the target because of him," I mutter.

I shake my head.

"It has to be related to the email. They've been following us the whole tour. It makes sense I would have been followed to a nail salon."

I thought it was public enough, but apparently not. I get up with renewed determination and climb the stairs. Banging on the door with as much strength as I can at the weird angle, I scream.

"Let me out, you coward! You made me miss my daughter's birthday! At least fight me face to face!"

My dad taught me how to take down a grown man. Have I practiced what he taught me? No. Not in years, but I'm kind of hoping it's muscle memory. I will not rot down here, or worse.

"What's wrong? Is my dick bigger than yours? Or are you terrified of vaginas?"

Shit. What if the ringleader is a woman and I'm just assuming the two guys that took me are in charge?

"This chick just said she has a dick," I hear right outside the door.

"And it's bigger than yours!" I yell as loudly as I can.

The handle squeaks and stops.

"Don't open it! The boss wants to talk to her before we take care of her," Man One says.

"She needs to learn to shut the fuck up. I'm sure the boss won't mind if I rough her up a little," Man Two counters, but from the sound of smacking flesh, I don't think Man One agreed.

I take a deep breath and count. One. Two. Three. Then I grab the handle, which thankfully turns, and push the door open. The two men are punching each other but stop when they see me jump out of the storm shelter.

I don't stop. I don't look around. I just run.

"Hey! Get back here, you bitch!" one of them yells. I

don't turn to look. I just run into the cornfield in front of me and hope I can lose them in it.

Keeping my head down, I move my legs as fast as I can, taking turns at random. The sun is starting to set, and I know my red hair is like a glowing beacon. It's not long before I'm panting and cursing the amount of corn. Where the fuck is the end to this?

The shouts from the men get quieter, so I take a moment to slow down. I don't stop, but I do slow to a walk. All my darting has them going in the wrong direction.

Or they're going in the direction help would be, and I went the wrong way.

Hot, fat tears stream down my cheeks before I can stop them. I wipe at them furiously.

No. I'm not going to lose it. Not now. My feet are sore and covered in mud. I can't even see the purple sparkles on my toes anymore.

Wait. Mud!

The men's voices are coming closer, and I know they'll spot my hair, and if they don't, my yellow shirt isn't exactly conspicuous. I whip it over my head and coat it in mud, shivering as I put the cold, muddy fabric on my body.

I wince as I do the same to my hair and skin, doing my best to hide any color that won't blend into a field of corn. Then I stay in my crouch and wait, listening to the idiots continue to bicker, easily keeping me aware of where they are.

They pass by a few minutes later. I stay still, watching their feet through the stalks. They're now considering running from whoever their boss is, but they don't think they'd make it. Interesting.

This is so stupid, I think. So fucking stupid. Not giving myself time to talk myself out of it, I follow them.

thirty-five

CAL

"FOUR FUCKING HOURS AND NOTHING!" I yell, pulling at my hair and pacing the length of the shared space in the suite my dad had booked.

"Harrison just landed, and he's been working during the entire flight," Jo says, staying calm every time I have an outburst.

"His tech guy has been tracing the emails. They're from the same account," Willa points out. We didn't find any other emails that were threatening. We didn't find anything in Ezra's file either.

We have nothing. Nothing to tell us where Harlow is. Nothing telling us who took her. I'm ready to rip apart this entire state to find her. The only thing stopping me is the little girl asleep in the next room that has been asking for her mama.

Kai and Belle are back at the buses in case she somehow makes it back there, but they're also contacting anyone they've ever known back in our hometown, trying to see if they can confirm Senator Wolfe is still in Maine.

Harrison burst through the door a few minutes later. He doesn't say hello, he just gets right to work.

"The email bounced around so many IP addresses that my guy is still working on pinpointing its origin," he says, taking a seat on the ugly floral couch and opening his laptop. "But I've been following Harlow's drug theory." His swallow is audible as he says his daughter's name. "I gathered enough information and submitted it to the DEA yesterday."

I stop pacing and look at Mav. The initial shock of his dad being some drug king pin has worn off in the weeks since Harlow had the theory. He seems more resigned than upset.

"How bad is it?" he asks.

"I won't lie to you. It's bad. I don't have access to a lot of information, but from what I did find, your family either owns a lot of the ports in Maine or somehow has control of them. He's funneling drugs in through them and using his power to wipe records."

"Then how did you find anything?" Jo asks.

"He's panicking. We're getting close to something. I'm not even sure what anymore, but it made him sloppy. I got security camera footage of him at one of the docks. He was exchanging money for something at two in the morning."

Harrison's phone rings. "What did you find?" he asks the person on the other end.

"The email was just used again. It looks like it sent from a cell near you in Nebraska."

"Where?" everyone asks at the same time.

"Oh. Uh. Hello. Didn't realize I was on speaker," the man on the phone says.

"Where is she?" I demand.

"I don't know if it's the exact location. I don't have the content of the email. But it pinged at what looks like an abandoned farmhouse on an unnamed road off Market Street. I'll send you the coordinates."

Harrison's call ends, and he checks the coordinates. He stands like he's heading for the farmhouse, which is where I will also be going, but he stops.

"What is in the email?" he asks, his voice shaky for the first time since he got here.

Jo pulls it up on her iPad and pales. Willa grabs it from her and gasps. I take it from her hands.

You were warned. She paid with her life. Back off or who knows who will be next?

There's a picture of Harlow curled in a ball at the bottom of a narrow set of stairs. Blood is pooling underneath her, and her eyes are closed.

"No. This is photoshopped." I toss it on the couch and head for the door, waiting for Harrison. But when I turn to tell him to hurry the fuck up, he's sitting on the couch with his head between his legs. "Let's go, Harrison!"

He doesn't move, and I go to him, pulling on his arm, but he doesn't budge. "Give me the coordinates then, and I'll go alone!"

Harrison stands. "No. I'll go collect her. You stay with your daughter. You don't need to see this." His eyes are red, and he's not trying to hide his tears.

"I'm not giving up on her. Let's go! She needs us. She isn't dead!" I scream, heading for the door. If he won't tell me where she is, I'll look for any and every dirt road off Market Street until I find her.

"Callahan," Harrison starts.

"No! You can be a coward all you want, but I'm going to find her and bring her home. Alive! You may have given up on her, but I won't."

"You think I gave up on her? She's my daughter!"

"She's my fucking wife, and I *will* get her back!" I shout, startling everyone. The shock seems to momentarily have dried their tears.

"Your wife?" Mav asks, having recovered the quickest.

"We got married after that party in Vegas. We were going to throw a party when we got home and surprise everyone," I explain quickly. "Now give me the damn coordinates and let me go get my wife."

"I think he's right, Harrison," Jo says, not having been able to take her eyes off the picture of Harlow. "This blood doesn't look right."

Harrison doesn't even look. He just nods and grabs my arm, pulling me out the door with him. "We're talking about this after we get Harlow back," he says sternly.

"Yes, sir."

I'M CROUCHED in the corn as close to the house as I could be without anyone seeing me. The mud I caked on myself is starting to dry and get itchy, but the sun is gone, and I feel safely hidden.

The two idiots are pacing in front of the house. One of them had a genius idea to send a picture to the podcast email. Judging from the frustration coming off them in waves, they didn't get whatever reaction they were looking for. If I wasn't trying to hide, I would laugh.

It's been hours since they grabbed me. It was around three in the afternoon when they showed up outside the nail salon. It's dark now. I don't know when the sun sets in August in Nebraska, but my best guess is it's at least eight, maybe closer to nine. Which means my dad and Jo have had at least five hours to find me. And Jo will have been on top of the emails. She definitely saw whatever those two sent.

"Boss is calling. I told you that email was a bad idea," Man One says, slapping Man Two on the back of the head. "You didn't send it to that other email first so they can send it around the earth first or whatever." I recognize Man One as the guy that was in front of the town car. Man Two must have been the one who grabbed me. They both have a similar build and seem to look alike from where I'm standing. Brothers would be my guess. They're even dressed the same. Except Man Two has a blue shirt instead of a dirty white one.

"You did not say a damn thing about the email being a bad idea!" Man Two argues, rubbing the spot on his head.

"Hey Boss," Man One says, answering his phone. "Well, Sal thought sending them a picture would get them to back off," he pauses. "Of course, we still have the girl. She's in the storm shelter where you told us to put her," another pause. "Move her? That wasn't the deal. The deal was we get the girl and take her here. Then you pay us, and you deal with her after."

Okay, that's interesting. These are just paid hands, which I kind of figured out from the rocks in their heads. But I was also toying with the idea of crazed Shattered Halo fans or weird anti-podcast people.

I can almost make out the voice on the other side of the phone with the way they're screaming. It almost seems familiar, but I'm not willing to get close enough to confirm that.

"Double?" Man One's eyes go wide and Man Two, or Sal apparently, nods and then frantically shakes his head. "You got it, boss."

"How the fuck are we going to do that? She's lost somewhere in the miles of corn!" Sal yells, throwing up his hands.

"We just need to find another redhead and hope she passes."

"That won't fucking work, Mikey, and you know it," Sal argues.

Man One, Mikey, just shrugs. "If we beat her face, it might. Boss won't know until the swelling goes down and we'll be in the wind by then."

Both of their heads suddenly snap, looking up the dirt path and pulling their guns. I follow their line of sight.

No.

It's the black SUV Cal rented. I recognize the rental company's plates on the front and the mermaid magnets I let Cora put on the driver's side.

No, no. This can't be happening.

The SUV flies in and screeches to a stop, sending dirt and rocks flying. I squint, trying to see what's happening. All I hear is yelling.

Then I hear the crack of a gunshot and run.

thirty-seven

"STAY in the car and stay down!" Harrison yells, pulling a gun from the back of his jeans. I don't respond. I don't bother knowing it would be a lie.

I am not staying in this fucking car while my wife is out there somewhere, potentially hurt.

Harrison opens his door and immediately ducks behind it. I do the same with mine.

"Cal!" Harrison yells, but nothing he can say will stop me. I can see the door for the storm shelter and it's open. Maybe she got out. Maybe she ran and is at the police station as we speak.

Or maybe she's still in there and can't get out. I need to make sure.

I know it's potentially stupid. I know how much danger I'm putting myself in. I know I could be taking both of Cora's parents from her.

But what choice do I have? Belle and Kai will care for Cora like she's theirs and hopefully when she's older, she'll understand. Understand that her dad loved her mom so much that he was willing to give his last breath to get her back for her. To get her back for both of them.

I duck down, using all the dust the car kicked up to stay hidden. I make my way as quickly as I can, around the two men aiming their guns and shouting at Harrison, and to the open shelter door. It's pitch black down there.

I look back. They haven't noticed me. I grab my phone out of my pocket and carefully make my way down the stairs, only turning the flashlight on when I get down there. It's empty. Turning the flashlight off quickly, I run back up the stairs. She's not down there, but there wasn't any blood either. I was right about the photoshop. I didn't actually look at the picture long enough to know one way or another. My brain just wouldn't accept it.

"What the fuck do you think you're doing?"

I spin on my heel to see the guy in the blue shirt pointing his gun at my chest. I slowly lift my hands, ready to negotiate. They're probably doing this for money. I'll give them every cent. But before I can hand over the details of my bank account, blood splatters from the man's shoulder, causing him to drop the gun.

The noise from the gun and the blood causes my vision to blur around the edges. Images from that night in the prison flicker in front of the endless cornfields in front of me. I gasp and clutch my chest, trying to force enough air into my lungs to scream.

A brown animal darts out of the corn and heads straight for me. My eyes widen, and I start to back up, trying to get away from the bear or whatever animal lives out here.

"Stop!"

I look to see the other man holding a gun up to me, with

Harrison gripping a bleeding leg at his feet. My eyes flicker back to the animal charging me, but it's closer. I would know those green eyes anywhere, glowing with white hot anger and icy fear in the light from the SUV's headlights.

"Harlow," I breathe, forgetting my father-in-law bleeding on the ground and the man holding a gun, and run to her. I need to get to her. I need to protect her from these men and beg her forgiveness for failing her.

Harlow is inches from me as she throws her entire body into my arms. I wrap her in my arms just as the crack of another gunshot disturbs the night air, followed quickly by a second shot. I swing my head to Harrison, thinking he was shot again.

But Harrison is standing, holding a gun over the man with the white, now red, shirt. I let out a sigh of relief. It's over.

"Cal," Harlow whispers in my arms before she slumps.

"Harlow!" I say in alarm. I put her on the ground gently. Maybe she just passed out from an adrenaline dump.

She's covered from head to toe in mud. Harrison is by my side a moment later, helping me look over his daughter. It takes us a minute to find it, the mud and darkness making it difficult. The pool of blood on the ground underneath her is hard to miss.

"She's been shot," Harrison says. I see what he sees, a weeping wound in her back. I rip my shirt off and press it to the wound, trying desperately to staunch the bleeding.

Harrison is on the phone with 9-1-1 detailing what he needs and Harlow's condition.

"Please, baby," I beg. "Cora needs you." I'm crying, letting the tears fall onto the side of her face. "I need you."

My brain is slow to catch up to what happened. I'm still pressing on her wound, crying and begging her to open her eyes when I realize what happened.

She jumped in front of me. She jumped in front of a bullet. For me.

"Why did you do that?" I ask her. "Why? Don't you know my life isn't worth yours?"

Harrison directs the police and ambulance down the dirt road. I refuse to take any pressure off where Harlow's life is slowly draining from her. The medics let me in the ambulance with her, not willing to fight me on it or realizing that the pressure needed to be kept. I'm not sure which, nor do I care.

"Come on, Firecracker. You have to stay with me. I love you. Cora loves you. She needs her mom, and I need my wife," I tell her. "I love you." I just keep repeating it the entire drive to the hospital, the entire run into the emergency room and right before they finally took her from me.

I kept repeating it when Harrison led me to the waiting room. I repeat it while my friends try to give me coffee, and my sister hugs my numb body. I repeat it when the police come to question us and when the doctors come out to tell us she made it through surgery.

I repeat it like a prayer or a spell as I take the seat next to her bed. I repeat it for the days that followed when she doesn't wake up.

I'm repeating it right now, ten days later, as I ignore the doctors telling me she may never wake up.

I will never stop repeating it. Not until she wakes up and shows me those perfect green eyes.

THE FIRST THING that hits me is the smell. Antiseptic that always has an underlying smell of urine.

The next thing that hits me is the noise. The beeping of machines and barely audible crying.

The last thing that hits me is the bright light as I peel open my heavy eyelids.

It takes a few blinks to get my vision to clear. Fluorescent lights in the ceiling, monitors showing vitals, and scratchy blankets.

Yup. I'm in a hospital.

"Come on, Firecracker. You have to stay with me. I love you. Cora loves you. She needs her mom, and I need my wife."

I turn my head to see Cal at my bedside, his hands clasped like he's begging, tears flowing freely onto the blanket.

I open my mouth to tell him how much I love him, but nothing comes out. My mouth and throat are so dry it feels like I swallowed an entire desert. Instead, I reach for him; the movement taking more effort than that one time I thought running a half marathon was a good idea.

The moment my fingers brush his, Cal's head whips up and his eyes lock onto mine. He's a mess. His eyes are red and puffy, his face is covered in a messy almost-beard, and his hair is sticking up in every direction. The dark bags under his eyes advertise how little sleep he's gotten.

"Harlow," his voice cracks on a sob. He reaches out a shaky hand, gently stroking my face. "Is this a dream?"

I shake my head and slowly lift my hand, patting my throat, hoping he understands. His eyebrows fly up, and he grabs me a cup of water, holding the straw as I take a drink.

"Slowly," he says, his eyes still locked on mine with so much adoration and fear shining in them it makes me want to cry.

"Cal." My voice comes out as a croak, but it's enough for him to collapse next to me and sob. His hand is gripping my hand so tightly it almost hurts, but I grip his hand back with as much strength as I have. "What happened?"

Cal kisses my hand, his tears mixing with his lips. "You jumped in front of me," he says, pulling my hand to his chest and holding it there. "Never do that again."

I snort. Cal shakes his head at me, but a small smile teases the corner of his lips.

"What's the last thing you remember?" he asks, helping me take another sip of water.

"Corn," I say, and it's his turn to snort.

"You're awake!" An older nurse says and clasps her hands together. "Oh, we so hoped you would. Your husband here, he never gave up hope, and he would kick out anyone who said otherwise. You got yourself a keeper right here, young lady," she says with a wink. She has the kind of eyes that older people have where you can't tell if they're sparkling because they're happy or if they're chronically watery. I smile, though, fully aware of how lucky I am to have Cal in my life.

She takes my vitals and calls the doctor in. They fuss over me for longer than I'd like. Cal holds my hand the entire time, not giving a single shit that he's in the way.

"Cora?" I ask when they finally leave us alone.

"She's back at the hotel with everyone else," Cal says, his thumbs rubbing the back of my hand. "She really misses you."

"I'm sorry I scared you," I tell him, my voice still raspy.

Cal leans forward and kisses me softly. "You can't ever leave me, Harlow. I barely survived you laying in this fucking hospital bed and your heart was still beating. If it stopped . . . if you were gone," he chokes.

"I'm here Cal. I'm not leaving you. I love you too much for that."

"I love you too. So fucking much, Firecracker."

We stay like this, his head in my lap, and my hand clasped against my chest until my eyes feel heavy, and I fall asleep.

***

The next time I wake up, my room is swarmed with people. Cal is still in his spot next to me, but my dad is on my other side. Belle, Kai, Mav, and Willa are standing by the window. Jo and Jason are at the foot of the bed with Cora.

"Mama!" Cora yells when she sees I'm awake.

"Hi Cora girl," I say with a smile. "Mama missed you!" The anxiety I felt every time I referred to myself as her mom has vanished. That feeling of being an imposter or that I didn't earn the title is gone.

Her pudgy little hands reach out for me, and I reach for her. Jason brings her over and gently puts her on the bed next to me. Cora immediately scrambles onto me, causing me to hiss when her foot hits my middle. I remember what happened. I just didn't want to talk about it with Cal yet.

The doctor told me I had been in a coma for twelve days. My gunshot wound is healing well, but they had to make another incision in my front to get the bullet out from where it lodged itself underneath a rib. It's still sore and a baby foot directly to it doesn't feel great. Cal goes to grab her from me, but I hold her tight and glare at him. He shakes his head and laughs but keeps her bum and legs above my stomach as I hold her to me. She clings to me just as tightly.

"I missed you so much, my girl," I tell her, kissing her cheek and smelling her hair.

"Mama," she sighs in contentment.

My dad squeezes my shoulder and kisses my temple. "You scared the ever-loving shit out of me."

I bark out a laugh. "I'll try not to get kidnapped and shot next time."

The mood in the room sobers, and I allow Cal to take Cora from me.

"What happened, Harry?" Jo asks, squeezing my foot.

I tell them everything that happened from the moment I stepped foot out of the nail salon until I woke up in this hospital bed. Everyone's eyes just kept getting wider and wider. Which would be comical in any other situation.

"Like father, like daughter," my dad sighs, sounding both impressed and exhausted.

"Okay, we can all admit the mud was really smart, though," Mav says.

"I thought a bear was coming after me," Cal says, causing everyone, including me, to laugh.

"A short and skinny bear on two legs?" Willa asks.

"Does Nebraska even have bears?" Kai asks Belle, who shrugs.

"Keep laughing. It was dark, she was covered in mud, and I wasn't exactly thinking straight," Cal defends.

"So, have we figured out who or why any of this happened?" I ask.

"Michael and Sal Anderson, brothers who were hired to take you and transfer you to an undisclosed location, were given five thousand dollars in cash and promised another five at the handoff," my dad says, and I frown. "What?"

"Only ten grand?" I say, knowing it's pretty stupid to be offended, but I think I'm worth a lot more.

My dad sighs and pinches the bridge of his nose. "Michael, or Mikey, is no longer living," he continues, pretending I didn't speak. "And Sal is claiming he wasn't the one who took the calls. They were supposed to meet whoever paid them at the farmhouse for the exchange, but plans changed. He didn't know what caused the change, either."

"It just feels so sloppy," Jo says, crossing her arms, that familiar line forming between her brows as she thinks. "They didn't seem too smart, and that seems risky."

"I think they shared a single brain cell and left it at home that day," I say seriously, but Kai bursts out laughing.

"Oh shit," Willa says, staring at her phone. She grabs that control thing that all hospitals have attached to the beds and puts the TV on.

"Holy hell in a handbasket," the nurse says as she comes into the room, probably because of the amount of people in here. No one looks at her, our eyes are glued to the screen.

Senator Wolfe is front and center giving a press conference. His dark hair is perfectly slicked back, and his expensive looking blue suit is as wrinkle-free as ever, but it's his eyes. The panic is shining through.

"These allegations are unfounded. I can assure everyone here today and all the good people of Maine that I have been working tirelessly to rid this community of the drugs plaguing us. I have never and would never conspire to infect the state with more poison. I look forward to proving these allegations false and finding out who is trying to undermine my position as your senator. I will not be taking questions at this time. Thank you."

"So they didn't arrest him?" Mav asks, looking at his feet. I can't imagine what he's feeling right now.

"It's a scare tactic. Someone, the DEA, if I had to guess, leaked that they were looking into him and had substantial evidence against him. They want him to panic and mess up so they can catch him," my dad says.

"And what happens if they do? They arrest him, and we're still no closer to finding Ezra," Belle says. "I know getting drugs off the street is important, and I'm sorry if this sounds selfish, but Ezra is important too."

"Can we, I don't know, negotiate? Get time off his sentence if he tells us where Ez is?" Willa asks.

"There isn't an open case," I say sadly. "As far as the law is concerned, Ezra is dead and has been for almost seven years."

"Going through the senator isn't the right play. He won't give us anything. The more he sees us poking, the more he's going to react," Jo says, gesturing to me. "Obviously."

"So we're going to just assume this was him and not anyone else?" Cal asks, not looking convinced.

"It was him, but I don't have a strong enough way to connect it," my dad said, looking down at his phone.

"You suddenly seem sure," I say.

"My guy got into Mikey's phone. He was texted the drop location from a burner phone. It was a private airstrip. He also found the plane you were supposed to be on."

"Okay," I say, waiting for the bomb to drop.

"The plane was supposed to fly to Maine, Harlow," my dad says.

I sigh and look around the room. Everyone is exhausted. You can see it in their eyes, in the way they're standing, in the way their shoulders are drooping in defeat.

"What's going on with the tour?" I ask. We're still in Nebraska, and we're definitely not supposed to be right now.

"We postponed the shows for the second leg," Cal says. "Logan was going to cancel them and take the hit once he found out what happened to you, but we told him no. I knew you'd be pretty upset if we did."

"I'd be more than upset."

Cal chuckles and shakes his head. I look at Jo while

everyone else starts discussing when to resume the tour. I know she's thinking the same thing I am.

We need to go to New Hampshire, but with the tour postponed, it's going to be harder to convince Cal. I also refuse to let this ruin Cora's birthday.

I just need to get out of the hospital and home first. Then I can regroup.

HARLOW WAS PLANNING a birthday party for Cora the moment we landed in Boston. The doctors cleared her to go home two days after she woke up, against my insistence that she wasn't ready. The glare Harlow shot my way when I tried to get her to stay is one for the record books. And clearly it worked since I'm standing in my backyard that has been transformed into a watermelon wonderland.

My wife is standing in front of a sign that says "Cora is One in a Melon," directing Willa and Belle on where she wants the balloons placed on the balloon arch. The balloons are in two different shades of pink and a light green. Honestly, everything looks amazing. There's a long row of tables with watermelon tablecloths and decorations scattered on the top. A caterer should be here any minute with the food.

Since we still don't have definitive proof of who took Harlow, we're keeping the party small. Which is something I tried to point out during the planning process, but Harlow had already called my cousin Millie and invited her and Logan along with their infant daughter. I'm lucky she stopped there.

"This seems like a lot for a baby. Is that a ball pit?" Kai asks, as he comes to stand next to me. Harlow bought a kiddie pool and filled it with green and pink balls. Cora is going to love it.

"There's a watermelon shaped sprinkler too." I tell him. I don't mention the custom watermelon sugar cookies, watermelon themed drinks and snacks, or the two-tier watermelon cake.

He sighs and looks to the sky. "Belle is going to want to be this over the top when we have kids now."

I spit the watermelon water I had just put in my mouth and look at him. "Don't talk about knocking my sister up. What is wrong with you?"

Kai laughs and slaps my back. "We live together, dude. What did you think we were doing?"

"I don't know! Taking cooking classes and learning to crochet?"

"We practice making babies," Kai says with a smug look on his face. I tackle him to the ground. He grunts and forces a roll so he's on top. "She likes it like this too."

I punch him right in his stupid face.

"Fuck!" he groans and rolls off me.

"What are you doing?" Belle asks, running to Kai and glaring angrily at me.

"He started it!" I defend. Harlow has her hands on her hips as she stares down at me. She's not mad, but curious. Willa shakes her head and gets back to the balloon arch. She's used to us.

"Explain," Harlow says.

"He kept bragging about fucking my sister!" I say indignantly, pointing at Kai. Harlow snorts and Belle turns her glare to Kai.

"Really, Malikai?" she says, and he shrugs, smiling like the smug fucker he is.

"I see some things never change."

I turn to see Millie walking into my backyard. Her hair, so similar to Belle's, is pulled back into a ponytail. They're even both wearing jean shorts and pink shirts. The two of them look more like siblings than Belle and I do. Belle squeals and runs to hug Millie. I get up off the ground and dust myself off, then take my turn for a hug.

Holding out my hand to Kai, I pull him up. "Sorry," he says, but the smile tells me he is absolutely not sorry.

"You wouldn't like it if I bragged about fucking your brother. Which I did. Often," Mav says deadpan, walking by us with an armful of presents. Kai's face is a mixture of shock and disgust, making me laugh so hard I have to bend over and grab my knees to catch my breath.

By the time I'm able to get myself together, Logan is standing in front of me with a baby strapped to his chest. He's smiling at me, holding out his hand for a shake. I take it and shake. I'd hug the man if there wasn't a fragile baby in the middle. Hell, I might kiss him to thank him for how he's handled us postponing the tour.

"Thanks for inviting us," he says. "It's Valerie's first birthday party invite, and Millie was thrilled."

"You guys are always welcome here," I say honestly. Harlow meets my eye, and I gesture for her to stand with me. "This is my wife, Harlow," I tell Logan once she's by my side.

Logan's eyes flare slightly before he composes himself, ever the distinguished businessman. "It's wonderful to meet you, Harlow," he says, shaking her hand. "I'm Logan and this is my daughter, Valerie."

Harlow gushes over the new baby as Millie walks up to us. She quickly introduces herself to Harlow and the two take off to get Cora ready, chatting about surprising people with husbands as they walk away.

"That's going to be dangerous for us, isn't it?" Logan says, watching them disappear into the house.

I laugh. "She's already best friends with my sister and best friends. It was inevitable for her to scoop Millie into her circle too."

"So. Wife?" Logan asks, hitching one eyebrow.

I shrug one shoulder. "I knew the moment I met her. She filled a hole in my heart that I didn't even know I had. Making her my wife just made sense."

"When you know, you know," he says, looking wistfully in the direction Millie went.

"Are you going to explain that one?" Willa asks, arms crossed and looking annoyed. She's in a pink shirt and jean shorts too. Harlow told everyone to wear pink, and it seems we all went for a pink shirt and jeans of some variety.

I smile. Willa hates not knowing things, so this is really pissing her off. "No. I think we're going to keep that moment to ourselves. Something perfect and special that's just ours."

Willa narrows her eyes as she studies me. She must find what she's looking for because she nods and walks away.

"Birthday girl is coming!" Jo shouts. Everyone turns to watch as my wife carries our daughter into the backyard. Millie and my dad follow closely behind them, but I only have eyes for my girls. Harlow, Cora, and me are all in pink shirts that Harlow painted black ovals on, and green shorts. She thought it was going to be a fight to get me to wear it. One day, that woman is going to realize I would give her anything she asks for.

They make their way to me, and I put my hand on Harlow's waist, pulling her to me and kissing her lips and then Cora's head.

Fuck. I'm one lucky asshole.

"I'm exhausted," Harlow says, flinging herself on the couch and wincing.

I hold my tongue. The party was a lot, and I'm not entirely sure Harlow was supposed to be holding Cora, but telling her otherwise would have been very dangerous for my health. Instead, I move her legs and sit under them, take her sandals off, and rub her feet.

"*Oh.* Oh god, Cal. Keep doing that," she moans and throws her arm over her eyes.

"You need to stop making those noises, Firecracker," I groan, and readjust myself.

"I can't help it. It feels so good," she says and gasps when I press my knuckle into her heel.

"Harlow," I warn.

"Right there, Cal!" she screams. I know what she's doing. She's technically able to have sex. I was there when she asked the doctor. But I've been too worried about hurting her.

"Fuck it," I mutter and make quick work of removing her shorts and panties.

"Finally," she says, reaching for me.

"I'm going to eat your sweet pussy and that's it," I say, and she pouts. "That's all you're getting for now, baby. I can't hurt you. I won't."

"You won't hurt me, Cal."

"You're sore from the party and don't pretend you aren't. Let me take care of you," I whisper, kissing my way from her foot all the way up her leg until I'm close to where she wants me.

"Okay," she says on a breath, arching her back, trying to get closer to my mouth.

"So impatient," I say, kissing everywhere except where she wants me to.

"Callahan, if you don't put your mouth on my clit right now, I'll be taking care of myself," Harlow huffs. She's adorable when she's frustrated.

I pause, considering my options.

"And I won't let you watch," she adds, knowing exactly where my thoughts just went. So I do as she asks and suck on her clit, earning me a moan.

I lick and suck until she's panting and begging for more. She tangles my hair in her hands and grinds against my mouth.

"Cal, I need more. Please," she whimpers. I insert two fingers and watch her face as she moans. "Make me come, husband."

I growl into her soaking wet pussy. She knows exactly

what it does to me when she calls me husband. I suck her clit back into my mouth and curl my fingers. She comes on a cry, pulling my hair so hard it hurts, but I don't care. Having my wife fall apart on my face is one of the best things I could ever experience.

Once Harlow releases her death grip on my hair, I crawl up her body, being careful to keep my weight off her and kiss her. "I love you, wife."

"I love you too," she says, taking my hand in hers. "We need to get rings."

"Oh, I bought you a ring, baby. I had it custom made. It just isn't done yet." We're wearing the cheap bands we got when we got married, but we definitely need upgrades if the green circle underneath them is any indication.

Harlow frowns. "How do you feel about tattooing your finger?"

I snort. My Firecracker is a jealous woman, and I fucking love it. "I'll tattoo your name across my forehead if you want me to."

"Your finger is fine. I like your face too much to mar it like that."

"I'll make an appointment tomorrow," I tell her, getting to my feet and picking her up in my arms.

She laughs. The sound will never get old, especially after not knowing if I would ever hear it again.

"I was kidding. I'm getting you a ring," she says.

"Whatever you want, Firecracker."

I'm making a tattoo appointment the moment I wake up.

"ARE you taking me into the woods to murder me?" Cal asks, looking out the car window. "You couldn't find closer woods?"

I laugh. We're renting a cabin in New Hampshire a few towns over from Green Peak General Store. It's a cute A-frame at the end of a dirt driveway surrounded by tall trees. It's late summer, so the leaves haven't started to change, and the weather is still warm. I bet it's pretty in the fall when all the leaves are shades of reds, oranges, and yellows.

When I explained to Cal that I wanted to come speak to the owner, he was understandably irate. But once I showed him the letter and explained the weird phone call from his granddaughter, he saw what I was getting at. He still didn't want me to go but knew he couldn't stop me.

Cora is back at home with Jason, and Jo is working on rescheduling all the tour dates and was too busy to make the trip. Belle and Kai came with us. They're staying in a cabin down the road from this one. We invited Mav and Willa, but

Mav said he didn't want to follow dead ends again, and Willa wanted to stay with him.

I hate being separated from Cora again, but we need to figure this out. I don't feel safe leaving the house anymore, and I know Cal is freaking out about going on tour again.

The police found old records of Belle's ex, Brad, having interned for Senator Wolfe. Making it not a huge jump to assume it was the senator that sent Brad after Belle. Going with that assumption, the next most plausible assumption is that he went after me too. The connection being both of us digging into Ezra. We need to end this before he goes after Willa next, or even his own son.

"I wouldn't need to bring you to the woods to kill you," I tell Cal, keeping my voice serious even though I want to laugh at the horrified look he's giving me. "Although, I guess it would save me a body disposal trip."

"I got your name tattooed on my finger!" he yells, pulling the platinum band I got him off his ring finger and wagging it in my face. "They would know it was you!"

I can't keep my laughter in anymore. "I would never kill you. You, Callahan Elizabeth Griffin, are my entire soul and at least thirty percent of my daily entertainment."

Cal's face quickly went from relieved to offended. "Thirty percent?" he says, clutching his chest like I just broke his heart.

"Your dad is pretty funny," I say with a shrug.

"My *dad?*" He's screaming now. Cal is dramatic, so messing with him is so much more fun than it should be.

"Have you noticed how handsome he looks with his new haircut?" I'm lucky we're parked in front of the cabin because I think Cal would've driven off the road by now.

"Firecracker, don't for one second think I won't kill my dad if he touches you," Cal says, white knuckling the steering wheel.

"You won't kill your dad."

"He's had a good run," Cal says and shrugs.

I snort and shake my head. I can't tell if he's joking or not, but it doesn't matter. "I only want you, husband. No need to commit patricide."

Cal grabs my neck and pulls me in for a punishing kiss. "You're mine, wife. Mine."

"Yours."

"This town is fake," Cal says, looking around at all the adorable buildings with suspicion. They're all separate and look like they may have been small houses at one point. They even have window boxes with colorful flowers spilling out.

"I was thinking the same thing," Kai says, looking around like something is going to jump out at him.

I exchange a look with Belle. We should have left them behind.

The town is adorable. All the stores are on the main street, which is aptly named Main Street. They have a general store, post office, mechanic, pharmacy, bakery, and a small boutique. We're currently walking with iced coffees in hand from the bakery on our way to the general store.

Kai is in front of Belle and me, with Cal taking up the rear. They're constantly looking around for bad guys or bears. I'm not sure. No one knows we're here. I didn't call ahead to the general store, and it's not a public date for a concert. I even put the cabin reservation under a false name. I don't think anyone has even recognized us. That's a nice change.

"Why does everyone keep waving at us?" Kai asks.

"It's a small town. We grew up in a small town. It's exactly the same," Belle points out, rolling her eyes at his back.

"This is a fake small town," Kai defends. I just snort.

"I think it would be the perfect backdrop for a Christmas movie," I say.

"See!" Cal says. "Fake town."

"Beautiful morning for a walk," an older man with stark white hair says as he passes us, waving.

Kai turns and starts gesturing wildly at the old man's back. "See!" he whisper-shouts.

"We're here. Behave or stay outside," I tell the guys, making direct eye contact with both of them.

Kai grabs Belle by the hand, and Cal pulls me into him by the waist. "You two stay with us or you haven't seen how dramatic I can be," Cal says.

"I was there the day you lost in fantasy football and had to get your legs waxed," Belle says. Kai barks out a laugh, clearly having seen the same event.

Cal glares at the back of her head as she walks into the store.

"Did you get it on video?" I ask as we follow them in.

"Of course. I'll show it to you later," Belle says, smiling over her shoulder.

Cal grumbles something about traitorous siblings when we're greeted by a cheerful voice. "Welcome to

Green Peak General Store, home of the famous Peaky Buns!"

The man who offered the warm greeting is sitting behind a wooden desk with a golden old fashioned cash register. There are jars of jams and jellies lining the counters and a basket of individually wrapped cookies.

"Your store is adorable," Belle says.

"Thank you so much! It's been in my family for over a hundred years!" This must be Joseph Pitts III. He's tall and skinny, with brown eyes and gray hair that's parted to the side and slicked back. He's wearing a shirt with the general store's name in front of a mountain. There are variations of the shirt in different colors hanging from racks in the store.

"What's a Peaky Bun?" Cal asks, walking around Belle and Kai, where they're looking through brochures of different activities in the area and pulling me with him.

"Oh! Let me get you one! The only way to explain is to experience!" Joseph practically runs to the back of the store, where there's a small amount of grocery options and what looks like a bakery display case with a too-small cafe. He's back a moment later, holding two bread buns and a small container of a brownish butter. At least I think it's butter.

Cal and I each grab one and slather the sweet-smelling butter on them. They're warm, and I groan when I bite into it.

"It's a simple milk bun, but the secret is the maple butter. The maple syrup we use to make it is made right here in town," Joseph says, clasping his hands together and smiling gleefully.

"Can I try one?" Kai asks. Joseph's smile gets even wider

until he turns to look at Kai. Then his smile drops and his face pales. "Are you alright?" Kai asks, alarmed.

"You're back!" Joseph says, composing himself.

My eyes bounce between Joseph and Kai before meeting Belle's eyes and seeing they're just as wide as mine. Cal tightens his grip on my waist, the only indication he's made the same connection. It's the same assumption Jo and I had from reading his email. This man thinks Kai and whoever worked here are the same person. We just weren't sure if he would when he saw Kai up close.

"I . . . Uh," Kai stutters.

"Don't tell me you don't remember me, Ethan. I'm Joseph. It's been a few years, but I'd like to think you liked working for me," Joseph says, chuckling.

"Ethan Paul?"

We all turn at the new voice. A teenage girl with straight black hair down to her waist and the same shade of brown eyes as Joseph just walked through the doors to a backroom. She's wearing one of the store shirts and a green apron around her waist.

"You probably don't remember my granddaughter, Fiona. She was only twelve when you left," Joseph says, pulling Fiona over to him from where she was frozen by the door.

"How old are you now?" I ask. Kai is just staring at them with an unreadable expression on his face.

"Sixteen," she says, looking at Kai suspiciously.

"Don't mind Ethan," I say quickly. "He got into an accident. We're trying to get his memories back."

"An accident? Oh goodness! What happened?" Joseph asks.

"He, uh, skied into a wall," I blurt.

"A wall?" Fiona asks, not believing me for a second. I can see it in her eyes.

"Yeah. He dodged a tree and hit a wall," Belle adds. "Anyway, we're trying to make stops at all of his old haunts to try to jog more memories."

"Oh dear! Come come. Have a seat and we can talk," Joseph says, ushering us to a small table by the bakery case. Once we're all seated, he folds his hands and sets his eyes on Kai.

"You came to live here about," Joseph taps his chin as he thinks, "I'd say at least six years ago."

That tracks with the timeline. Maybe this is the first stop Ezra made.

"You seemed terrified of something. I never did find out what, but you were asking for a job and a place to stay. So I set you up with a job here and let you stay in the apartment upstairs."

"That was very kind of you," Kai says, clearing his throat.

"You were the best worker I've ever had. Don't tell my granddaughter," Joseph says in a whisper loud enough for Fiona to hear. She rolls her eyes and then continues her suspicious looks at Kai.

"When did he leave? Do you know where he went after?" I ask.

"You became close with a boy from a neighboring town. I don't remember which one. Our town is a through town, you understand. Lots of folks come through here and a lot of them are regulars, but they don't live here." Belle pales at his words. Sure, Ezra could have become close as friends with another guy, but there's a chance it was more and that would break Maverick.

"Do you remember his name?" Kai asks.

"You really don't remember?" Fiona asks, not hiding her suspicion from her voice.

Kai meets her eyes and shakes his head.

"I don't remember. He played a sport, I think. So he came through here more often, going to and from games," Joseph says, tapping his chin some more as he thinks.

"*Ethan*," Fiona says, making it clear that she absolutely does not believe that Kai is Ethan, "left town four years ago, and we haven't heard from him since."

"Well, duh. He can't remember you," Cal says, and I snort.

"Who are you to him?" Fiona asks. I like her, even if she's not on our side right now.

"His best friend," Cal says proudly.

"You punched me in the face a week ago!" Kai argues.

"You kept talking about banging my sister!" Cal shouts.

Joseph looks utterly shocked, but Fiona leans forward, suddenly more interested.

I roll my eyes and Belle smacks the table with her hand. "You two need to stop."

"You're my sister! I didn't object to you two dating because I can see how happy you are together. And I know he'll treat you like you deserve, but I refuse to be told you have naked time together," Cal says, crossing his arms and leaning back in his chair.

I laugh even though I try not to. So does Fiona.

"I changed my mind. I like you guys. Even you, fake Ethan."

"That's mighty rude, Fiona," Joseph chastises.

She snorts and looks at us. "I know you're Harlow Ray, and Callahan and Bellamy Griffin. Just like I know you're Malikai Irons and 'Ethan' is Ezra Irons."

"Uh. No. I'm, uh, Mark?" Cal says. I pat his leg. I can see in Fiona's eyes that she knew who we were the moment we walked in the door.

"Shattered Halo fan?" I ask.

"True crime. I'm looking forward to your podcast," she admits.

"Are you the one who answered the phone when I called?" I ask her. She flinches before nodding.

"I just started following the case. When you called, I was worried you'd bring press and who knows what else here. I didn't even realize Ezra was Ethan. The image I have in my head from when I was younger doesn't really match with him," she says, pointing at Kai. "But when my granddad insisted that Kai was Ethan when we saw you doing that live performance on the morning show, I realized he was right."

"You knew he was my missing brother, but didn't say anything?" Kai asks her, the accusation clear in his tone.

"Ethan was hiding from something. How was I supposed to know if you were the something or not?" she says, crossing her arms defiantly. "I remember how much he flinched every time the bell over the door would ring, signaling someone coming into the store."

"That's fair," I admit.

"You're the one I emailed?" Joseph says, looking at me,

but giving a side look to his granddaughter. I don't think he knew about the phone call.

"I am. We planned to come and ask you some questions, but you threw us with the Ethan stuff," I explain.

"We're identical, in your defense," Kai says.

"I'd say," Joseph says, taking a napkin from the dispenser in the center of the table and dabbing his forehead.

"You really don't know where he went or who the boy was?" I ask Fiona.

"I was young when he left, and I don't remember him saying anything about where. His dad showed up a few months after he got here and they moved into a house a town over from here," Fiona says and then looks at her grandfather. "Granddad, do you remember when his dad sold the house?"

"Gerald didn't sell it. He was renting from Bea over at the post office. I think he moved right around when Ethan, uh, Ezra, moved."

"Maybe he left a forwarding address for his mail," I say to Belle. I'm assuming Gerald is actually Gavin, but I could be wrong.

"Oh, he didn't. I asked so I could mail Eth-Ezra his things," Joseph says. The poor man is struggling with the name change.

"What things?" Kai asks, looking close to tears. I can't blame him. If Ezra really was here four years ago, that means we have proof of life beyond anything we've had so far.

"I still have it in a box out back. Fiona?"

"I'm on it," she says, getting up and going to the back room.

"I apologize. I had no idea you were looking for your brother when I sent that email," Joseph says.

"Don't apologize. You were just trying to get in touch with a boy you knew and got his twin instead," Kai says, emotion clogging his voice.

"Can I ask what happened? Fiona loves things like this, but I don't follow it at all."

I give him a brief summary, saving Kai from having to do it. As it is, he looks down at his hands as I explain everything.

"Here you go," Fiona says once I finished my story. She sets a white box on the table. The side says 'Ethan' in black marker.

I think everyone at the table holds their breath as Kai reaches his hand in. He pulls out a picture and stares at it for less than a second before he bursts into tears. Alarmed, Belle grabs the picture and Kai at the same time. She hugs him tightly and gasps when she looks at the picture.

"Let me see," Cal says, snatching it from her. I look at it with him. "Holy shit."

It's Ezra in front of this exact store with his arm around his dad. They're both smiling at the camera.

"Holy shit!" Cal yells, jumping up from the table. "He's alive." Cal slumps back into the chair just as quickly as he left it and cries. I hold him to me, tears falling from my own eyes.

"Thank you," I say to Joseph, who is smiling with watery eyes.

"I wish I could tell you where he was now."

"You have no idea what you have done for us," Belle explains through her tears. "This is the first time we have proof he didn't die like the police said he did."

"That case is bullshit," Fiona blurts.

"You've got that right," I tell her.

"Was this from a disposable camera?" I ask, flipping the picture over. Printing pictures isn't super common with the invention of smart phones and digital frames.

"It wasn't. Ezra had a fancy camera. He took it with him everywhere. He turned the closet in Bea's rental into a dark room. I remember her complaining about it after they moved out," Joseph says.

Fiona nods. "He really liked photography. He even sold some of his photographs before he left. Granddad let him display them in the store window."

Kai takes a shaky hand and continues to go through the box. There are more pictures of the area and landscapes, a few stray t-shirts, and some DVDs. Kai tips the box and pulls out a black frame.

"Is this the boy?" he asks Joseph, turning the frame so everyone else can see it. It's Ezra standing with a blond boy in a baseball uniform. Although calling him a boy isn't accurate. He's in his twenties, from what I can tell. They're smiling and look happy.

"That's him!" Joseph says.

"Can I see that?" I ask, and Kai hands it over. I examine it more closely. "WM University?"

"Oh, that's the local university. White Mountain University. They have a great baseball team," Fiona says.

"Thank you for everything," I tell them, standing and taking Cal with me since he won't let go of my waist. Belle quickly puts everything back in the box, taking my signal to leave.

"Please let us know if you think of anything else," she says, shaking Joseph and Fiona's hands.

We all say our goodbyes and exit the store.

We're close. So close. I can feel it.

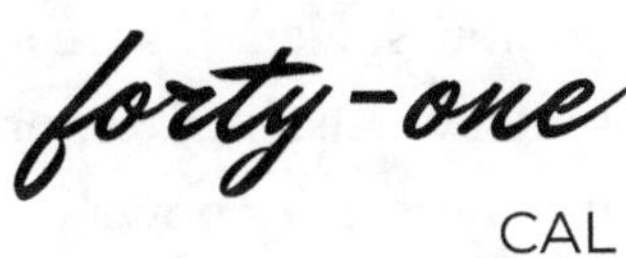

CAL

HARLOW IS in our cabin on a video call with her dad and Jo. So Belle, Kai, and I decided to start a fire in the fire pit. We've all just been staring at the flames in silence. There are plenty of chairs, but Belle is on Kai's lap, and he's clinging to her like she's his life raft.

I've opened and closed my mouth so many times I know I look like a fish. There are no words to help Kai or to express all the feelings I have right now. I wish I could grab Harlow and cling to her in the same way, but she's busy. Not only that, but it's been her determination that got us this far. I fought her on coming here, but she was right to insist.

"I'm sorry," I blurt eventually.

Kai and Belle both look at me with matching frowns.

"I tried to stop this trip. If I had . . ."

Belle shakes her head. "Do you really think you could've stopped Harlow?"

Kai snorts, and I glare at him.

"I mean, she's my wife," I say, like that means I have any control over her.

"I think that just makes you her bitch," Kai says. I'd glare at him, but he's smiling.

"I was her bitch before I married her," I grumble.

Belle throws her head back and laughs.

"He's alive," Kai whispers after the laughter dies down.

"Has anyone told Mav?" I ask.

Kai shakes his head. "I want to hand him the picture when we see him tomorrow. I asked Harlow to tell Jo to keep it to herself for now."

"You know, I overheard Harlow talking about the case once, and she said something that stuck with me," I say. Making sure to pause for effect.

"Which is what?" Belle asks impatiently.

"Breadcrumbs."

"Are you sure she wasn't making chicken?" Kai asks.

"No, you asshole. She said that she has a theory that Gavin left you breadcrumbs to find them. That he didn't love one son more than the other. Just one of you was in danger, so he had to leave the other."

Now it's Kai's turn to do his best fish interpretation.

"Because Gavin Irons would not have left a picture of his legally dead son behind," Harlow says, stepping out into the yard and sitting on my lap. I hug her tightly to me and feel her chuckle.

"What did your dad have to say?" Belle asks her.

"He's mad we went without him, but happy with what we found out. He's going to go through alumni and team records for the university. I didn't see anything with a quick Google search, but I also didn't have a name. My dad will have a name by the end of the day."

"Then what?" Kai asks.

"Then we track down Mr. Tight Pants and ask him some questions," Harlow says and Belle laughs.

"His pants were pretty tight," she agrees.

"No more looking at pictures of men with tight pants," I declare.

"Seconded," Kai says immediately.

Harlow and Belle laugh.

"You can't stop us," Harlow says, her eyes twinkling with that mischief I love so much.

"Too late. The motion has passed," I say, slamming my hand down on the arm of the chair like a gavel. We all break out into a fit of laughter that's only interrupted by the ringing of Harlow's phone.

She answers and wanders around the yard as she speaks, just out of range to hear what she's saying. Then she comes running at us.

"Hurry up! We have a call!" she says, running by us and straight into the cabin. The three of us look at each other for a beat and then get up to follow her.

HARLOW

"THANK you for agreeing to this on such short notice," I say.

"That's Jasper Wentworth," Cal says to Kai. The awe in his voice is clear and completely unhelpful right now.

"If you two can't get your shit together, you need to leave," Belle hisses at them.

"Absolutely no problem at all," Jasper says. "Shattered Halo is my favorite band."

Cal gasps, and I pinch his leg, making him yelp.

"Sorry. My husband is also a large fan of yours," I tell Jasper.

Jasper Wentworth is the boy in the picture with Ezra. I sent my dad the picture right after our call, and he immediately recognized him. He asked Jo to reach out through official channels for the band, thinking correctly that it would get him to speak with us quicker. Thirty minutes might be a record.

"He's a two-time world series pitcher and the best the

Nashville Chickadees has ever seen!" Cal says, practically vibrating next to me on the couch.

"What's with the bird names for teams?" Belle asks. Off-topic, but good question.

Jasper just laughs, and it's deep and charming as hell.

"What did you guys need to talk to me about so urgently?" he asks, doing a better job of keeping on topic than I am.

I hold up the picture of Ezra and Jasper without saying another word. Looking at the picture now, it's pretty obvious that's Jasper, assuming you've ever seen him. I'm guessing Cal and Kai were too focused on Ezra, alive and smiling next to him to put it together.

If Shattered Halo is Jasper's favorite band, then he knows who Kai is and what he looks like. He definitely knows who Ezra is. I watch his face closely. He's not giving anything away.

"I can't tell you what you want me to. I don't know where he is right now," Jasper says.

"When was the last time you saw Ezra?" I ask.

Jasper sighs and looks down.

"Please. I need to find my brother," Kai pleads.

Jasper's head snaps up and meets Kai's eyes. They stare at each other, not breaking eye contact until Jasper nods.

"I figured out who he was pretty quickly since I'm a fan," Jasper says. "He swore me to secrecy, and I never said anything. But he talked about you all the time."

Kai's eyes water, and he nods.

"You and Maverick," Jasper amends and smirks. "Man, did Ezra love Maverick. Probably still does. Wherever he is."

"You haven't seen him recently?" Belle asks, tears in her eyes too.

"I got signed to the Chickadees four years ago. Talked Ezra into coming with me. He is, was, my best friend. I knew enough of his situation to know he was hiding, but I didn't want to leave him behind." We're all silent. I don't think any of us are breathing as we wait for Jasper to continue. "He changed his name again, and I ended up getting him a job with the team. He was with us for two years."

"And you don't know where he went after that?" I ask.

Jasper shakes his head. "Something spooked him. I don't know what. I tried to get him to tell me, but he wouldn't. He left in the middle of the night one night, and I haven't heard from him since."

"What name did he use while you worked together?" I ask him.

"Evan Roger," Jasper answers.

"Well, he's sticking to 'e' names. That's a pattern," I say mostly to myself.

"And first names as last names," Cal adds.

"Thanks for your help. Let us know if you think of anything else," I say.

"Yeah and let me know if you want to go to a show. I'll get you some backstage passes," Kai says. Jasper perks up and smiles.

"I'd love that, man. Same goes for you guys, if you want to come to a game."

The guys all exchange numbers while Belle and I snicker at them. Once the call ends, Kai lets out a sigh.

"Two years. He was alive at least two years ago," he says, then turns to me. "I can never repay you for this, Harlow. You've brought me closer to finding my brother in a matter of days than I have been able to do in years."

"Thank me when I find him," I say.

Because I will.

I will find Ezra Irons.

forty-three

CAL

"CAL!"

I spin on my heel and find Maverick running in my front door, his eyebrows high on his forehead and eyes wide.

"What? What happened?" I ask, meeting him in my living room. I hear feet racing down the stairs at the same moment Mav collides with me.

"Cal!" Harlow yells, Cora in her arms clapping. The large round yellow diamond sparkling on her finger. The gold band is engraved with tiny fireworks. I got her a matching wedding ring of yellow diamonds and another band of green peridot, Cora's birthstone. I plan to add another band for every baby she'll give me.

"Cal!" my sister's voice comes from my front door.

"Why the hell is everyone yelling my name?" I yell back, throwing up my arms in frustration.

"Turn the TV on," Willa says, coming in from the back door with Jo.

"I need to take your fingerprints off my locks," I mutter,

doing as she says anyway. After what happened with Harlow, I decided fingerprints were better than keys, so I swapped out all the locks. The problem with that is my friends also insisted their fingerprints needed to be in there in case of an emergency. I disagreed, but Harlow argued the point with no clothes on. Which was such a good argument, I agreed. But now they're always in here like they don't have their own damn houses.

"Holy fucking shit on a cracker," I say.

"Yeah. Whatever that means," Kai says. No idea where he just came from, but my mind is too riled from what I'm seeing on the news to care.

Senator James Wolfe of Maine arrested on charges of drug trafficking, importing a controlled substance, money laundering, racketeering, and election fraud with more charges pending.

"Holy cracker shit or whatever Cal said," Kai says.

"They got him," Mav says, his face still showing how shocked he is. He collapses on the couch, and Harlow collapses right next to him with Cora snuggled into her. "Kidnapping wasn't in there."

Harlow shrugs. "As long as he isn't a threat to any of us anymore, that's all I care about."

"What about Ezra?" Mav says, audibly swallowing. When we showed him the picture and told him about the call with Jasper, he collapsed onto the ground and sobbed for almost an hour. Now he's more determined than I've ever seen him. The proof that Ezra has been alive this whole time lit a fire under his ass. His house is always clean now, and he's always put together. It's like he's a whole new person.

"We have his trail. We just have to keep following it," Harrison says, coming into the room.

"Where the hell did you come from?" I ask.

"Front door."

"Your prints are in the system too?" I ask, second guessing how many requests I grant Harlow while she's naked.

"Door was open," he says, looking disappointed in me. I glare at Kai, who was the last one in here.

"Sorry, man. I rushed in here." He at least looks guilty, which makes me feel a little better. My father-in-law is one scary motherfucker, and I don't like when he looks at me like that.

"I don't know what to do with myself right now," Mav says.

"I think we can relax?" I say, also unsure.

"You go back on tour in two weeks," Jo points out.

"Are you excited, Sunshine?" Mav asks her, grinning like an idiot.

"I have calls to make and emails to answer," she says, pretending Mav hadn't spoken and leaves.

"I think I'm growing on her," Mav says, leaning back into the couch and smiling. We all laugh at his delusion but let him have it anyway. He has a look of a man who's had a huge weight lifted off their shoulders.

"What are your plans for the first podcast episode?" I ask Harlow. It's coming out next week. It coincides with the date that was supposed to be our last show in Boston before we had to move everything. The girls didn't want to wait, thinking a delay before they even start wouldn't help them gain listeners. We did our interviews as soon as we got home from Green Peak.

"We already recorded it," Harlow says. "We went heavy on his disappearance and probable interference with the case. We asked the public for help specifically regarding that and asked them not to inundate our email with Ezra sightings."

"That's smart," Harrison says.

"We don't want people searching for him while we do, but I knew changing the topic of our first episode would either bring negative attention or get people's curiosity so high that they interfere inadvertently."

"So you kept it, but with a specific focus. That's a great idea," Willa says.

"Thanks," Harlow says, blushing.

"So, uh, not that I'm not glad you're here, Harrison, but why are you here?" I ask.

"I just wanted to deliver the good news myself," he says. "Police were able to find enough evidence to connect the men who kidnapped Harlow to Wolfe. Those charges are pending the district attorney reviewing them, but you can sleep easy knowing the guy that caused you pain is behind bars."

Harlow sighs in relief, and slumps in her seat, her posture mirroring Maverick's. Cora giggles and squishes Harlow's cheeks together, making her laugh.

"There's more," Harrison says. "The guard at the prison that shot Brad and then herself. I found wire transfers from an offshore account for hundreds of thousands of dollars. She willed it all to her sick mother."

"Jesus," Willa mutters.

"I was able to trace those accounts back to Wolfe."

"So he did it. All of it," Mav says, his expression unreadable.

"It would appear that way," Harrison confirms.

"Now what?" I ask, genuinely not knowing what to do with myself.

"Now we find Ezra," Harlow says with so much confidence I believe her.

And if anyone can do it, it's my wife.

I DON'T BOTHER HIDING in the shadows this time. I'm right where Cal can see me while he's on stage. He glances over during every song and smiles at me. His eyes stayed locked with mine for the entirety of Firecracker. I swear my heart is about to burst from all the attention he's giving me by the end of the show. That or my panties are going to go up in flames.

The fans with backstage passes are on the other side of the stage and are slowly making their way over to an area that Nate has designated for them if they want to meet the band. I decide to join them and eavesdrop on what they talk about. Nate notices me but says nothing. I don't think he ever says anything unless it's barking out directions.

"Do you think they told him the wrong side of the stage? He kept looking in the opposite direction from us," a girl with neatly curled green hair says. I'm standing behind the group, hoping no one will notice me. I don't think I'm overly recognizable normally, but Cal has posted a few pictures of us, and these people are super fans. It would ruin my fun if they noticed me.

"He's married," her friend with bright blue curls tells her.

"It could just be a publicity stunt. You know, to clean up his image or something," the green-haired one says with a hint of desperation.

I get it, girl. Callahan Griffin is a catch. A fucking hot one at that. I would be sad too.

Her friend shakes her head, making her blue curls bounce, and sighs in a way that tells me this isn't the first time they've had this discussion. "Maverick is still single," she offers.

Maverick is the most unsingle single person there is. Not that I can tell them that. It would be hard to explain. Actually, it would be impossible to explain since Mav is still waiting to find Ezra before announcing there was or is something between them.

The girls start bouncing on the balls of their feet and squealing through clenched teeth as the band makes their way over. I only have eyes for the tall one with floppy dark hair and deep brown eyes.

"Callahan is so hot!" I yell.

"He is *so* hot," the green-haired girl says without turning to look at me.

"His ass is perfect!" I add, trying not to laugh.

"I want to touch it so bad!" she says. I snort and try to cover it up with a cough. Normally, women fawning over Cal make me irrationally jealous. But this is actually kind of curing me of it.

"Hi everyone. Thanks for coming out to the show," Cal

says politely. The crowd starts shouting over each other about how much they love Shattered Halo and the band members. Willa catches me in the crowd, and I quickly put a finger to my lips, begging her not to say anything. She smirks and continues signing a man's forehead.

By the time Cal gets over to the side I'm standing on, I'm pretty convinced the green-haired girl is going to faint. I think she held her breath the entire time. Her friend was definitely here for Belle, if the nervous rambling she did when Belle signed her album was any indication.

"What's your name?" Cal asks her, holding the head-shot she handed him and waiting so he can personalize it for her.

"Her name is Ginny," her friend answers for her, nudging her with her elbow.

"Thanks for coming to the show, Ginny," Cal says, giving her a polite smile.

Poor Ginny squeaks, and she looks like she might be physically shaking.

"Callahan Griffin has a giant dick!" I yell, trying to distract her so she doesn't faint. But also so Cal sees me, and I can see the look on his face. His eyes snap right to mine, and he sighs, pinching the bridge of his nose.

"Firecracker," he mutters. "What the hell are you doing over here?"

"Nate said this is where the fans go," I say innocently, making my way over to him. I stand in front of him and let him pull me in for a heated kiss. He's always worked up after shows, and I reap the benefits.

"This isn't where you go," he says, pulling away and giving me one more kiss on the forehead.

"Hi, I'm Harlow." I introduce myself to Ginny. "I'm Cal's wife. Sorry."

"Why are you sorry that you're my wife?" Cal says, deeply offended.

"I took you off the market," I explain.

Cal sighs again and looks to the ceiling for answers.

"Oh, uh. Thank you?" Ginny says, completely confused. She's breathing and stopped shaking. So at least it worked.

Cal finishes signing her things and pulls me along with him while he finishes with the rest of the crowd.

"I don't think that's for publicity, Gin." I hear as we walk away.

Cal nips my ear as he leads me out of the stadium they just played and into the car Nate called for him. We don't have to leave tonight, which means the buses are staying parked, and we're all staying in a hotel. Cora is staying overnight in Jason's room to give us time alone.

"I've been so fucking hard for you since I saw you watching me on stage tonight," Cal says, kissing the side of my neck.

"Cal," I say, trying to push him away. "Wait until we don't have an audience." The driver is staring straight ahead and pretending he can't hear anything. He definitely can though.

"Baby, I had to strap my dick down with my belt and hope my shirt covered it for the whole damn show. I can't wait."

"If you keep it in your pants until we get to our room, I'll do that thing you like," I tell him. He freezes for a minute and then sighs, leaning back into his own seat.

"Fine," he grumbles and squeezes his eyes shut. I'm pretty sure he's naming presidents under his breath.

It takes less than five minutes to get to the hotel, but with the way Cal hops out of the car and pulls me with him, you'd think it had been hours. He's practically running to our room, dragging me along with him. I'm laughing so hard I'm having trouble keeping up, so he lifts me into his arms and continues to run.

"You're ridiculous," I tell him.

"I need you so bad, Harlow. I'm about to burst in my pants." There isn't a hint of humor in his voice. But there is desperation.

"Why are you so worked up?" I ask him, kissing his neck.

"I had a moment, after seeing you mixed in with the fans, where it felt like all this was a fever dream, and you weren't really mine," he says, smacking the key card against the reader and kicking the door open.

"I'm right here, and I'm yours," I tell him, kissing along his jaw.

"I need to be as close to you as I can. Inside you. I need to claim you," he says, putting me on my feet and tearing both our clothes off. He pounces on me the moment I'm naked.

He kisses me so deeply our teeth clash and our tongues fight for dominance. Cal is feral with his desire and his urgent need for me, and it's making me feel the same way. Our hands are everywhere, grabbing and clawing.

"Please, Cal. Take me. Prove to yourself I'm yours," I say against his hot skin as I kiss his chest right where his heart beats.

Cal groans and brings me to the bed, our chests pressed together, and my back already sticking to the sheets. He reaches down to check how wet I am and lets out a more animalistic groan.

"Always so fucking wet for me, Firecracker," he says right before he slams himself into me. We both moan so loudly; I'm sure the rest of the hotel can hear us. "You feel so good."

Cal's pace is brutal, but I'm right there with him, meeting his thrusts with my hips.

"You are everything to me. Everything. Do you understand?" he says, his voice coming out in pants as he continues to work us to the edge. I meet his eyes and see a madness there that is only for me. I'm his love, his obsession.

I put my hands on his cheeks and nod. "You're mine, Callahan," I tell him, breaths coming just as heavy. "Mine."

Cal claims my mouth. "Yours," he says against my lips. He reaches down and circles my clit with his thumb. My orgasm hits me so hard and so fast; I'm screaming. "You're fucking perfect," Cal says in my ear as he thrusts into me one more time and yells out his release.

He kisses me slowly after that, lovingly. Pouring every ounce of his affection into each touch of his lips against mine.

"I love you so much, baby," he says, nuzzling into my neck and hugging me against him.

"I love you too."

"Are you okay? Was I too rough?" he asks once he catches his breath. His eyes are filled with concern as he looks up at me.

"I'm a little sore, but I loved every minute," I tell him honestly. "I might hide with your superfans more often."

"Harlow," he says, frowning. "Don't do that to me."

I laugh. "I won't, but you have to admit the sex was really hot."

"Every moment with you is perfect, but this was on another level," he concedes.

Cal kisses his way up my side to my neck and then over to my mouth. "Already?" I ask, feeling his erection where it's pressing into my hip.

"I'm always hard around you, Firecracker," he says, kissing me again. "But I remember you promising to do that thing I like."

I laugh again and push him off me. "A promise is a promise," I say, laying on my back and pushing myself until my head hangs over the edge of the bed. I open my mouth and wait. Cal groans and quickly makes his way to stand in front of me.

He slowly pushes himself into my mouth. This is the only way I can take him to the back of my throat, which makes it his favorite. I love the sounds he makes, but the position causes all the blood to go to my head, so he doesn't get it often.

"Fuck. I love your mouth almost as much as your pussy," Cal gasps as he hits the back of my throat. He grabs my hands and places them on his legs so I can tap out if I need to. "Ready, baby?"

I nod and mumble around his length. He pulls out enough to let me take a deep breath and then fucks my mouth. I swipe my tongue back and forth over the underside of his cock as he drives in and out.

"Fuck yes, baby. You're so fucking good at that," he moans. "I'm not going to last. I never last like this."

I moan around him, getting just as turned on by this as he is. I reach across my body and rub my clit.

"Fuck, Firecracker. That's it, baby. Does sucking my dick make you wet?"

I moan again because that's all I can do and rub faster. I can feel Cal swelling in my mouth, so I know he's close, and I'm right there with him.

"Come with me, baby," Cal moans, leaning forward and pinching both my nipples. I shoot off like a grenade, practically screaming around his cock. He holds off long enough for me to stop screaming before he empties himself down my throat. He pulls out slowly and then helps me into a sitting position.

"You have utterly and completely ruined me," I tell him, using his body to keep myself sitting.

Cal barks out a laugh and scoops me up. He places me gently on the bed and tucks me in before getting in on the other side and pulling me into his chest. I sigh in contentment, my head resting over his heart so I can hear it beating.

forty-five

CAL

"IT'S BEEN LESS THAN AN HOUR."

"I know," Harlow says, pacing in front of the couch. Melt the Ice released their first episode this morning. I've already listened to it, and I think they did a great job. Jo was serious as always, and Harlow brought more lightheartedness to the show while still keeping to the serious nature of the topic.

"What are you worried about?" I ask, pulling her to sit on my lap.

"Negative impact. Hurting Ezra." Harlow looks past me and out the glass door into our backyard, lost in thought. "Oh fuck! What if this makes him run again?"

"Fuck!" Cora says cheerfully from her spot on the floor.

Harlow looks shocked but recovers quickly. "Good job, Cora girl! Duck!"

"Duck!" Cora repeats and we all clap.

"That was close," Harlow mutters as I laugh.

"Why would he run?" I ask.

"In the off chance it wasn't Wolfe," she says. "I know all

evidence points to him, but if there's even a slight chance it wasn't, this could spook Ezra."

"I don't think he'll run," I say after thinking for a moment.

"You don't?" Harlow asks, looking like she doesn't believe me.

"I don't. He's had to have seen the news about his dad, and I'm sure he'll listen to the podcast. He's going to know what we're doing. He's going to see we'll never stop searching. When it's safe, he'll come out of hiding, or you'll find him before that."

"You think he'll listen to my podcast?"

"I know he will. Ezra has a curious mind, kind of like you. He'd be too interested to ignore it." I kiss her forehead and she leans into me.

"Let's hope someone has a credible tip," she sighs. "Because I have no idea where he went after leaving Jasper in Nashville."

"We're getting tips on the site already," Jo says, walking in through the back door. "Well, it looks like the app is actually the preferred method at the moment."

"And you need to come over here to say that?" I ask grumpily. I don't get a ton of alone time with my family, and I was enjoying it, even if Harlow was freaking out.

"There's one that stands out that I think we need to look into," Jo says to Harlow, ignoring that I even spoke. Which is typical. Jo hands her phone over to Harlow, who reads whatever is on the screen. Her eyebrows shoot up, and she looks at Jo.

"Holy shit."

"Shit!" Cora echoes.

"Good job! Fish!" Harlow says, giving me a guilty look before turning back to Jo's phone.

"Do we think this is real?" Jo asks.

"It could be," Harlow says, biting her bottom lip.

"The submission is anonymous, but maybe we should ask your dad to try to find the person," Jo says.

"If we do that, we might be putting them in danger. And even if we aren't, it goes against the entire point of it being anonymous."

"Can someone tell me what the fudge you're talking about?" I ask, trying not to swear since apparently Cora picked today to be a parrot.

Harlow hands over Jo's phone so I can read the submission.

I know for a fact that Ezra witnessed a murder. The murderer saw him and that's why he ran. Murderer is still at large, so he can't come home.

"One of your theories is that he witnessed something bad. This would confirm it." I hand Jo's phone back to her and shrug.

"The texts from the unknown number confirmed as much too," Harlow says. "But if they're still at large, it's not Wolfe."

"That's also assuming this is a real tip," Jo says. "Are you sure we can't ask your dad to find this person?"

"If we get desperate, we might have to. But this narrows down what we think he saw. We could look into missing people from that time frame in that area," Harlow says.

"Not murders?" I ask.

She shakes her head. "Do you remember hearing about any unsolved murders back home?"

"What if it was on or near campus? We don't know when this happened," I say. "I don't remember any murders, but there's probably missing people. We went to college in Bangor."

"Shit. That adds a lot more cases to look into," Jo says.

"I'll mention it to my dad. I think he was looking into something in Nashville, but I'm sure this will interest him."

Harrison went to Nashville to ask questions around the area where Ezra used to live and work. Jasper helped him out as best he could with locations, but it wasn't a lot to go on.

Jo's shoulders sag as she deflates like a sad balloon. "I got ahead of myself with that," she says.

"It could lead to something, and it could not. It's going to keep happening. We knew that. Don't beat yourself up about it," Harlow tells her.

"I didn't tell Maverick, so if you could keep this to yourselves," Jo says.

I frown, and Harlow cocks her head. "Why?" I ask.

"He's been happy lately. He even leaves the house without anyone forcing him to. I don't want to bring him back down with something that could turn out to be false. I promised to keep him in the loop, and I will. Just with facts, not speculation."

"I'll keep it to myself as long as you promise to tell him the moment you have anything to back up that claim," I say, and Harlow nods her agreement.

"I promise," Jo says, looking relieved.

"What's going on with you two?" Harlow asks.

Jo meets her eye and gives her a sad smile. "Nothing. We

can't ever be anything, Harlow. He loves Ezra, and you're going to find him. I won't be a placeholder for his real love."

"Okay," Harlow says quietly. Jo holds her gaze for a moment more and then leaves the way she came.

"Do you think it's really nothing?" I ask.

"No. I think Jo has feelings she's denying, and Maverick probably isn't helping. We all see the way he follows her around like a lost puppy."

"She's right about Ezra though?" I point out.

"Is she? We're going to be coming up on seven years since Ezra went missing. There's no way he isn't an entirely different person now. Not to mention, there's a very good chance the person Maverick is in love with is the memory version of Ezra that never really existed."

I suck in a breath, ready to argue, but then I let it out. She could be right. I know she's at least partially correct. Seven years of living while looking over your shoulder for danger has to have changed Ezra. There isn't a single scenario where it wouldn't. I'm not sure Maverick has come to terms with that, or even willingly understood it.

Harlow lets out an exhausted sigh and slumps into my arms. "I think we should just find him first and stop speculating."

"Works for me."

"IT SMELLS GOOD IN HERE," Harlow says, wrapping her arms around my waist and pressing her cheek into my back.

"Get your apron on and help me," I say. I'm cooking Thanksgiving dinner and Harlow asked to have it here. By that, I mean she told me we were having it here, and she had already invited everyone. I pretend to be upset about it, but she knew I wasn't.

"What do you need to do? I saw you put the turkey in the oven, and you assigned everyone else the sides and desserts," she argues.

"Not all of them. We still need to make a pumpkin pie and the stuffing. Plus, we should probably have a backup mac and cheese ready since Willa volunteered for that, and her cooking would make prisoners cry."

Harlow grumbles under her breath but lets me go and puts on her apron. "What do you need me to do, chef?"

I smack her ass, and she laughs. "Pumpkin pie recipe is

out on the counter. I use store bought pie crust, so you just have to make the filling."

Harlow gasps, and I narrow my eyes at her. "Store bought crust? The blasphemy!"

"You realize the Midnight Macaroni I make when the girls are upset is just boxed stuff I add extra cheese to?"

Harlow slaps her hand over her heart and widens her eyes until they're comically large. "It can't be."

I take her by the waist and spin her towards me. "Make the pie, Firecracker." I plant a kiss on her lips and let her go.

"Yes, chef!" she says, and I laugh. No one makes me laugh like this woman.

We work in tandem for the next few hours. She gets the pie and stuffing done before helping me with the mac and cheese.

My house is loud with the sounds of the people I love the most. Cora's laugh rings loud above it all from where she sits in her highchair and shoves mashed potatoes into her mouth with her tiny fist. We're finally using the dining room table Belle forced me to buy when I first moved into the house. I ignored the smug grin she sent my way when we first sat down to eat.

I sip my water and watch everyone from my place at the head of the table. Cora is to my left and Harlow to my right. Our friends and family fill in the other seats with my dad sitting at the other head.

Harlow reaches for my hand and squeezes. "I love you," she says. Happiness radiating from her face.

"I love you too, Firecracker."

The doorbell rings, breaking my eye contact with my

wife. I frown, looking around the room. Everyone is here. Harrison and Jo included.

"I'll get it!" Willa says, leaping from the table and running to the door. Harlow's gaze follows her, and she looks just as confused as I do. I turn toward my sister, but Belle's expression mirrors everyone else's.

Willa returns less than a minute later, followed by a tall, broad man in dark jeans and a navy button-up shirt that he's rolled at the sleeves, letting his tattooed forearms peek through. He has light brown hair and green eyes, a shade darker than Harlow's. But it's not his appearance I'm focused on. It's his arm around Willa's shoulders.

Willa clears her throat, but it's unnecessary since the room is silent. Not even Cora is making noise right now.

"Everyone, this is Declan," she says. "My husband."

HARLOW

"CAN you believe Jasper actually came to the show?" Cal says with stars in his eyes.

"That was over a month ago," I point out again.

"I know, but Jasper Wentworth came to my show," he says, looking like an excited little kid. I laugh at him and kiss his cheek. "And he got me tickets to the season opener in April!"

I looked into that game since Cal won't go without all of us, and I helped Jo book the hotel and flights. "You know that game is against Boston, right?"

Cal rubs the back of his neck. "Yeah. Do you think he'd be offended if I went to his game in the opposing team's jersey?"

"You think you'd be offended if he wore an opposing band's shirt to your concert?" I counter. Cal frowns.

"I'm going to be cast out of New England if I wear a Chickadees jersey," he says, looking a little panicked.

"Why don't you just wear Shattered Halo merch?"

Cal's shoulders slump in relief. "That will work."

"Glad I could help. Now, I have to go over some files that were submitted to the platform with Jo," I tell him. "I'll be back in time for Cora's bedtime."

"Okay, wife," he says, kissing me longer and with a lot more tongue than is appropriate for a goodbye.

"You're not convincing me to stay and have sex on the new couch." We had to get a new one after Cora got into some markers I didn't hide high enough. My girl is growing a lot faster than I like.

"Aww. Come on, Firecracker. It'll be fun," Cal says, trying to pull me closer to him.

"Yes, it will. Tonight," I say, freeing myself and quickly walking to the door.

"Fine," he says, pouting. "I'm going to go over to Mav's. Kai is already there. So that's where I'll be if you need me. Or you miss me."

I snort and shake my head.

"I love you, wife," he says, smiling sweetly.

"I love you too, husband."

I quickly make my way out the door and down the sidewalk to Willa's house. The temperature has turned cold quickly, and I can smell winter in the air.

Jo is at the door when I get there. "I think we got something!" she yells and turns to run into the house. I follow quickly behind her, stopping to discard my shoes at the door. Willa and Belle went out to dinner. They invited us, but I was already cooking dinner for my little family and Jo was busy. So it's just us here right now.

Willa's house is brighter than the others. She has large windows throughout the bottom floor and all the walls are white where you can even see the wall. She kept the natural wood on the window frames and the beams on the ceiling. The warm brown leather sectional and thick blue rug in the living room are inviting. I haven't been in too much of the house, but I imagine it's the same style.

I take a seat on the couch next to Jo and wait while she pulls her laptop onto her lap. She has an audio clip on the screen that was submitted anonymously.

"I was a reporter at the time of Ezra's disappearance," I read the note accompanying it out loud. "I've kept this recording as insurance, but I think you could use it more."

"Ready?" Jo asks.

"They don't say who the recording is of?"

"Nope."

"Have you listened to it yet?" I ask her, turning to see her looking annoyed.

"Woman, can you ask all your questions after I play it?"

"Right. Yup. Play it," I say, miming zipping my lips.

Jo hits play, and I listen.

"You got rid of the boy?" a voice comes through. It's muffled, and I can barely make out what they're saying.

"I told you I did." That one is Senator Wolfe.

"Then why is his brother trying so hard to find him?" comes the muffled voice again.

"It's his brother. What the fuck were you expecting?" Wolfe.

"You could've left a fucking body," the muffled voice hisses.

"You told me to make sure no one could connect it to us!" Wolfe.

The other voice makes a strange noise and the recording ends.

I frown. "Can you play that again?" Jo nods and plays it again.

"We can assume this is about Ezra, and Wolfe is clearly the one being recorded," she says. "But I doubt it was obtained legally, and we don't know who the other voice is. Whoever that is was calling the shots."

"Senator Wolfe didn't kill Ezra. We know that, but now it seems like it was either on purpose, or he was covering up his fuck up."

"Who is powerful enough to use a senator as a puppet?" Jo asks.

"He was just a judge at that time," I say.

"Judges still hold a lot of power."

We sit there long enough for the sun to set and come up with nothing.

"Two things. We need to know what Ezra saw, and we need to know who that voice is," I say.

"So we need to find Ezra," Jo says.

"We're doing that, anyway. I just hope he's willing to tell us when we find him."

Jo nods, going to put her laptop away, but I stop her. "Play it again."

She does without questioning me.

"Again," I say after it ends. She frowns but plays it again. There's something in that voice. I know it.

"What are you thinking?" Jo asks after the third replay.

"One more time," I say, ignoring her question.

My jaw drops as everything clicks. I shoot to my feet and run out the door, not bothering to put my shoes on.

"Harlow! What the hell? Wait up!" Jo calls, chasing after me.

Thank god all their houses are close together, or I would

lose a toe. I charge up the front steps and into Maverick's house.

He comes around the corner at the sound of his door opening, and I almost crash into him.

"Harlow? What's wrong?" he says, seeing my face.

"Firecracker!" Cal says excitedly as he comes into the foyer too. Then he sees me and rushes to my side. "What happened, baby?"

"I'd really like to know that too," Jo says, panting as she finally catches up.

"It's not your dad," I tell Mav.

Everyone is frowning at me, both confused and concerned. I ignore them, trying to explain as my brain sorts through everything.

"Your dad. He's a pawn or a scapegoat, or maybe just a cohort. All those charges. I don't know how many he actually did," I poorly explain.

"If it wasn't him, who was it?"

"It's —" I say, but then the front door slams open, and we all turn to see a woman walk in like she owns the place. Maverick's frown deepens and turns angry.

"What the fuck are you doing here?"

bonus chapter

HARLOW

"What's this wild plan you have?" I ask, my hand clasped firmly in Cal's. I'm smiling so hard my cheeks hurt, but I can't help it. I love this man, and he makes me so happy.

"You'll see, Firecracker," he says, then kisses me.

"Keep your eyes on the road!" I screech. We're driving somewhere in a rental car. Cal quickly pulls over.

"I'm doing this wrong."

"I don't know what you're doing, so I have no comment," I say and laugh.

"Will you marry me?" he asks, grasping my hands in his and looking into my eyes. My knee-jerk reaction is to laugh, but I can see the sincerity in his eyes. He's serious.

"Really?" I ask, my voice breaking with emotion and tears coming to my eyes.

"Really, Firecracker. I love you with every part of my heart and soul. Any moment spent without you feels like all the breath has been sucked from my lungs. I need you more than the air I breathe, Harlow. And I love you more than my heart can handle. So yeah, Firecracker. I mean it when I say I want to marry you."

"Okay," I whisper.

"Yeah?" he asks, grinning like a fool.

"Yeah. Let's get married."

Cal throws his hand in the air and whoops before kissing me. Then he turns back to the wheel and starts driving again.

"Wait. Right now?" I ask, as Cal pulls the car into a drive-through marriage chapel. I didn't know that was a thing, but it must be efficient.

"I don't want to live one more minute without you being my wife," Cal says, pulling up to a speaker and ordering the premium package like we're going through a car wash. I look around, double checking that it isn't actually a wedding themed car wash. When we pull up to the window and are handed forms to fill out, it becomes apparent that it's an actual wedding chapel.

I fill out my part of the form and hand over my license. Cal's hand is grasped firmly in mine, and we're both smiling like idiots.

And I wouldn't have it any other way.

The woman dressed like Dolly Parton reads us our vows and hands over cheap silver bands. The entire thing takes less than five minutes. I lean over to squish my face next to Cal's while she takes a picture and informs us it will be sent to the email provided before shutting the window.

Cal takes my face in both of his hands and kisses me fiercely. "I love you, wife," he says against my lips.

"I love you too, husband," I say, loving the sweet taste of the words on my tongue.

"Let's go back to the hotel and consummate this," he says, putting the car in drive as I laugh.

I smile like an idiot the entire drive back to the hotel. My eyes unable to stay off the ring on my husband's finger, marking him as taken. As mine.

"Hurry up," Cal says, pulling me through the lobby and towards the elevators. I laugh at how rushed he is.

"Is there a fire I should know about?" a deep, sexy voice asks, stopping us both in our tracks.

"Just made the need for a honeymoon suite official," Cal says, wiggling his ring finger in the face I would recognize anywhere. It's on enough tabloids and magazines to cement his existence into my brain.

"Asher Cross," I squeak. "You're so famous." I'm so starstruck, my brain has decided to take the night off.

Cal turns to me looking absolutely insulted. "I'm literally a rock star."

"But that's Asher Cross," I argue.

"Firecracker," Cal growls. Asher starts laughing and holds his hand out to me. I shake it, still feeling like I'm in a dream.

"I'm Harlow Ray," I tell him.

"Harlow Griffin," Cal says, pulling me in tightly in a possessive hold. I laugh. He's not in danger of me running off with Asher Cross.

"It's lovely to meet you Harlow," Asher says, a smirk on his face as he glances back at Cal. "Were you this starstruck when you met your husband?"

I snort. "No. We met in the woods when we were younger, and he wasn't famous. He was busy trying to talk my friends into a threesome."

"Foursome. And you were busy telling me my singing sounded like birds being murdered," Cal says.

"I said you were pitchy!"

Asher laughs and it's deep and warm. "I'll let you two enjoy your night. It was wonderful meeting you, Harlow."

"Uh, can we keep this between us? I haven't told anyone that we're married, and we'd like to do it on our own terms," Cal says to Asher.

"Of course. You have my word."

We shake hands and Asher leaves us at the elevator.

"Time to make it official?" I ask as Cal crowds me the moment the elevator doors shut. His lips are on mine a moment later, and he's pulling me into him.

"I fucking love you," he says against my lips.

"I love you too," I tell him. "Forever."

Patrice Ashley is an author of romantic suspense. She loves writing and reading more than she likes leaving the house. If she isn't doing that, she's playing with her daughter and spending time with her husband. Patrice lives in New England and loves doing basic things like looking at the leaves change while drinking a pumpkin spice latte and wearing brown boots.